Face to Face with the Führer

Face to Face with the Führer

by Gill James

Chapeltown Books

British Library Cataloguing in Publication Data

A Record of this Publication is available from the British Library

ISBN 978-1-910542-99-6

This edition published 2022 by Chapeltown Books
Manchester, England

Cover illustration: © Ashleigh James

Contents

London 1976

She looked at the young man curled up in the doorway. He seemed to be sleeping peacefully, at least. She would try her best not to wake him. She must get inside though. This meeting was really important.

It was getting worse. It showed up more at this time of day anyway. They got lost in the crowds as the day wore on. Somebody should do something.

This one looked about the same age as she was then. Goodness, something like this – or worse – could have so easily happened to her.

It wasn't as bad, now, as it had been then. Not yet. It was similar enough though. It was as if it was all starting over again. Nobody had really believed it was going to happen back then either.

Could she do this? Well, she'd have to try. Gingerly she stepped over him. This sort of thing wasn't so easy any more. She cursed. Why did people have to get old?

He stirred slightly. The smell was awful. Then, to add to the bad body odour, he farted. It was a bad one and suggested an upset stomach.

No wonder with the sort of food he probably has to eat.

She fumbled in her handbag and found her purse. She slipped out a large note, looked over her shoulder to see that no one was watching and posted it into his begging tin. He nodded and grunted.

Don't you dare spend it on drugs or alcohol, young man.

She knew she shouldn't do it, really. There were systems in place to deal with these people but they just weren't working fast enough. She'd always preferred a more direct method. Wait for the authorities and you'd wait forever. Sometimes you needed to stop them anyway. The authorities aren't always right.

She pushed open the door. In seconds the world of the young man was left behind. Now she was in the plush foyer of the five-star hotel where she was to meet the reporter. She recognised the soft notes of Vivaldi's Four Seasons – wasn't that Spring playing? Nice.

She sat down on one of the overstuffed armchairs. Goodness, the carpet was so thick here and the parquet area round the reception desk so polished.

She watched some of the guests going up to the desk. All furs and smart shoes. Not her scene really. Not anymore. She smiled to herself. Actually, though, no less than she deserved after all of that.

A waiter, all in black and white, made his way over to her. "May I help you, madam?"

"Can you bring me a pot of black coffee, please?"

"Certainly, madam."

She was getting into her stride now. Yes, she would be able to tackle that reporter, she was sure.

The coffee arrived. She took a sip. It was very good. This was the life most certainly. Now then, what should she tell him when he arrived?

AH Linz 1904

School was over for the day, thank goodness. He would get away from the idiots as fast as he could. They used to be okay and when they'd all been little they laughed at his jokes and egged him on when he played the fool. He was grown up now. He hadn't got time for their childish games. He had a battle to fight.

Soon he was charging on his fine stallion. He would trample the bastards down. Just see if he didn't. God help them if they got in his way. God wouldn't help them, actually. God would only help the righteous and upstanding, those made in his own image, his chosen people. Did he count? Germans did surely? He was almost German. They were right on the border here.

He charged again and grunted.

He didn't see the customs official making his way up the path. He hurtled straight into him, almost toppling him.

"Shit, Adi, why don't you grow up?"

He froze. He knew what would happen next. He watched as his father slowly removed his belt. He waited for the first blow. He'd learnt to shrink the pain by looking at it until he could shut it out altogether. He counted. He was spot on. Ten strikes today.

"Klara," shouted his father. "You'd better come and see to the boy. Don't let him play these stupid games if you don't want to clear up the mess afterwards."

At least he knew his mother would be kind to him.

Berlin 1905

Chapter 1: a broken toy

Käthe watched Rudi playing with his clockwork train. He wound it up and then let it go across the parquet floor. It chicker-chickered at first quite fast and then slowed. He rushed after it and then wound it up again. Käthe held her breath as he turned the key. He was quite strong for his age but hadn't got all that much control. Any moment now he would overwind it and it wouldn't go anymore.

It was a beautiful thing with its shiny black body and tall chimney. It pulled along a bright red carriage and a dark blue one. It was really the mechanics of it that fascinated her, though. Those little cogs that made the wheels you saw on the engine go round. She would love to have a closer look at it. Every time she tried to though, Rudi snatched it back angrily. "It's mine, not yours. It's not a girl toy."

Oh she wished people would buy her engines to play with and not silly dolls. She didn't even really want to play with it, though. Rather, she longed to figure out how it worked.

The train slowed again and then bumped into the leg of Mutti's chair.

"Careful," said Mutti.

Rudi snatched it up.

"Is it all right? Let me look." Käthe held out her hand ready to take the toy.

"Not for girls!" Rudi started winding it up again. He put it down on the floor but this time it didn't go as fast as before. Then it stopped quite suddenly.

Leo now picked it up and tried to wind it. Nothing happened. He shook his head.

Rudi snatched the toy back and rushed over to Mutti. "Mutti, it's broken."

"Oh dear," said Mutti. She hated these new mechanical toys, she always said. They broke so easily and then the children were always disappointed. Käthe loved them, though. They were so much more interesting than the ones that she and Leo had had when they were younger.

"Give it to me. I think I might be able to mend it," said Leo.

"I don't suppose you can," said Käthe. "As usual it will probably be me who fixes it." Her older brother was useless.

"Let's hope one of you can," said Mutti.

"I tell you what," said Vati, "why don't the three of you go down to the workshop in the cellar and see what you can do? Mind, only Leo should handle the tools."

"I can use them as well!" Käthe felt her cheeks go red. Leo wouldn't have a clue.

"I know you're very deft," said Vati. "But only Leo has big enough hands to hold them properly."

Käthe frowned. "He might have big enough hands but it doesn't mean he knows how to make them work," she mumbled.

"What did you say?" Leo was now scowling.

"Nothing," said Käthe.

It was stuffy in the cellar. The air was stale. Even with the light on it seemed gloomy. There was no window to the outside. Dust motes floated in the air. Käthe loved it though. It was like a real workshop. With its big wooden bench it would make an ideal laboratory.

If only they'd let her do science experiments down there. She imagined herself mixing powerful chemicals together, or looking at something through a microscope or even dissecting a rat.

They wouldn't of course. All of the residents in the flats shared the cellar and there were all sort of rules about what you could and what you couldn't do down there.

Leo put the engine on the bench.

"I'll get the tools, shall I?" Käthe went towards their locker.

"No, I'll do it. I've got the key." Leo went to put it into the lock.

Trust you. Of course, Vati wouldn't dream of giving the keys to a girl.

Rudi was darting between the two of them. "Can you fix it, Leo? Will I be able to play with it again?"

"I should think so. But not if you keep on rushing about like that. I need to concentrate."

I could do it without having to concentrate.

Leo took the tool box out of the locker and brought it over to the bench. He took out a small screwdriver. He unscrewed the case that housed the mechanics. She had to admit it – he was being extremely careful. "Beautiful, isn't it?"

It so was. All those tiny cogs and levers. Leo poked at them. He shook his head. "I can't quite work out what's wrong though."

"Let me have a look." She pushed him aside.

"I don't think you'll be able to see anything I can't."

"Poof," said Rudi jumping up and down so that he could see up on to the bench. "What do girls know about engines?"

"You'd be surprised."

Leo sighed.

Käthe peered into the inside of the engine's workings. Suddenly she saw it. "There it is look. That little lever's snapped."

"Where? I don't see it."

"There." She poked at a fractured piece of metal with the corner of the screwdriver.

"Okay, I see." Leo pulled a face. "What can we do about that?"

"Can't you fix it? Can't you fix it?" Rudi charged at Leo.

"I don't know," muttered Leo. He pushed Rudi away.

Käthe prodded it again. If only they could pull it out, they would be able to solder it, and hook it back in. Then she had an idea. "I'm just going to go upstairs. I know exactly what we need."

Both Leo and Rudi stared at her as if she'd gone mad.

"Mutti, I need your sewing-box," she said as she arrived back in the lounge.

"Goodness. You're not going to try to sew it back together, are you?"

"Don't be silly, Mutti."

Annoyingly, her mother was trying not to laugh. It wasn't funny. This was a really practical solution. "I need your needle-threader and a couple of needles perhaps as well."

Mutti raised her eyebrows. She got up out of her seat and walked over to the other side of the room. She picked up her sewing basket and brought it to where Käthe was standing. She grinned. Her eyebrows went up a little bit further.

Don't laugh at me. Käthe rummaged in the basket.

"The needles and the needle holder are in the top pocket," her mother said.

Käthe found them. "Good. Thank you. I'll look after them."

"I know," said Mutti.

Käthe took the threader and a few needles and made her way back out of the lounge.

"What was all that about?" she heard her Vati say after she'd closed the door.

"I don't know," said Mutti. "But I wish she'd be a bit happier."

Vati laughed. "Oh at her age. And she's frustrated that she's not a boy."

Huh! I don't mind being a girl, thank you very much. It doesn't mean I can't be an engineer or a scientist. At least, it shouldn't.

When she got back to the cellar, Leo and Rudi were still poking at the engine.

"Do you think Käthe will have a good idea?" Rudi said.

"She does sometimes. Very occasionally."

Very occasionally? Oh, she'd show them.

Rudi noticed her. "What you going to do, sis?"

She pushed the two of them out of the way and bent down over the crippled engine. She held her breath and her tongue poked out as she fed the needle-threader into the mechanism.

"She's going to sew it," said Rudi. "She's bonkers."

"I don't think so." Leo laughed.

Käthe was so surprised she almost dropped the threader. Then she realised her older brother wasn't trying to say she wasn't a complete idiot but rather that there was no way she would be able to sew an engine back together again. "No, of course, not," she snapped.

The threader made contact with the broken lever and lifted it

15

slightly. She used one of the needles to hold it in place. "There. We can solder it now."

She turned to face her brothers. They were gawping at her. "Well, then," she said, "get to it."

Both boys jumped. Leo grabbed the soldering iron. He'd at least had the gumption to get it ready in the furnace while she'd been upstairs. Rudi just dithered and looked anxious.

"There look," she said, pointing to the broken bit of metal. She slipped the threader off and held the little bar steady with her needle as Leo applied the solder. "Smooth it down. If it's lumpy it won't work and it won't go back in."

"Yes, ma'am." He looked as if he was going to snap his feet together.

"Don't you dare click your heels while you're doing this or you'll just make a mess." Käthe tried her best to look stern.

Leo nodded and concentrated on the solder. A few seconds later, he leant back. "What do you think?"

Käthe looked at his work. Yes, it did look nice and neat and tidy. She nodded.

"Will it work now?" said Rudi.

Leo blew on his handiwork. "Hopefully in a few seconds." He peered into the engine. "Yeah. I think it's ready." He screwed the cover back on and wound the toy up. The right noises came from the engine. He put it carefully down on the floor and it chicker-chickered away as if new.

"Hooray," cried Rudi. "You mended it."

Käthe cleared her throat.

"Käthe helped," said Leo.

Helped? I did most of the work. Cheek.

"All finished?" said Mutti when they got back upstairs.

"Yes," said Leo. "I managed to repair it."

"I helped," said Käthe.

Leo glared at her. She pulled a face at him.

"Mmm," said Mutti, "I think a walk in the park will do us all good. Go and get your hats and coats."

Käthe looked at Leo. He frowned and shook his head. Then he turned to his mother. "But, Mutti, we can't. It's the Sabbath."

"Well, if it's the Sabbath you shouldn't be playing with your toys and you certainly shouldn't be mending them."

Vati put a hand on Leo's shoulder. "That's all about to change. Mutti and I have decided to convert to the Evangelical Church."

"Why?" asked Leo.

"It's more modern. We want to be a proper 20th century family."

Käthe noticed Vati look at Mutti with a question her eyes. Mutti shook her head. There was something more to this and they weren't saying.

"Come on, then," said Vati. "Put the engine away now and get your hats and coats. Let's go and meet the Christians in the Tiergarten."

Käthe's heart thudded as she got ready to go out. They were going to become a modern family. Did that also mean a family that approved of women working? Of women becoming scientists?

Yes, that was certainly what she wanted to do. It now looked as if it might be possible. Just think of it – discovering something new and becoming famous. Did she want to be famous? She wasn't sure. It was the thrill of being the first to know something that she wanted. And it was all so interesting, looking at the way things worked.

"Come on, daydreamer," said Vati. "We're waiting."

AH Vienna 1908

Unbelievable. These people had no idea when they had raw talent in front of them. But here it was in black and white: the Vienna Academy of Fine Arts would not be offering him a place to study art.

He folded the letter up and swallowed the lump in his throat.

Would it have been better if he'd applied earlier? Would they have had him when he was eighteen? There's been no chance though. His father had still been alive then.

"You need a proper profession, Adi. This arty stuff won't make you a living," he said every time the topic was raised.

Well, he would show them. He had his paints. He could buy some postcards and paint landscapes and portraits for a few coins. He would live cheaply until he was recognised as a great artist.

One day. He would be great one day.

He had some decorating skills as well. He could always paint houses for people if he needed the cash.

He could do this. He could really do this.

Berlin 1912

Chapter 2: the desire grows

"I'll need my table back now, thank you, missy," said Imelda. "I need to get the lunch on."

"Just two more to do," said Käthe. "I'll clear up quickly, I promise."

She now added the tenth coffee filter and started counting as they fell to the kitchen table. Yes, she got up to five again. It had been five every time except for once; that had been when Imelda banged the kitchen door and caused a draft.

"Ready now?" Imelda was standing with her hands on her hips.

"Yes, yes, all done." Käthe sighed. If only she could use that lovely bench down in the cellar. It didn't make sense. Mutti and Vati had said she couldn't use it because it belonged to everybody but now Leo had got some of his experiments set up there. It wasn't fair. Still, at least tomorrow she would be able to do the experiment that involved dropping a marble into flour. Imelda had her afternoon off and it would be easy to take over the kitchen.

She gathered up her papers, returned the coffee filters to the packet and made her way up to her room. She sat down at her desk and looked again at the chart she had produced. It looked good. It proved that weight made no difference to the rate at which objects fell but there was a little variance just to prove that there might be other factors to consider. Now, she should write it up properly. She opened the exercise book where she was recording all of her experiments. She smiled to herself as she saw her neat writing and precise little charts. Then she sighed again. Was there really any point to this? Would anybody ever see her work? Anyway, this was her least favourite bit about doing experiments.

She looked over to her bookcase. Oh yes. There was that book about the planets. Perhaps she could read that a bit until lunch time.

It was a heavy book but that was one of the things she liked about it. It was solid. She loved the illustrations in it as well. She carefully leafed through the pages. Each drawing was covered with a sheet of tissue paper. Some of the pages were glossy and the light caught the pictures. Others were slightly embossed, making the lines stand out more clearly. Her favourite was the picture that showed the relative sizes of the planets. Jupiter was huge. Mercury was tiny. And good old Earth – just right. Of course also, just the right distance from the sun to be able to maintain life.

Life? Could there be life on other planets? Mercury and Venus would be too hot. Surely. Jupiter and Mars too cold? But didn't that depend on what sort of life? Life didn't need to be exactly like the life that she knew on earth, did it? Would we ever learn to travel through space? That would be something.

She started rereading the chapter about how the planets circled the sun and how the moons of those planets that had them circled the planets.

We're just moving all of the time.

It was amazing. Twenty-four hours to turn around on our axis. 365 days to circle the sun. Well, strictly speaking, 365.25. Day and night. Winter and summer. Why twenty-four? Why sixty minutes to an hour? Why sixty seconds to a minute?

The front door opened and she heard footsteps in the hallway.

"I'm back," she heard Leo call.

She heard Mutti open the drawing-room door. "Good. We can serve up lunch now."

It was always the same. The whole household ran according to the needs of the menfolk. She wished meal times would depend on her activities sometimes.

There was a knock on the door.

"Lunch will be ready in five minutes. Do make yourself presentable, Käthe."

What for? My two brothers, my mother and a servant? Oh, it was all so dull, trying to be a respectable young lady. She almost wished she was back at school.

She stood up and looked in the mirror. The grey flannel dress suited her mood. That would do wouldn't it? Surely. She pinned a stray hair into place and sighed. She made her way into the hall. Leo's briefcase was standing open under the table. It was just too tempting. She bent down and looked through the papers. Goodness,

21

this was exciting stuff. Some of it though seemed really complicated. But what was this? A brochure about various courses? She took it out, stood up and started reading through it.

The door to the dining room started opening.

Käthe hastily stuffed the brochure under her bodice. It was a good job she was wearing a two-piece today.

"Come on, Käthe. We're all waiting." Mutti was frowning.

Lunch was as boring as ever. Leo and Rudi argued. Mutti insisted on knowing exactly what Leo had been doing and what he intended to do that afternoon. She checked up on Rudi's private study. All she said to Käthe was. "It's a glorious day today. You should go out for a walk. You're looking very peaky." That at least gave her an idea.

She waited for a few seconds after Leo had left and then pulled on her hat and coat. When she stepped out onto the street she could still see him. She didn't really need to follow him to the university; she actually knew the way. She just wanted to see what life was really like for him.

She kept her distance. He really mustn't see her.

As they got nearer to the university she noticed him stopping to speak to young men she presumed were other students. Once he stopped to talk to an older man. One of his professors, she supposed. He seemed so engrossed and animated. It must all be so interesting. Why couldn't she do this?

Finally he went into one of the buildings. Other students flocked in, all of them carrying briefcases or satchels. They were all men, of course, though at least none of them stared at her. It was almost as if she wasn't there. Soon, they had all gone into one of the classrooms. It was almost totally silent on the corridors. Such a contrast to the street outside. A smartly-dressed gentleman with a bushy beard swept past her, nodding curtly at her as he went into the room her brother had entered a few moments before.

It was odd. They could see her and yet they weren't treating her as if she was unusual, even though she didn't belong. *That had to be good, didn't it?*

"Can I help you?" said a voice suddenly.

Käthe turned to see another young man. He held a clipboard and appeared to be counting something.

"I was wondering where I could find out about courses."

The young man put his clipboard down on a nearby table. He folded his arms across his chest. "Now that would depend on what sort of course you were interested in."

"Physics," said Käthe. She was sure, wasn't she?

"Upstairs. The second door on the left. I'm going that way in a few minutes. When I've finished here. I can show you the way." He took up his clipboard again.

I'm sure I could find it on my own. It seemed a bit impolite, though, to say so. Anyway she might be able to find out something if she chatted to this man for a while. However, he didn't say a word as he counted all of the light bulbs in the corridor.

He wrote something down on his clipboard and sighed. "See, we have to account for everything." He turned and looked at Käthe. "Come on then. Let's go and look. There is another young lady, you know. So, if you do come here to study you'll have some company. I expect she'll be glad to have another young woman around as well."

"There's something I'd like to talk to you about," said Käthe as Imelda cleared the dessert dishes from the table that evening.

"Oh?" said Leo.

Yes, I do have something to say. Of course all of the conversation over dinner had been about her brothers' plans. And just little bit about what was going on at Vati's factory.

She took deep breath. "I want to go to university."

Mutti and Vati exchanged a glance. Leo looked at Rudi and shrugged.

Mutti leant forward and put her hand on Käthe's. "Why do you want to do that?"

Leo shook his head and raised his eyes at Rudi.

Vati grinned.

Chapter 3: persuasion

"You're mad. It's not just fun and games, you know. It's hard work."

Hard work would be better than this boredom. In a few minutes he would finish breakfast and leave for an exciting day of physics and engineering or whatever it was that he was studying. What would she do? Twiddle her thumbs and try to be a young lady.

"I'm not scared of hard work." She'd helped set up the laboratory in the cellar hadn't she? She'd taught herself physics as well. And she'd sat up night after night with Rudi when he'd been little and ill. No, she wasn't afraid of hard work.

"Anyway, it's not the right atmosphere for a woman."

What on earth did he mean? "How come?"

"We're all men, aren't we? Sometimes, some of the things we talk about…"

"And what about that other girl?" Now she'd got him.

"How do you know about her?"

"Ah!" She tapped the side of her nose. "She gets on all right, doesn't she?"

Leo shrugged. "She's a bit special." He blushed.

So, she was special, was she? "Really?"

Leo took out his pocket watch. "Look, I'd better get going."

Hmm.

He made his way out of the room.

What now?

She didn't have to wait long. As soon as Leo had left, in came Rudi. He was up so late today. Was he ill again? She hoped not. Maybe he'd just got too used to taking it easy.

He lifted the lid off one of the dishes. He pulled a face. "Yoghurt and muesli. Again." He sighed and took a piece of the now cold toast. "Is there any coffee?"

"I expect that's cold as well."

"I'll ring for Imelda then."

"Don't be so idle."

He stared at her, his mouth open.

She leapt to her feet. "Oh, forget it. I'll go."

Imelda wasn't in the kitchen when she got there. It didn't take her long to make the coffee. The water boiled in no time and there was a satisfying smell as the grounds infused. At least she knew how to make coffee. Would either of her two brothers? Would Mutti and Vati? Would this skill come in useful one day?

She made her way back to the dining room with the pot of hot coffee. Rudi was sitting at the table, grinning at her.

"Good on you, sis. That's what I like to see."

What did he like seeing? Her working? "You know, one day you'll have to do something for yourself. That will come as a shock."

Rudi licked the butter off his fingers. "I do plenty for myself, thank you very much. You should try it. It's amazing what you can find out just by reading books."

Käthe suddenly felt bad. Perhaps Rudi too would have preferred to attend the university just like Leo did. He couldn't though, because of his poor chest. He just shouldn't mix with too many people. They all dreaded him catching TB. It must have been just as frustrating for him as it was for her.

"Here you go." She poured the coffee into Rudi's cup.

"Ta, sis." He grinned at her.

Perhaps she would just carry on teaching herself. It might be the only way. She stacked up the dishes from the sideboard on to the waiting tray. She would check with Imelda if she could get on with the baking powder experiment.

The maid was in the kitchen when she got there. Her sleeves were rolled up and she was up to her elbows in soapy water. "I don't know what Master Leo does with his food. It just clings to the plate when he's been at it."

Käthe wasn't sure either. "It's not a pretty sight, when he eats." He always shovelled his food in so quickly you would think the world was about to end.

"Always so much work with you young people." Imelda looked really cross. A stray hair was hanging across her face. She pushed it aside and tutted. Not the moment, then to ask whether she could carry out the baking powder experiment. That was a shame. She wouldn't be in Imelda's way but she would have to get her permission to help herself to a little baking powder. That wouldn't be easy with her in the mood she was in now. She daren't just take it, though. Imelda counted everything.

"We try to be good," said Käthe.

Imelda sighed and stopped scrubbing. "You probably do. But there's still a lot of work to do."

Was she softening? Might this be the moment?

Too late. The door opened and in came Mutti. "In the kitchen again, Käthe?"

"I've got nothing else to do."

"Well, we'd better fix that. Go and get your hat and coat. We're going out."

Ugh. It was probably going to be some boring coffee morning with some of Mutti's stuffy friends. She suddenly thought of the elegant buildings she'd visited the day before. How exciting it had been. But what would she face now?

Berlin 1913

Chapter 4: a funny little man

The café was crowded. All of the customers were just like her and her mother: although not all that rich, they were able to afford nice clothes and had enough time to sit drinking expensive coffee all morning. But it was so boring. Oh so boring.

"Why have we come here?" Käthe jogged her mother's arm.

"Because it's what we do," said Mutti. "Now, pay attention and join in the conversation when the others arrive."

"Who's coming?"

"The usual crowd."

Käthe sighed. No one under the age of thirty-five, then. "Can't I go out for a walk instead?"

Her mother frowned. Then she shook her head. "I suppose it won't hurt. Make sure you're back here for 11.30 though. And try and be dignified. Remember, some time you are going to have to take your place in society and behave like a well-brought-up young woman."

Käthe rescued her coat from the stand and made her way out into the busy street. This was better. The air was fresh and the temperature mild. The sun was shining. Berlin was alive. Watching busy people going about their business was so much more interesting than listening to her mother's friends and their dull talk.

She found herself drifting towards the university again. Young men carrying leather briefcases walked and cycled past her. Many of them seemed to be daydreaming. Some were even frowning in concentration. It must all be so interesting, what they were learning. Why couldn't she?

A crowd was gathering outside one of the impressive buildings. She noticed there were several ladies like her mother and young women like herself amongst them. A young man thrust a leaflet into her hand.

"Talk on the work of Professor Einstein, soon to become a member of the faculty," she read.

There was a photo of the professor on the flyer. Gosh, what a funny little man. He had wild eyes and hair that looked as if it hadn't seen a comb in months.

"Who is this Professor Einstein?" she asked.

"Why don't you come in and listen to the talk? It's free."

Käthe glanced at the other people entering the hall. Yes, lots of students, obviously but also plenty of people who looked as if they'd understand an awful lot less than she did about science.

Why not? If she was late for Mutti, Mutti would just have to wait. She went in.

Käthe looked round at the other people in the hall. They were mainly men and just like the ones she'd seen the day before. So, most of the women had chickened out, had they? But there were some women and in fact she recognised some of her mother's friends. Ha! They'd be missed too at the coffee morning.

Everyone was chattering and there seemed to be a good deal of excitement.

"I hope we'll be able to understand what they talk about," she heard one woman say.

"I've heard that Professor Einstein himself is very down to earth. He explains things so that ordinary people can understand them. I hope these people do," her companion replied.

"I'm not quite sure I agree with his ideas, but the academy seems to approve," a man said.

Well this might be the ultimate test. If she could understand this scientific talk as well as the students in this hall, then she would have a really solid argument to support her idea of studying at the university.

A man walked on to the platform and the chattering stopped. Käthe felt a tingle of excitement creep up her spine.

"Good morning, ladies and gentlemen." He also looked like a professor. He had that slightly distracted gaze that suggested his mind was actually elsewhere. "It is my great pleasure to introduce you to the work of Professor Einstein who will be joining us shortly at the institution."

Käthe listened fascinated as the man told them all about Einstein's work. An hour and a half went by in what seemed like a few minutes. This was all so exciting. The universe isn't quite what we might expect. It's not quite as we know it. There were so many new possibilities. This settled it. She had to go and study at the university. She just had to persuade them.

"Goodness," she said to no one in particular. "Nothing is quite what it seems."

"It isn't is it?"

Käthe jumped.

"I'm sorry. Did I startle you?"

She turned to look at the speaker. He must be about the same age as her brother. He didn't look like a student, though. He was dressed a little more smartly but he didn't look rich either. He might be an office worker or something. He smiled pleasantly.

"I was just thinking out loud," said Käthe. "I wasn't really expecting anyone to listen."

"You are right though. What this new professor suggests will turn the world on to its head."

"It's fascinating, isn't it?"

"It is." The young man sighed. "I wish I could study it but alas I have to work for my living."

"And I'm not allowed to, because I'm girl."

"That shouldn't stop you." He took out his pocket watch. "But I must go."

"What *is* the time?"

"Quarter past twelve."

No. Mutti would be long gone. "She'll kill me," Käthe muttered.

"I doubt that very much."

Well, he was right. Mutti wouldn't kill her – just go on and on about her being irresponsible. Anyway, she could do what she always did. Walk round to Vati's factory and either spend the afternoon with him or if he was too busy he'd send her home in a carriage.

"Where do you have to get to?" Perhaps he worked somewhere near her father's firm.

"I work at Freidrichbaumachinentechnik, Thomas Strasse."

Unbelievable. "You must know my father. Ernst Lehrs."

"You're Ernst Lehrs's daughter? Goodness me. I work directly for him. I'm a clerk in his office."

"Never!"

"Look, I'd better get going now."

"He won't curse, will he?"

"Not at all. It's just that he did give me half the morning off to come here and there's a stack of work to do."

"I'm coming with you."

Chapter 5: at the factory

It was a brisk twenty-minute walk from the university to the factory in Thomas Street. They could have caught a tram but it would have meant changing twice and at lunch time they went quite slowly as everyone was going out to eat.

They found plenty to talk about. Christian Bauer came from a poorer family but had done so well at school that he been taken on by Freidrichbaumachinentechnik as a filing clerk and had made his way up quickly to become an administrator in her father's office. Science was his hobby. There was plenty to talk about there.

"You walk very quickly for a girl," he said. He had suggested they take a cab but she didn't like to ask him to pay for one. She didn't have enough cash and anyway he might not have liked a woman paying.

"I always wear sensible boots, that's why," she replied. That was something else that Mutti nagged her about constantly. She absolutely refused to totter about on little heels.

"But you look like an oaf, not a young lady in those boots," her mother said.

Christian nodded. "Very sensible. The markings of a true scientist. You really should go for it."

Christian was such a nice young man. He would make a great brother. Not like the pair of buffoons who claimed that title at the moment.

In no time they were walking into her father's suite of offices.

"Goodness, my favourite daughter and my favourite clerk called Christian arrive at once," said Vati. "How do you know each other?"

Käthe explained and Vati nodded.

Christian hung up his coat and disappeared into the side office.

Vati sighed. "What is it this time, Käthe? What have you been up to now?"

"Mutti's usual boring Kaffeeklatsch. It's all so dismal, Vati."

"Yes but these things are important. You have to learn to behave like a young lady."

32

Käthe stamped her foot. "I really think there is more to life than that. I want to be a scientist. I want to go to the university like Leo does."

"Couldn't you be content with studying on your own like Rudi?"

Käthe shrugged. "I want to do the experiments. I want to talk to the other scientists." She just had to tell him about the talk as well. "Vati, it was fascinating. This Albert Einstein... he has so many new ideas and he'll be part of the university. Please let me go, Vati."

"I don't know, Käthe. We'll need to discuss it. There's no need for you to have a career. We have enough money and sooner or later some suitable young man will want to marry you."

"Ugh! I can't think of anything worse."

Vati stroked her hair. "You'll probably think differently when you meet him. Anyway, what are we going to do with you until then?"

"Can I stay here for the afternoon? Is there anything I can help you with?"

Vati shook his head. Then he threw his hands up into the air. "I suppose you can look through the accounts again."

"Oh yes please." She's spent several hours doing that a few weeks ago. It had been fascinating. She'd recognised some patterns and had been able to give Vati some ideas about when to promote some of his stock.

"All right then. I'll get a message to your mother. And then I'll set you up with some of the paperwork."

One of her father's other clerks set out a pile of ledgers on a table and soon she was engrossed in looking at all of the figures. She spotted a few errors which she pointed out to her father.

"It's a good job you saw that," he said. "Or we might have had problems later."

"You should employ me to check you accounts," she said.

"You'd get bored with it all after a while."

"Not as bored as when I had to keep on going to those coffee parties."

Her father had to talk to some important clients later that afternoon so she was left on her own for a while. She found it fascinating, though. She could see that the firm was doing well. She was beginning to get an idea of what caused the peaks in their success. She couldn't wait to tell her father. She spotted a few more mistakes though and she looked forward less to mentioning those. When the door opened and he burst back into the room she didn't get a chance though.

"Well that was most satisfactory," he said. "We must celebrate. We have just secured a gigantic order. We'll need to take on more staff." He put his hand on Käthe's shoulder. "You do realise, don't you, that we've had no lunch. I think we should make do with cake, don't you?"

She wanted to tell him what else she'd found in the figures but it was clear he wasn't going to listen to anything she had to say. He opened the small cash box that stood on his desk and took out a few notes.

"Go and ask everyone which cake they would like. I'll get Frau Drescher to make some coffee. Then go to the Konditorei at the end of the street and buy cakes for everyone. Don't try to carry them back, mind. Get them to send a boy."

Well nobody could say her father wasn't generous. That was for sure.

Christian agreed. "He's really kind, your Vati. Apfelkuchen for me please. And I've had an idea."

"Oh?"

"You should write a paper and send it to the university. Show them what you're made of. If they like it, you can ask if they'll let you study there. If they say yes, you can make your case better to your parents."

"What an earth can I write about?"

"One of your experiments? Or an essay about the implications of Professor Einstein's ideas?"

She couldn't think what to say.

"Well, don't you think that would be a good idea?"

Of course it would. "Yes. Yes, it's a great idea."

She hardly noticed the walk to the cake shop and she certainly didn't remember ordering the cakes. She did notice, though, that there was a bit of confusion as there were too many slices of Beinenstich and not enough Käsekuchen and in fact there were almost twice as many cakes as people. No one complained however. She decided, though, it might be an idea not to mention the mistakes on the ledgers. She would just correct them quietly.

Chapter 6: a letter to the university

At last she was able to get into the kitchen and get hold of the baking powder. She'd not entirely been able to keep her plans from Imelda, though.

"Does it absolutely have to be baking powder?" the maid had asked. "Won't cornflour or plain ordinary flour do? The quantities you're talking about for baking powder will be so expensive."

"I'm afraid it really must be baking powder," Käthe answered. "It's so much lighter. The heavier flour will skew the results. I promise I won't use the whole tin."

Imelda huffed and sighed. "It's a good job money's no object, then." She tutted as Käthe made her way out of the kitchen.

Leo was out so Käthe could use his basement laboratory undisturbed.

She poured enough baking powder to fill the lid of the coffee jar. It would look like the surface of the moon by the time she'd finished. Not that she was all that sure exactly what the surface of the moon would look like. She could only go on the artists' impressions she'd seen in books.

This was all about simulating the effect of a meteor strike. The idea was to drop a marble from various heights and measure the size of the crater it made each time.

She used Leo's long ruler. She smiled to herself as she thought how cross he would be if he knew.

Soon, though, she didn't have time to think about Leo. She was so absorbed in what she was doing. She kept a graph that related the height from which she dropped the marble to the size of the crater. It should now be possible to predict what size crater would be formed according to the length of the drop. She made a few predictions. Then she verified them by repeating the experiment.

It worked. It really worked.

This could be so useful for something. She was pleased. It was all about kinetic energy. She was mapping this. She really understood it. Why shouldn't she go to university?

Hmm. The baking powder was really getting mucky now and it was beginning to look more like a bomb site than the surface of the moon. Time to pack up.

She tidied away the items she'd borrowed from Leo's supply, gathered up her papers, put the spoiled baking powder into a paper bag and went back to the flat. She had just returned what was left to the kitchen and thrown the spoiled stuff away when the front door opened.

In came Leo. "You're looking pleased with yourself," he said.

"I am. I've just been plotting the kinetic energy of a marble dropped into a tray of baking powder. It really worked. After taking a few measurements, I could work out the rest. Either way. I managed to establish how big the craters would be if I dropped the marble from a certain height. And how high up I needed to let it go to make the crater a particular size. I checked a few of them. They were spot on."

The corner of Leo's mouth twitched. "That's such basic stuff, Käthe. We don't even do things like that anymore at the university."

"Oh." After all that effort.

"I can't think why a girl would find that so interesting. Haven't you got some sewing to do or something? Shouldn't you be looking for a husband?"

Käthe felt as if her head was about to explode. How dare he talk to her like that.

"I'm not at all interested in that sort of thing. I want to know how the world works."

Leo shrugged. "I suppose that's one thing you've got right. It's quite boring at times. It's not always exciting."

Oh, what was he talking about? Anything was better than the monotony of staying at home all of the time. Rudi did okay. He was positively encouraged, though, to keep on studying. She was criticised when she tried to do it. No, she was determined to get into that university. "I was going to send the write-up of the experiment to your faculty. See if they'd let me become a student." She felt her cheeks go bright red.

37

Leo chuckled. "You can't be serious. This is what a child might do. You'd have to come up with something better than that."

"Well, what do you suggest?"

Leo shrugged. "Oh, maybe an essay about some of the new ideas."

"They wouldn't prefer to see that I can write up an experiment?"

"Well, even if that was good it wouldn't be enough to get you on to a proper course."

"What do you mean?"

"You just haven't got the qualifications. And Vati would have to pay and I'm not sure he'd be willing to."

Well, she'd see about that. If she could get them to offer her a place she was sure she could get Vati to pay.

Leo sighed. "There is one thing you could do, I suppose."

"Oh?"

"You could register as a guest reader."

"What's that?"

"You just attend the lectures and seminars you fancy. You can even go to some of the practicals. Of course you have to get permission first for all of it. You just pay an appropriate amount. You don't have to take any exams. Ideal, I would have thought, for you."

That would be something at least. She was still a bit puzzled, really, about why a woman shouldn't join the university properly and go and have a career as a scientist. At least, though, if she could get the university to allow her to do what Leo had described and if Vati would pay… "So you think an essay might be better?"

"Yes. You went to that talk about Einstein, didn't you? Why not write about some of his ideas?" He fumbled in his briefcase and brought out a pile of papers. "Here, borrow my notes as well."

"Thank you." My, things were looking up.

Leo nodded and made a little movement with his feet that looked a bit as if he was clicking his heels. Then he scooted off to his own room.

Back in her room, Käthe looked at her notes again. She was really pleased with them. They were neat and tidy. The tables were

38

clear and her results were all that she could have wished for. But perhaps Leo was right. Perhaps she should show that she understood some of the new ideas.

The talk about Professor Einstein had been fascinating but she hadn't taken any notes. She hadn't really known what was going to happen. She could remember a lot of it. Maybe Leo's notes would help. She started reading them. It was quite difficult to decipher his handwriting but some of it gradually made sense.

Yes, she remembered it now. This theory of relativity. The ball game on the train. If you threw a ball and it travelled at fifteen kilometres an hour and you were travelling on a train that was going at forty kilometres an hour, the ball was actually travelling at fifty-five kilometres an hour. The same thing with a fly in a carriage. Time was relative. Never mind the difference between observed and elapsed time. Goodness, didn't she know about that? Observed time at Mutti's coffee mornings dragged and dragged and dragged.

Everything was relative, then. Nothing was what it seemed. Except the speed of light. That was the one constant. Ah! So what of all of these careful measurements? Measurements are only ever approximate. We can never be totally accurate. So her experiment wasn't valid, then? Could any experiment ever be? Maybe the one that measured the speed of the ball on the train… or maybe not.

It was all so interesting. Yes, yes, yes. She knew exactly what she could write.

She sat down at her desk, took up her notebook and made a plan. Twelve points. She would make twelve points and write a paragraph about each.

She filled her best fountain pen, took out her pack of good quality writing paper and began.

The time elapsed and wasn't observed. In fact, she was amazed to see that by the time she had finished almost three hours had gone by. Her wrist ached. A hard lump had formed on her middle finger and her fingers were covered in ink.

She sat back and read it through again. Yes, that would do. That would do very well indeed.

There was a tap at the door. "Dinner, Käthe. Have you changed?"

Oh, back to the middle-class conventions. "No, just coming." As she slipped off her day dress and walked over towards the wardrobe to find something a little smarter or at least clean, she caught sight of her experiment notes. Such a waste. Wouldn't they be impressed with her attention to detail? Shouldn't she send that after all?

She was too excited to eat properly. Her mother and her two brothers didn't seem to notice. It was the usual dinner-time ritual. Leo and Rudi dominated the conversation. Vati made his usual jokes and Mutti bubbled away at her two precious boys.

Vati was the only one who took any notice of her. "Käthe, you're very quiet. You've hardly touched your food. Is something the matter?"

"I'm trying to make a decision."

"Oh? Is it anything we can help with?"

The others were now staring at her. "I've got two ideas. One of them is very practical and down to earth. The other is exciting and a little fantastical."

Leo cleared his throat and rolled his eyes at Rudi. Rudi at least had the grace to ignore his older brother.

"Hmm." Vati put his hand in front of his mouth and frowned slightly. "You know, sometimes people come to me with fantastic ideas. Yet at times they seem so far-fetched I ask them to go away and write out a proper business case for them. Occasionally they manage it. At other times they don't. I tend to take on the ones that do. In other words, those people who can prove that their ideas can work and know how to put them into practice. Perhaps you should suggest both to whoever is interested."

"Perhaps I should."

Leo shook his head and raised his eyebrows. Käthe glared at him. Her appetite suddenly came back and she tucked into her roast beef.

The sun was shining as Käthe walked towards the post office the next morning. It felt almost as if the world was telling her this was a good idea.

She'd thought about taking her package directly to the university but Vati had advised against it. "It's better to post whatever it is. The people in the office are trained to make sure everything gets to precisely the right person."

She'd been very careful not to tell him exactly what was in the package and where she was sending it. She was relieved that he'd seemed equally careful not to ask her too many questions. She was thankful for that.

It had taken her another two hours to write up her experiment. She'd also added a suggestion for how to conduct an experiment to show relativity in time to her essay about Einstein's theory. She'd been so eager to get on with it all that she hadn't bothered changing into something more suitable and had got ink all over her smart dress. There would be comments made about that sooner or later. Never mind, this was what was important now.

This was it. The clerk in the post office carefully weighed the package. He told her the price and she handed over some coins. He smiled at her. "Thank you, Fräulein. It will be with them later today or first thing tomorrow morning. Good day to you."

She'd done it. Now all she had to do was wait. The worst they could do was say no.

She stepped back out into the bright sunshine. There now. She was a very modern woman. She had just taken her first step towards freedom.

Berlin 1914

Chapter 7: war

Käthe was in her room looking again at the book about the planets, trying to take her mind off waiting for a reply to her letter. It had only been a few days. She must be patient. It seemed to be taking forever. If she were truthful, though, even Mutti's coffee parties were a bit of an distraction.

She was surprised then to hear the front door go and Vati calling out in the hallway. He was back already? It was only just after four, surely. He was already talking animatedly to Mutti. Was there something wrong? She hoped nothing bad had happened at the factory. She opened her door.

"Käthe, you're here," said Vati. "Come into the drawing room. There's something I need to tell you. Is Leo home yet?"

On cue the front door opened. Käthe noticed he looked a little pale. And he was home early, too. Rudi then also appeared in the hallway.

"Good," said Vati. "We're all here now. Come along. This is really important."

Seconds later they were all sitting down in the drawing room. Mutti's face looked pinched. Did she know something already? Or was she just worried about what Vati might be about to tell her? Leo's eyes were gleaming. He looked almost excited about something. Did he already know what Vati was going to tell them? Rudi just looked surprised. He always was the calmest.

"I'm afraid," said Vati, "that we are at war with England. They have just declared war on us."

"Dear gods," said Mutti and put her hand up in front of her mouth.

Leo nodded. So he had known.

Rudi whistled.

"Why?" asked Käthe. "What have we done?"

"Well you know we've been trying protect ourselves from the Russians for some time."

"Have we?"

Leo tutted. "Don't you ever read the newspapers?"

"No actually. Why would I?"

Leo raised his eyebrows and shook his head.

"There's no need for her to," said Mutti. "Vati tells us all the important news."

He hadn't said anything about this though had he? So this hadn't seemed so important. Why was it suddenly so important?

Rudi nodded. "All because of the assassination of Archduke Franz Ferdinand of Austria. He was heir to the throne of Austria-Hungary. That happened back in June, didn't it Vati?" So Rudi had been keeping up with the news.

Vati nodded.

She still didn't understand how this was leading to a war, though. It didn't make sense. "But why is England wanting to go to war with us? And why are the Russians threatening us as well?"

"Because the assassin was Yugoslavian and the Russians are protecting them. We gave an ultimatum to their king."

"Oh." Käthe was pleased to see that Mutti was looking just as puzzled as she felt.

Vati sighed. "We have now marched into neutral Belgium and Luxemburg and we're moving towards France, so England has jumped in to support them."

"So, what does it mean, Ernst?" Mutti's hands were clenched tightly. She must be really scared. "Will there be problems at the factory?"

"Not initially, I don't think." Vati was still standing.

He was doing that to look confident, wasn't he?

"I think everybody is hoping that this will all be over quickly and that we can come to some sort of amicable agreement soon." He'd turned away from them. His hands were resting on the mantelpiece and he was staring at the fire. They couldn't see his eyes.

Then he turned back to them. "Maybe some of our young men will have to go and fight?"

"No!" Mutti looked as if she was about to cry.

"They won't have Rudi. But Leo might have to go."

A smile was playing around at the corners of Leo's mouth. He wanted to do it. He wanted to go and fight.

"Don't worry too much," said Vati. He put an arm around Mutti's shoulders. "Everyone thinks it will be resolved quite quickly. I just came home early to tell you because I didn't want you hearing it from someone else."

"Vati, will you bring the newspaper home so that I can start reading it?" asked Käthe.

Vati chuckled. "I don't see why not but I don't really recommend it."

Leo laughed as well. "Trying to get educated are we?"

Rudi began to giggle.

"Don't be so mean," said Käthe.

"Children!" Vati warned. Then he turned to Mutti. "Let's leave these young people to their fights while we change for dinner. Let me try and put your mind at rest."

Mutti and Vati made their way out of the room.

Rudi pulled a face. "Do we need to get changed as well?"

"No," said Leo. "That was just an excuse to get away from us."

Rudi snorted like a horse. "It's all right for you," he said to Leo. "You'll be able to go and fight. They'll all think I'm a coward."

"Oh, it's all right, is it? I can go and get myself killed." Leo's eyes were flashing angrily.

She hated it when they quarrelled. "Stop it, you two. It's supposed to be a war out there not in here."

Both of her brothers turned and looked at her. "It's all right for you. You're a girl," they both said at once.

"You really think that? You think we women like it that we're not allowed to do our bit? And what do you think it would be like for me and Mutti, waiting at home, not knowing what was going on?"

"Well Vati won't have to fight. He's too old and too disabled."

"No, but no doubt he'll be doing something for a war effort. And what will he do at the factory if he loses all of his workers?"

Leo smirked. "I don't suppose you'd be able to take over."

"Why shouldn't I? Why shouldn't I be able to do what men do? I bet I could even hold a gun better than you can."

Both of her brothers burst out laughing.

"Oh you're impossible, the pair of you. I'm going to go and help Imelda."

"Come on, sis, we were only teasing." Rudi was grinning at her and she almost felt like forgiving him but then he started tittering again. Leo had by now lost all control.

"Agh! Men!" She ran out of the drawing room and slammed the door.

Imelda looked surprised when she walked into the kitchen.

"Those two are driving me mad," Käthe said to the round-eyed maid.

"Teasing you again, are they?"

Käthe nodded.

"It's only because they're nervous. Worried they're going to have to go and fight."

"Oh, so you know about the war?"

"Yes, I most certainly do." Imelda stopped her chopping and looked straight into Käthe's eyes. "It's always the same. Big men in high places make stupid decisions and then ordinary young men have to go and get themselves killed."

"Vati said it probably won't last long."

"Hmm. I hope he's right but I doubt that he is." Imelda banged the saucepan down on the table. "Now, Fräulein Käthe, if you want to make yourself useful, go and lay the table."

It was peaceful in the dining room. It was oddly soothing setting out the cutlery and napkins neatly. She could still hear Rudi and Leo talking in the room next door but she was glad that she couldn't make out what they were saying.

Chapter 8: going to be a soldier, going to be a student

It was a waiting game now. Käthe knew that. It wasn't helped by this dratted war. She couldn't get her head round it. The Archduke and his wife and been assassinated. Why did that mean they were at war? Not that there was much happening just yet. Well, there was a bit. The students and the staff at the university were looking worried all of the time. Oh yes, she made a point of walking past the buildings most days. Would all those men be asked to go and fight?

Rudi caught her standing by the mailbox. "What are you waiting for? You won't get call-up papers, you know. Not even Leo will. They're not actually calling people up yet."

She was hovering there just as she did every day. She liked to check the post before the others saw it. She didn't want them knowing her business.

"Does Mutti know you're riding that bike?" She'd got to have something to hold over him – just in case.

"No, and you're not to tell her."

Käthe shrugged. "All right." Yes, Mutti was a bit of a pain the way she fussed over Rudi and his poor chest. It struck her that he seemed to do pretty much anything he wanted to and that was more or less the same as all of the other young men did. She didn't really care. But she'd keep his secret just in case she needed him to keep one of hers. "So what's happening with this war, then?"

"Not a lot as far as I can tell."

The postman arrived at the moment. "Lehrs?" he asked.

Käthe nodded.

He handed her a large envelope. "One for you, young lady, I think."

Her heart skipped a beat as she saw the postmark. It was from the university.

Rudi had seen it too. His eyes grew round. "Why are you getting post from the university?"

She didn't get time to answer him, which was just as well because she didn't know what to say. Leo arrived. "Hey, you two. I've got news. Come on up straight away and I can tell you both at the same time as I tell Mutti and Vati."

She exchanged a glance with Rudi, then they both followed Leo up the stairs. Rudi shrugged and shook his head.

He made his way into the drawing room. Rudi and Käthe followed. Mutti and Vati were sitting talking quietly.

"Mutti, Vati," Leo bowed slightly and softly pushed his heels together. "I need to talk to you. Quite formally."

"I think I know what's coming," Käthe heard Mutti whisper. Rudi didn't seem to hear her. "Very well," she said more loudly. "Rudi, Käthe, you'd better go to your rooms. We'll let you know if Leo has anything important to say."

"Oh, but I thought…" Leo looked over towards them.

"If it's what I think, it's better that you discuss it with Vati and me first." She nodded towards the door.

"I wonder what that's all about," said Rudi.

"I've a pretty good idea." Oh, yes. If it was what she thought it was, might there be a chance that she could go to the university in Leo's place? She was still clutching the letter. She didn't want to open it yet. It might be disappointing. She would wait.

Rudi went towards his room.

"No, wait."

She made her way to the kitchen and fetched two tumblers.

"Here." She handed one to Rudi.

"What am I supposed to do with this?"

"And I'm supposed to be the girl who's too stupid to be able to do any science? Put it to the wall and use it to help you listen, silly."

Rudi frowned.

"Go on."

They both put their glasses to the wall. Yes, it worked. They could hear the others' voices clearly.

"Well," said Vati gently. "What did you want to tell us?"

"I've decided to volunteer. I want to go to the front."

There was a long silence. Käthe couldn't imagine what was

happening. Observed time again. Leo eventually spoke: "Mutti, don't look so concerned. Most of my friends have already gone to fight."

"And that's a reason, is it? You do what your friends do? If they jumped off a cliff you'd follow them, would you?"

"Mutti, I'd be doing it for Germany."

"Can't you wait a while? Let the professional soldiers do most of the work first?"

"If I wait until then it may be more dangerous. The more people we have out there the better. Then this can all be over sooner rather than later."

There was another pause.

"Don't go. Just don't go," she heard Mutti whisper.

"I have to, Mutti."

There was another long pause then Mutti spoke again. "I understand. I do understand." Her voice was hoarse.

"It is good of you and brave. I wish I could do my bit." Vati sounded really serious.

"Ernst, you will. Your work at the factory. They'll need engineers. Surely." Mutti sounded almost cross.

"Yes, but it won't be the same as going to the front."

"I will be going for everyone. My uncles can't go. Neither can Vati. And Rudi probably won't be able to go later. I'm young and I'm strong. Please give me your blessing."

"He is so right, Clara. He really is."

No one spoke for the next few minutes. Then they heard the sound of someone slapping someone else's back.

"Take care, my son. I'm proud of you," said Vati.

"Will you give me your blessing, Mutti?"

Mutti didn't say anything.

She must have nodded, though because then they heard Leo say, "Thank you."

Käthe heard a soft clicking of heels and Leo came rushing out of the room. She and Rudi jumped. Leo glared at them but didn't stop to speak. Both of them tried to look as if they were making their way back to the kitchen.

Käthe was still clutching her letter when she arrived back at her room. It was a bit crumpled now. She took a big breath and opened it.

20 September 1914

Dear Fräulein Lehrs,

Thank you for your letter and your very interesting essay. Thank you also for the detailed explanation of a well-conducted experiment.

Unfortunately this isn't enough for us to offer you a place on one of our courses. It is highly likely in any case that as you are a woman a full-time degree course may not be in your best interest.

However we would be delighted to welcome you as a guest reader to any of the classes listed here. If you are interested in attending any of the practical sessions, please write to the tutor concerned.

Please find enclosed a copy of our tariffs.

We look forward to hearing from you in due course.

Yours faithfully,

Professor H Humboldt

Käthe studied the price list and the list of classes. Goodness, they were all so interesting but they weren't cheap. She wanted to do this thing definitely. It was just a matter of persuading Mutti and Vati. Of course, Leo had just completely upstaged her. How was she going to raise this?

"So what happens next, then?" asked Mutti. "How long before you're in uniform?" She poured Leo another coffee.

"I'm not sure exactly. Anyway, the first thing I'll do is go and talk to my academic tutor at the university."

"That would be polite." Vati nodded.

Could this be her moment? "Actually, talking of the university..."

"They're sort of expecting it really."

Oh. So they were ignoring her. Why did Leo always have to talk over her?

Vati nodded again. "I'd heard as much. I'm really rather dreading losing some of my good men. Young Christian was saying he wanted to volunteer."

Christian was going to be a soldier as well? This was madness. But with so many men going away...

"At least we don't have to worry about Rudi." Mutti smiled.

"Mmm." Rudi scowled. "Oh, I'll be doing war work one way or another. Don't you worry."

"What is it, Käthe?" Vati was actually looking at her. "There seems to be something on your mind."

Everyone was now staring at her. *Deep breath. Deep breath.* "I've been offered a place at the university."

Leo scowled. Mutti and Rudi frowned. Vati grinned.

"Well, not a proper place, really. As a guest reader."

Leo smirked. "It means she won't get a degree. They don't really trust her."

Why did he always have to be so mean? "It's not that. They liked my experiment notes and my essay."

"You actually sent them?" Leo's eyes grew wide.

"Of course I did. You know me. I always do what I say I'm going to do. No, they were more bothered about me being a woman. They don't think it's all that suitable for a woman to get a degree in science."

"Hmm. Cheek." Mutti was frowning now.

Käthe was surprised. Was Mutti actually feeling as indignant as she did? Käthe had always thought she was very old-fashioned. That was what all her coffee mornings suggested.

"Doesn't it just mean you can actually go to pretty well all of the classes you want to?" Vati was looking at her intently now.

Käthe nodded. "They charge, of course."

"Do you have a list of the prices?"

"It's in my room. Shall I fetch it?"

"Perhaps you, Mutti and I can study it this evening." Vati was grinning again.

Leo shook his head and raised his eyebrows. He got up from the table. "I'd better get on."

Rudi threw back his head and roared with laughter. "My big sister, going to be a scientist."

She glared at him.

"Much better than all of those coffee mornings," said Mutti.

Had she heard right? Again? Her mother actually approved?

"This evening then," said Vati, getting up from the table.

Chapter 9: the new student

Käthe took a big breath as she made her way up the steps up to the entrance hall. She checked the map of the university again. The lecture on Gravitational Forces was in room E13. The ground floor, then, and room 13 should be easy enough to find.

At least no one was staring at her. This surprised her. She'd not seen another woman after she'd left the street and started walking towards the university buildings. All those young men looked so much more comfortable than she felt. It must be so much easier to walk in trousers. She dressed as sensibly she could in a simple skirt that came to just above her ankles, a smart jacket, flat boots and a plain hat. But she was still so obviously a girl. The strap on the satchel that Vati had given her as a present was beginning to chafe a bit. She'd walked all the way from home in an effort to calm her nerves. Now though the leather and the contents of the satchel were weighing heavily. She hefted it back on to her shoulder and took a few determined steps forward.

She was relieved to discover that the rooms were numbered quite logically. She soon found number 13. Her heart was thumping in her chest as she pushed the door open. This was so exciting and a little bit scary at the same time. It was noisy inside. Everyone seemed to be shouting as loudly as they could and one or two of the young men were actually throwing balls of paper at each other.

She sat down at an empty seat. "This is the lecture on Gravitational Forces, isn't it?" she asked a young man who was taking a notebook and pen out of his briefcase.

The young man looked up and stared at her. It was almost as if he'd never seen anyone like her before. He carried on looking at her for several seconds. Then he looked away. "Yes it is," he mumbled.

A door that she'd not noticed at the front of the lecture theatre opened. An older man walked in. There was a sudden silence. All of the students stood up.

"Good morning, ladies – yes we have two with us today – and gentlemen. Please be seated."

The other girl was here? Where was this other girl? She looked around but couldn't see her. Perhaps she'd spot her later. She'd better concentrate on the lecture now.

The lecture was in fact enthralling. This was really an easy topic for her. Yet she still learnt a few things she'd not known before. She really wanted to ask the professor about the effect of the moon on the tides but she couldn't quite find the courage. Besides, many of the young men, including the two who had been fighting earlier, were asking what sounded like really intelligent questions.

The professor gave quite jokey answers, specially to some of the less clever questions and she found herself chuckling as well.

Then he suddenly sighed. "Go on, then, Fräulein Oppenheimer. What is it today?"

Someone about the same height and build as Käthe stood up. Why had the professor called him Fräulein Oppenheimer? He was wearing plus-fours and a cap from under which wispy ginger hair appeared. He took a pipe out of his mouth. "So. If the mass of B were one-half as large as it currently is while A's mass remains the same, how can we work out the gravitational force?"

Ah. So the professor had been right. There were two ladies present. Fräulein Oppenheimer had dressed like a man. The voice was definitely a girl's.

The professor scratched his head. "It would depend of course on us knowing the gravitational force between the two objects."

"Four newtons?"

"That will do. My answer, young lady, is work it out yourself."

Everyone laughed. The professor started gathering his papers together. "Ladies and gentlemen, that will do for today. I wish you a good day."

Everyone stood up. Käthe could see Fräulein Oppenheimer at the front of the lecture theatre now. It would be good be able to talk to her. She scooted down the steps as quickly as she could. As she arrived at the last one, her boot caught in the hem of her skirt.

She tripped and fell. She heard the ink bottle smash and watched in horror as an ink stain spread first of all over her brand new satchel, then through her skirt and finally on to the wooden tiles. She desperately tried to mop it up with the untouched part of her skirt.

Fräulein Oppenheimer had disappeared completely by now. One or two of the men were sniggering. One kindly helped her up and offered his scarf to help absorb the ink. The next group of students was beginning to arrive. She was going to be late for her next class which was going to be in the building next door.

"Oh, so this is what happens when we allow women into the faculty. Don't you think you've be better off at home knitting socks for our soldiers, dearie? Instead of ruining our beautiful parquet." Another professor had just walked on to the stage and was now glaring at her.

Käthe felt her cheeks burn. "I'm sorry," she mumbled. She gathered up her belongings and made her way out of the side door as fast as she could.

Once in the corridor, she had no idea where she was.

"What have you got next?" asked the young man who had helped her.

"Relativity Matters."

"Me too. Just follow me." He held out his hand to take her satchel.

She shook her head. "I'm okay, thanks. But yes, please show me the way." She followed him gratefully.

They rushed up the two flights of stairs to the second floor.

"This is it," said the young man. He opened a door marked 218. "You'll probably like Professor Gurwell. He's a good sort. He won't mind that you're late. Let's hope we get a seat. He's popular."

The room was certainly crowded but they did manage to find a couple of seats on one of the side rows at the back. Professor Gurwell was already there. The other students were just sitting down.

"Ah, Fräulein Lehrs. Herr Haas. Welcome to this course on relativity."

One or two of the other students turned to stare at Käthe including a very familiar person in green plus-fours and a red cap. Fräulein Oppenheimer glared at her. Käthe felt her cheeks going red again. This really wasn't a very good start.

She managed to extract her notebook and pen from the satchel and to look relatively composed. She even managed to become calm enough to wonder at that. *This is a real relativity problem. I look calm but I'm quaking inside. They probably don't have a clue.*

She was quite pleased that she didn't find the lecture too difficult to follow. It was fascinating, actually. Soon she'd forgotten about worrying what the others were thinking about her. This idea of one twin moving into space at the speed of light and coming back was intriguing. They would be defying time. One twin would actually travel through time.

"So," said Professor Gurwell, "which twin has aged the most when they met up again?"

Käthe couldn't stop her hand shooting up. "Surely they both age? They've both moved in fact haven't they?"

Professor Gurwell laughed. "An easy mistake." Some of the young men started to snigger. "Gentleman, have a care. At least Fräulein Lehrs has dared to offer an answer. Quiet please."

Käthe felt her cheeks grow red again.

Professor Gurwell grinned. "The twin who remains actually ages more. The travelling twin travels twice, out and back. This makes the aging difference, not the acceleration itself."

Käthe growled. This was a puzzle.

The professor laughed. "Never mind, Fräulein Lehrs. You'll get it soon."

She almost did. Not quite though.

"Ladies and Gentlemen, we must finish now."

Everyone started packing away. Herr Haas nodded politely to her and then hurried away. She'd embarrassed him and she'd embarrassed herself.

She slid her own notebook and writing materials into the now ruined satchel. This hadn't really been a good start.

"You're right to worry," said a female voice. "It's tough. You'll have to learn not to be cowed by it."

Close up Fräulein Oppenheimer was even stranger-looking. She was frowning and not quite getting eye contact with Käthe. That made her seem even more scary. "Okay. So you did well to answer that question." She pulled off her cap, scraped her hair back up and pulled the cap back on. She looked even more like a man now. "Gurwell's kind but not to be fooled. And he's as capable as the next of making up a trick question."

She held her hand out towards Käthe. Käthe took it tentatively and shook it.

"What might your name be?"

"Käthe. Käthe Lehrs."

"It won't be quite the same for you of course. Your father isn't the Dean of Living Sciences. Maybe I can show you a trick or two, though. Are you ready to learn?" At last she turned and looked at Käthe. Her eyebrows were raised and she was smirking.

Berlin 1915

Chapter 10: women behaving like men

"Oh, it's so boring sometimes." Fräulein Oppenheimer yawned and stretched. "I wish they'd let us do some of the exciting stuff." She kicked the leg of the low table in the undergraduate common room. "Why can't we go and learn how to shoot with guns and dig fox-holes? It would be better than being cooped up in here."

Käthe wasn't so sure. She didn't really fancy getting all covered in mud. She longed instead to be able to do more of the experiments. The two young women were only allowed into a very few of the laboratories.

"Too dangerous for girls," they'd said. "Besides, we can't afford to waste the expensive material on people who won't become scientists."

Käthe sighed. "Why do they think we aren't capable of becoming scientists? We're just as brainy as the men, aren't we? If not more so?"

Fräulein Oppenheimer laughed. "Oh you look so funny when you get cross." She shrugged and lifted her hands into the air. "You, know what it is: they just want us to get married and have babies. You'll find that you have to give into that sooner or later. I shan't, though."

"Huh!"

"It's just the way of things."

"Why can't we do both? Work and be wives and mothers."

"Nope." Fräulein Oppenheimer shook her head and pursed her lips. "They'll never have it. Well, I might get somewhere but you won't."

"Why won't I?"

"Because you're too much of a girl." Fräulein Oppenheimer got up out of her seat and went and stood behind Käthe. She patted her hair. "This is too beautiful. You need to hide, it like I do."

Käthe had been very proud of the little hat she'd found. It was plain and simple. It made her look very smart and like a business woman. Mutti had complained about it, of course. In the end, though, it hadn't really been all that useful. She just couldn't pile all of her hair up under it like Fräulein Oppenheimer did with her cap. She'd got away as well with a shorter, plainer skirt that was easier to move in and she still always wore boots rather than fashionable shoes but there was still much about the way she dressed that made her less agile than the men and Fräulein Oppenheimer.

"You won't get anywhere unless you begin to think like a man." Fräulein Oppenheimer took off Käthe's hat and put it on the back of the armchair. She scraped Käthe's hair together and then took her own cap off and pushed all of Käthe's hair into it. "There. Look." She propelled Käthe over to the window. "Can you see?"

Käthe could see her reflection. Yes, it did make her look more like a man.

"Only now you need the trousers as well." She jabbed at Käthe's arm. "We women must wear the trousers."

Footsteps came along the corridor outside. Käthe recognised straight away the slight limp accompanied by the tapping of a walking-stick. It was the Dean, Fräulein Oppenheimer's father.

"I'm going to make him listen." She snatched her cap back off Käthe's head, gathered her own hair up, pushed it into the cap, and rushed out into the corridor.

"Vati, just listen to what we have to say. We're sick of it. Fräulein Lehrs and I."

The door slammed and Käthe could hear no more of the conversation. She could hear some shouting, though. Mainly from Fräulein Oppenheimer. The Dean seemed to be keeping calm.

She'd heard Fräulein Oppenheimer arguing with her father quite often before. It went on and on. Then, nothing changed.

It would be a while yet. She may as well find herself something to do. She got out her latest notes on relativity and started rereading them. The year had gone so quickly but she realised she'd learnt a lot now. This had all been so hard to start with and now it was so much easier to understand.

The argument outside seemed to take its usual course. Fräulein Oppenheimer's voice got louder and louder. She stamped her foot a couple of times. Then she became quieter. Finally, the Dean went on his way, the walking-stick tapping on the floor as usual except now it seemed to be tapping a little more often as if he were, after all, a little irritated either with Fräulein Oppenheimer for going over and over the same old questions or because he had been held up and was now late for an appointment. Or both.

As usual, the door to the common room burst open and Fräulein Oppenheimer rushed in. "He just doesn't listen. He never listens."

Fräulein Oppenheimer flopped down onto one of the couches. She folded her arms across her chest and sat back so that her legs were stretched out in front of her, crossed at the ankle. Some of the women who wore the shorter skirts would cross their ankles but not the way Fräulein Oppenheimer was doing it. No, she was sitting the way that the young men did when they sprawled lazily in the comfortable chairs. "We've really got to do something soon." She suddenly stopped frowning and sat up. "I know. We'll just go and set up our own experiment."

"How can we do that?"

Fräulein Oppenheimer tapped the side of her nose. "I know where the keys to the labs are kept."

"You can't just take them, like that."

"Can't I? Just watch!" She made her way over to the door. She turned and stared right into Käthe's eyes. Then she rolled her eyes. "Are you coming or what?"

Käthe knew she daren't resist.

It wasn't difficult finding the keys. Fräulein Oppenheimer mumbled something to the secretary about having to fetch something for her father. As Fräulein Oppenheimer had suggested, Käthe distracted the woman whilst Fräulein Oppenheimer found the right key. They actually found one of the laboratories that was hardly ever used these days.

"It's filthy," said Käthe as clouds of dust flew up when they opened the door.

"Yes, but at least nobody ever comes here. I'm going to keep the key and just return the rest of the bunch. They'll never know." Fräulein Oppenheimer's eyes were gleaming.

Käthe sighed. "I guess the first thing we'd better do, then, is get this cleaned up."

"Little housewifey," said Fräulein Oppenheimer. She pulled a face. Then she shrugged. "I suppose you're right. Needs must."

There was a small store cupboard in the corner of the room and they found a mop, a bucket and some cleaning cloths in there. There was, thankfully, plenty of hot water.

Two hours later both of them were filthy as well but the laboratory positively gleamed.

"First experiment, then, next Wednesday when they're off at their military training. What do you think?"

Käthe nodded, though she did ask herself where they would get the materials.

Fräulein Oppenheimer must have read her thoughts. "It's all right. I know one of the laboratory assistants quite well. He'll let us have all of the supplies we need. He'll have to. Otherwise I'll be obliged to tell my father about what he did last year."

"Oh?"

Fräulein Oppenheimer grinned. "He almost set the lab on fire. He managed to put it out himself and repair the damage afterwards. But it could have been a lot worse. He'll want us to keep quiet so he'll give us exactly what we want."

It all went very smoothly. They'd chosen the Cavendish experiment. This was one, she knew, that all of the second years did.

"Can't we do something more exciting?" Fräulein Oppenheimer had said. "Wouldn't it be fantastic if we found out something new?"

Käthe had insisted that they do something more conventional to start with. "They probably wouldn't believe us unless they can see that we've done everything properly."

Fräulein Oppenheimer sighed. "Oh, all right then."

Käthe was surprised that Fräulein Oppenheimer had given in so easily. Of course, she'd now left Käthe to write up the results. She didn't mind really. It was very late now though and something puzzled her. She was looking at Cavendish's original paper. He'd made Earth's density to 5.480 ± 0.038 times that of water. Her results said 5.448 ± 0.033. Had she made a mistake? She recalculated. No, that was correct. Had they made a mistake with the experiment? They'd been so careful. Surely not? She was tempted to make the result fit. She shouldn't though. That would be wrong. Had all of this been a waste of time? Would they now think that she and Fräulein Oppenheimer were just a couple of silly girls who couldn't set up an experiment properly?

Oh well, so be it. Surely once they'd presented this, someone would give them some feedback on their work. All of the students made mistakes, didn't they? That was how they learnt, wasn't it?

She wrote her final sentence, ruled a line under her work, blotted it and inserted the paper into a folder. It was good work, she knew, despite what anybody else might say. She looked at the clock on the mantelpiece. It was after midnight. She had a lecture at eight the next morning. She must get some sleep now. She stashed the folder neatly in her satchel. She would hand the notes into the office immediately after her lecture. What would they make of it, she wondered.

Professor Gurwell nodded. "Hmm. This is very careful work. Very careful indeed. I wish the degree students took as much care."

Käthe and Fräulein Oppenheimer exchanged a glance. Fräulein Oppenheimer actually smiled. It made a nice change from her normal scowling. It was just one week since Käthe had handed in the write-up of the Cavendish experiment. At the end of their relativity lecture Professor Gurwell had asked them to accompany him to his office.

"I bet we're in trouble," Käthe had said.

"Of course we're not. He wants to congratulate us. Anyway, the Dean's daughter can hardly get into trouble, can she?"

The professor looked up at Käthe. "I'm presuming you wrote up the experiment, Fräulein Lehrs. I know for a fact that we can never read Fräulein Oppenheimer's writing."

"Huh!" Fräulein Oppenheimer blushed, frowned and folded her arms across her chest.

"It's true, though, Fräulein Oppenheimer. If you seriously want to become a scientist you must be able to communicate well in writing. This work by Fräulein Lehrs is excellent. Clear, well-argued, truly scientific and we can actually read her words."

It was Käthe's turn to blush.

Professor Gurwell smiled. "I see also that you have corrected Cavendish's mistake."

"We have?"

"Yes. He made a slight miscalculation. Francis Baily actually corrected it in 1821. But well done, ladies, for conducting the experiment so competently and being so honest in publishing your results. I won't ask how you managed to get the laboratory space." He now glared at Fräulein Oppenheimer. "Just don't rely too much on your father's position. It's good that our laboratories are being put to good use. After all, with the war on, they are somewhat underused."

"This, of course, is a major coup for womankind." Fräulein Oppenheimer poured the coffee. They were sitting in the Victoria Café. She had insisted they should celebrate with coffee and cake. Käthe felt a little uneasy. Was Fräulein Oppenheimer after all just like her own mother? Rather fond of the Berlin social life that she measured out in the quality of various cafés?

"Come on then. Eat up." Fräulein Oppenheimer took a mouthful of her chocolate torte. "Oh, it's divine."

Käthe just stared at her Bienenstich. Yes, of course she loved the creamy honey-flavoured filling and the pastry covered in almonds but this just seemed a little frivolous and a little too much like what her mother enjoyed.

"Don't be such a grouch." Fräulein Oppenheimer waggled her arm. "You know, I didn't think you were going to be able to do this. I think you are, though. I think you'll surprise them all and become a fantastic scientist. Knock spots off the best of the men – if there are any of them left after this silly war. And you manage to avoid being married off."

She was right. There was still some way to go. She would have to work really hard at avoiding being saddled with a husband and a house to run. And even if they were allowed to do experiments they still weren't going to be awarded a degree. Without that would they ever be taken seriously?

"We can do it, you know," Fräulein Oppenheimer whispered.

Käthe stuck her fork into the Bienenstich.

Chapter 11: showdown

"Oh for goodness sake, just look at you. You're pathetic."

Käthe was soaked through. She'd walked all the way as there had been something wrong with the electricity and the trams weren't working. They'd blamed it on the rain. Precisely when you needed them most they let you down. She was desperately holding her skirt against the radiator in the student common room.

Fräulein Oppenheimer was screwing her nose up at her. "I mean, just look at this." She pulled up Käthe's sodden skirt. "Just so impractical. If you're going to do this, then do it properly. Play them at their own game."

Käthe was getting really fed up with Fräulein Oppenheimer. What was the matter with her? Why did she always blow so hot and cold. One minute she was quite friendly. The next minute she was so scathing. Enough was enough.

"Do we really have to behave and dress like men in order to be equal to them? I actually quite like wearing a skirt." She didn't know whether that was true. She'd never tried trousers. She'd drawn the line at sneaking into Leo's or Rudi's room and trying on a pair of theirs. Even if she'd felt inclined to do that, there would be no way she'd get them past Mutti. She suspected Fräulein Oppenheimer was right, though, but she wasn't going to admit it.

"I actually think we do. You're not getting very far, are you? They're not exactly all falling over themselves to let you get at the proper work."

"Well, it's no different for you is it really? Just because you look like one doesn't mean you are a man."

"Oh, I think I'm getting quite a bit of respect." Fräulein Oppenheimer's cheeks were bright red. "But you're not."

"How do you figure that one out?"

"You obviously can't see the way they smirk at you behind your back."

"Well, if they do that, why on earth don't you tell me? I'd be able to stand up to them then." How dare they smirk at her? How dare they?

Fräulein Oppenheimer laughed. "I don't think you'd get very far with that."

"Wouldn't I?" This was infuriating. She could stand up for herself. She was always having to do it with Leo and Rudi. At least she was used to dealing with arrogant males. It was just this arrogant female that was causing trouble at the moment.

"Oh, you do make me laugh." Fräulein Oppenheimer was looking away now.

"Don't turn away from me like that."

"I can't bear looking at you, you're so pathetic."

"What do you mean by that?" Käthe was aware that she was shouting now.

"You're just another weak little female. I mean that stupid hat you wear. So, you've got a shorter skirt. So what? It's all the fashion now. You're a victim of fashion just like the rest of them. We really have to start dressing just for practicality like the men do."

"Most male animals are the flamboyant ones. Are you really that ignorant? What about peacocks? Mallard ducks? If it's the females in our species, then doesn't it mean we're actually superior? And shouldn't we flaunt it?" Käthe had no idea where she'd just got that from.

"Well, you're not even doing that though are you? Your attempt to be fashionable is half-hearted. Just look at those boots. Frumpy but still not all that practical."

"Do you really have to be so personal?"

"Oh, you're getting on my nerves. Why don't you give up the struggle now and go and find yourself a man to marry?"

"I most certainly will not. I am NOT going to give up my science. Not for you, or for anyone.!"

"Suit yourself. But I'm telling you, you won't get anywhere."

The door was suddenly flung open and there was Professor Gurwell.

"Ladies, what is going on. What is all this noise about?"

Käthe felt herself blush and looked down to the floor. "We were just having an argument."

"Hmm. Arguments are fine. In fact we encourage them. But we also expect you to be civilised."

Fräulein Oppenheimer was standing with her hands on her hips. "Then it's time this institution became civilised and allowed us women to work here properly."

"Well, you're ruining your chances of that, if you continue to behave in this rowdy manner. After all that good work you did with those experiments. Though I wish you'd been more honest about how you'd obtained access to the lab, Fräulein Oppenheimer."

"I'm so sorry," whispered Käthe. "We won't let it happen again."

"I should think not." Then he farted. He went bright red and didn't seem to know where to put himself. "Now, I must get on. If you'll excuse me."

He hurried out of the room leaving an obnoxious smell behind him. It made Käthe want to gag at first, then though she felt an almost irresistible urge to titter. Fräulein Oppenheimer was screwing up her nose and waving her hand in front of her face. Then Käthe was giggling. "What has that man been eating?"

Fräulein Oppenheimer nodded. "A scientist ought to know better." She shook her head and started laughing as well. Her face suddenly changed, though, and she stamped her foot and swore between gritted teeth.

Käthe had now stopped feeling angry and was only perturbed that something was making the indomitable Fräulein Oppenheimer lose her temper. "What on earth is the matter?"

Fräulein Oppenheimer struggled to regain some control and then blurted out, "Vati has found out about our experiments and is threating to make me leave the university. Mutti persuaded him to give me one more chance. I've probably just blown that. If Gurwell tells him about our argument…"

"Right then." Käthe's anger was back. She made her way to the door.

"Where are you going?"

"I'm going to see Gurwell."

"You'll never be able to persuade him not to tell Vati."

"Well, I'll have a damned good try."

"I wish you luck." She grimaced at Käthe. Then she looked down at the floor. "I'm sorry, by the way," she mumbled. "I shouldn't have said all of those things."

"As long as you didn't mean them."

Fräulein Oppenheimer shook her head and looked up. "And please call me Gerda now."

"You must call me Käthe." She nodded and hurried on out of the room.

Professor Gurwell looked at Käthe over the top of his spectacles. "You're asking me not to tell the Dean about your and Fräulein Oppenheimer's behaviour? You do realise that that sort of behaviour is not to be tolerated and that it is a disciplinable offense?"

"It really wasn't her fault, though. It was all me."

"I find that very hard to believe."

Käthe shrugged. "Really, it was. I provoked her."

Professor Gurwell sighed. "You are much too loyal to your friend."

Friend? He must be joking. Oh, just get on with the discipline and be done with it. "So, what will happen now?"

Professor Gurwell got up from his seat and wandered over to the window. He turned his back on Käthe and looked out on to the quadrangle below. "You know," he said, "I wish they'd work half as hard as you two do. That experiment you did the other day was really good."

"Well, why don't you let us do more of them then?"

"It isn't up to me. And you've probably ruined your chances now by going behind the Dean's back. Stealing keys was not altogether bright."

"But you liked what we did. Doesn't that count?"

"I had no idea that you'd stolen keys in order to do it, though. I really thought you must have got the Dean's permission."

"I'm sorry. We tried that. It didn't work. My father always says 'Do what you think is right and apologise afterwards.' "

Professor Gurwell turned back to her. "You know, the Dean was impressed with your work as well."

"Well, then."

Professor Gurwell sighed. "Yes, it seems it's just an argument between him and his daughter really."

"So what will you do?"

"I won't tell him about the scene earlier."

Käthe literally felt as if a weight was lifting from her chest. "Thank you. Thank you." She stood up ready to go. "There isn't any chance, is there, that we could get your permission to carry on with the experiments?"

"I'll see what I can do." Professor Gurwell frowned and then doubled up, clutching his stomach. He was clearly in pain.

Käthe rushed over to the professor just in time to break his fall as he collapsed on to the floor.

"Vati said you did really well," said Gerda. "You saved Professor Gurwell's life." They were walking along the corridor towards their afternoon lecture.

"That's a bit of an exaggeration." It was true, though, she had known exactly what to do. Years of practice with Rudi had helped. She hadn't stopped to think. She'd made sure that he was safe and as comfortable as possible and then she'd gone to get help. An ambulance had arrived shortly afterwards and taken him to hospital.

"Well he's out of danger now and should be getting out of hospital soon. It was a stomach ulcer about to burst, apparently."

Käthe was glad he was getting better. She was glad also that it had only been a stomach ulcer, for although that was bad enough, it could have been something much worse like a heart attack or a stroke. But would there be any more news soon as to whether they could carry on with their experiments or not? That's what she really wanted to know. And of course, whether she and Gerda were going to get into more trouble. She hadn't had any bad news from the university in her student pigeon hole though she guessed that was because Professor Gurwell was too ill to say anything. Once he got better, who knew what might happen. She hoped he'd keep his promise, though.

They arrived at their lecture room. Gerda paused with her hand on the door. "There's more news. Apparently when Vati went to see him the other day he put in a special plea on our behalf. He said that as you could show such presence of mind he thought we should be allowed to carry on experimenting. Vati's agreed to it though he has given me dire warning about being careful and being honest." She rolled her eyes.

They made their way into the lecture room.

Gerda pointed to the front row. "Will that do?"

Ah. She was being asked her opinion for once. Käthe nodded.

"I'm really looking forward to working with you more closely," said Gerda.

Well she wouldn't hold her breath about that.

Gerda grinned at her and suddenly Käthe wondered whether things were after all about to change. She could at least be hopeful.

Berlin 1916

Chapter 12: empty hallways

Everything was gloomy. It was one of those days after Christmas when the sun hardly shone. It was wet and cold and it wasn't even that nice crisp cold that could be so invigorating. Käthe was glad to arrive at the university building.

It didn't take long, though, for her to realise that it was almost as miserable inside if not exactly quite as cold. Her own footsteps echoed along the corridors. Where was everyone?

They must all be afraid of the cold. A couple of the older professors shuffled past her. Then a young man with a limp made his way slowly and painfully up the stairs that led to the library.

Of course. More of them must have gone to fight now. They'd said something about that, hadn't they, in the paper? Perhaps there would be more in today's. She must read it carefully when Vati brought it home tonight.

She shivered.

Oh, it was so useless being a woman. Most of the men were gone and they still wouldn't let her and Gerda be scientists. Not properly anyway.

"Hey, Käthe, wait up!" Käthe recognised the voice and the clatter of boots on the marble floor immediately. Gerda.

A few seconds later Gerda had hooked her arm into Käthe's. "Have you heard the latest? Come on, let's go and get a coffee and I'll tell you."

The common room was deserted as well when they arrived.

"They're building really big trenches." Gerda stirred another lump of sugar into her coffee, took a sip and pulled a face. "We should have gone to the café. The faculty's getting worse. They can't even offer us a decent cup of coffee now."

"Bigger trenches?"

"Yes, like whole towns. The English ones are all just mud. Ours are much better. They're on higher ground for starters and we've got concrete stairs and electricity. We're bound to win."

"You've been reading the papers?"

"Oh yes. Vati has nearly all of the dailies delivered to the house."

"And have they called up more men? It's so quiet here."

"Yes. They've pretty well all gone, now. All of them who can."

On cue the door opened and a very able-bodied-looking young man, came in.

"Except this one, apparently," Gerda muttered. "Hey you. What are you doing here? Why aren't you at the front with the others?"

The young man blushed. "I'm finishing my doctorate," he stammered.

"Can't that wait?"

"It's considered war work. My research could help us win the war."

"Really?" Gerda's eyes were flashing now. "You're better than your professors are you?"

"No... I... I think I'd better be getting back to the library."

"You're just a coward. Go on admit it."

The young man took a deep breath. "All right. Yes. I'm scared and I don't want to fight. Would you?"

"Yes, if they let me. But they won't. There might be a chance, though, that I could get down to some serious science work if yellow-bellies like you would have the decency to do the right thing."

"Yes. All right. Whatever you say." He turned and went out of the room.

"So infuriating." Gerda stamped her foot.

Käthe didn't know where to look. She'd got a brother who wasn't at the front as well.

She cleared her throat nervously. "I hope you don't think my brother's a coward."

"No, of course not. Rudi can't help it. And isn't he working for the ministry at the moment?"

Käthe nodded. She didn't understand Rudi's work at all but he was always telling her how important it was for the war effort.

"See, that's completely different. And it is so unfair that despite most of the men being away they still won't let us study properly. I've a good mind to volunteer for war work myself."

"You wouldn't, would you?"

"Just watch me. I'm going to see what I can find."

She gathered her things together and stormed out of the common room.

Käthe couldn't concentrate after that. There were no classes as such today, anyway. She didn't feel like working in the library and as there was no Gerda to bounce ideas off there was little point in staying there.

She wondered what it might be like at Vati's factory.

A few moments later she was on her way there.

"Yes, we're just beginning to notice it," said Vati. "The last call-up has left us short-handed. We've used up all those men who are too young, too infirm or too old. We've even called back some out of retirement. The next step of course is to employ you women." There was a twinkle in his eye. "Would you like a job?"

"Doing what exactly?"

"Well, I wasn't thinking the factory floor. Those are very dirty jobs. Heavy work for a woman."

What was he saying? She was as strong as her brothers she was sure. "Vati, you're as bad as the rest of them."

Vati chuckled. "I'm losing my clerks rapidly. Young Christian Bauer is off to the front tomorrow."

"So he is going then. I knew he was thinking about it."

"Well, will you?"

It would be a bit of an opportunity, she supposed. It would give her a chance to show she could do as much as the men. She wasn't getting very far at the university. They were still treating her and Gerda as if they were silly little girls, only there for their own amusement. Not that she wanted to give up her science, though.

"I don't want to stop my studies."

"I wouldn't ask you to. You could work part-time."

"Would you be able to give some work to Gerda as well?"

"You mean your friend who always looks and behaves like a man?" He rolled his eyes but then nodded. "I don't see why not. She'd be rather good, I would have thought."

"All right then." Suddenly it felt quite exciting. She stood up. "I'll go and see if I can find her."

"Good."

As she walked back towards the entrance, she noticed how eerily quiet it was. Hardly any of the machines were running and nobody was shouting across the factory floor as normal. What would it be like, she wondered, once it was full of women.

Berlin 1917

Chapter 13: where is Leo?

Käthe enjoyed the walk home that day. It had been a good day at the university. Today's experiment had gone well. The sun was quite warm now even though it was still February. Of course, there was still this war going on. They weren't hearing much about it, though. They hadn't had a letter from Leo for a while but they do say no news is good news, don't they? Surely, anyway, the whole thing should be over soon. She couldn't feel gloomy for too long. It was such a cheerful day and she's just done so well.

She found herself whistling. A gentleman going the other way frowned at her. Yes, if Mutti caught her doing that she'd be in trouble. Not at all ladylike. Well, neither was studying physics at a university. It seemed that the more you started behaving like a man, the better you did. So, not ladylike was okay in fact.

It was a bit cold. It would be good to get in and perhaps have a mug of hot chocolate. Mutti or Imelda might have made a cake. She quickened her pace a little and was soon feeling warmer.

She was soon at the flat in Pariser Street. She ran up the stairs, put her key in the lock and opened the door.

"I'm home," she called. No one answered. That was odd. Normally Mutti, Rudi or Imelda would call back. This time there was nothing but silence. She took off her coat and hat and hung them up.

The door to the drawing room was slightly ajar. She pushed it right open. There was no one in the room but there was a big trunk box on one of the small tables. A soldier's box? Leo? Leo was home.

There was a letter open. Surely that was the last one he'd sent home, wasn't it? A couple of months ago? Gosh. The box looked dirty and smelt musty. She picked up the letter and read it again.

19 December 1916

Dear all,

Life continues in the trenches. We are wet and cold and sometimes scared but otherwise mainly quite well. We have been "over the top" several times now and now have a better idea of what is expected of us there. We're getting good at fighting.

The big news is that I have been made into an officer. I am now an Oberleutnant and have several men under my command. I feel responsible for their well-being also.

We have all been awarded the Iron Cross, so if anything should happen to me you can be very proud. I don't think anything will happen, though. It's almost as if we're being kept in a protective bubble.

Let's hope it can all be over soon and that I can come back to you. Oh to go riding on the trams in Berlin again. That is the peace we must fight for. Take care all of you,

Your loving son and brother,

Leo.

Yes, a sign that all was still well with him. They'd been so pleased to get that letter. Why was he reading his own letters, though, if he was home?

Footsteps came along the corridor. The door burst open. Mutti and Vati came in. Where was Leo? Why was Vati home so early?

Then she could hear sobbing. Real agonised sobbing. What could be so bad that someone would have to cry like that? Was that Imelda in the kitchen? "Why's Imelda crying? Where's Leo?"

Mutti and Vati exchanged a glance. Vati put a hand on her shoulder. "He's missing, presumed dead."

No.

Her legs turned to jelly and she sank to the floor. She wanted to say something but the words seemed to be stuck in her throat and her head wouldn't let her string them together in any coherent way.

Vati helped her up. Mutti put her arms around her shoulder but she brushed them off. "I need to be alone," she whispered.

Somehow she managed to stagger to her room. The apartment seemed to tip and buckle and she felt sick. She flung herself onto the bed and folded herself up into a ball. She bit her lip until it bled.

She wished she could sob like Imelda had been doing but she couldn't. Leo was gone. He was missing, presumed dead.

Later, much later, there came a tap at the door.

"Yes," she whispered.

The door opened and Vati came in.

"Will he come back?" she asked. "He's only missing, isn't he?"

Vati shook his head. "It's not too hopeful. Most men who are reported missing are in fact dead."

Now she felt the tears rising in her eyes. She didn't want to cry in front of Vati, though.

He put his hand on her shoulder. "You must be our scientist now. Now that Leo has gone."

"What about Rudi?"

Vati shrugged. "We never know about his health and he is working so independently. Besides, he's a mathematician. That's not quite the same. You are discovering the most exciting things now. Keep on working hard, won't you?"

She couldn't speak but managed to nod. This was what she wanted, wasn't it? But not at the cost of losing her brother. Not even Leo. Sure, he could be a real pain in the neck sometimes but he was still her brother.

"Good girl." Vati squeezed her shoulder again and then left the room.

So, now it was up to her. Would she be able to do it? She swallowed hard then took a deep breath.

Chapter 14: women at work

"It's very cosy here, isn't it?" said Gerda.

"That's one word for it." Cramped was what came to Käthe's mind. She bumped her leg again on the desk. That would be another bruise, then. The two of them had taken over Christian's work and there were now two chairs where there had been one. "I hope nobody's going to say that it takes two women to do the work of one man."

"That's stupid. We're both working part-time. It's more like two part-time women equal one full-time man. Or maybe even a bit more."

Käthe nodded. Her friend had a point. Someone might ask why they didn't work at separate times. They could actually do that now but they'd chosen to carry on working together even though they didn't need to any more. It had been good to do that at first, so that they could help each other to understand what was involved. Anyway, their timetables at the university meant that they were free at the same time. And if some of the men who were still there got a bit uppity, there was strength in numbers.

Gerda slapped the folder she'd been working on down on to the table. "Well, those are all the invoices ready to go out."

Käthe grinned. "And I've got all of the client accounts up to date."

"We're doing well."

"We most certainly are."

It really hadn't been that easy to start with, even though Käthe was used to looking over the accounts. There were all of those office routines to get used to. Some things needed to be done by a certain time. In some ways they were the easiest. Then, though, you had to keep the other processes ticking over or when you eventually needed some information you just couldn't find it.

Christian had always kept his desk so tidy. At first with them there though it had been total chaos. There had been files everywhere. Some had fallen to the floor and spilled their contents.

Vati had looked at it all and chuckled. Thank goodness he hadn't been cross. "I think I'm missing Christian," he'd said.

Käthe had almost felt like crying and even Gerda had looked away.

"Ladies, I'm sure you'll get this sorted eventually. Don't be afraid to ask for help it you need it."

Käthe had sighed and Gerda had snorted. "We're getting to the bottom of things. We're not hiding anything."

Now, though, it was different. There were just two folders on the desk and they would be filing them away any moment now.

"Is this tidiness a sign of success, do you think?" Käthe waved her arm over the desk.

"I should hope so, otherwise it's boring."

The door opened and Herr Schäfer came in. He was about the same age as Vati and walked with a stick. He was one of the few men left at the factory now. Some men his age had gone to the front but he was obviously too frail to go. Gerda frowned slightly when she saw him.

She hoped Gerda would have a go at Herr Schäfer,. He'd always been so kind to her when she'd visited the factory. He was such an important worker, too. He really helped to keep the factory running smoothly. Just as well his bad leg had kept him at home.

"Good morning, ladies," he said cheerfully. "I'm here after the invoices. We need to get them posted today."

Without saying a word, Gerda handed him the folder. Now her part of the desk was empty.

"And are the client accounts up to date, Fräulein Lehrs?"

Käthe nodded.

Herr Schäfer came over to the desk and looked at the papers she'd been dealing with. His eyes grew round and he nodded. "Well done, ladies." Then he pointed to one of the papers. "Though I can see you've been having trouble with the number 5."

"Yes, the key keeps sticking." Käthe could type really fast now but that made this pesky key even more problematic. She smiled to herself when she remembered how slow she'd been to start with.

"I'll get young Gottfried to come and take a look. Thank you, ladies."

Gerda shook her head after he'd left. "He didn't need to seem so surprised. And who the heck is Gottfried and why is he here?"

"He's seventeen and he's a trainee mechanic. Don't you be nasty to him when he gets here."

"Me? Nasty? I wouldn't dream of it."

Gottfried arrived a few moments later. He was a tall, thin young man and his clothes seemed to hang off him. His once white shirt was grubby and his hands were mucky.

"Right, then ladies, which one of these here beasties is playing up?"

Käthe pointed to her typewriter.

Gottfried bent down over it straight away. "Oh yes. I get it." He took a small oil can out of one of his jacket pockets." He fiddled around with the stubborn type bar and then dotted some oil on it. "That should do it. Like to give it a try?" Käthe slotted a piece of paper into the typewriter and typed a few 5s. She nodded. "Seems good."

"Now try it with some other keys."

She typed a few random words. The key didn't stick anymore but some oily marks appeared on the paper. "Yes, it's good but it's greasy."

"Soon fix that." He took a rag out of his other pocket and wiped the part he'd oiled. "That should do it."

Käthe tried a few more random letters. "Perfect."

"Glad to be of service, miss."

Gerda stood up and walked over to Gottfried. She put an arm around his shoulders. "You know young man, you're just the sort of person they need at the front. You'd be excellent at repairing the machines and guns. So what about it?"

"I'm only seventeen, miss, but yes, I'll be joining up as soon as they'll let me. I guess they'll have to wait until I'm twenty unless they bring the age down."

"You're pretty tall. They'd be glad to have you. I bet they'd believe you if you lied about your age."

Gottfried blushed. "I'm not very good at lying, miss."

"A good job too. Vati needs you here working at the factory. Don't tease him, Gerda. Take no notice of her, Gottfried. She's just after more jobs for the women."

"Well, Fräulein Lehrs, Fräulein Oppenheimer, that's one good thing about this war. It's got more of you ladies working in the factories and a very good job too. You make them much more cheerful places and the work gets done quicker."

"Well, well, we have another fan." Gerda patted Gottfried on the back. "Thank you, young man."

"You shouldn't have teased him like that," said Käthe after he left. "Poor lad."

"I know, I'm awful, aren't I? And he said such lovely things about us."

"Yes, and so did Herr Schäfer."

Gerda sat down again, slumped down into her seat and crossed her ankles. "He was complimentary about our work, wasn't he? Seems they really all appreciate us these days. But why are they all surprised all of the time? Why shouldn't women be as good at work as the men? Mind you, could you imagine them being able to cook?"

Käthe giggled when she thought of the time Vati had burnt a boiled egg when both Imelda and Mutti had the 'flu. Then she thought about Leo and guessed that the men in the trenches had to cook sometimes. She wondered how he would have got on with that.

As Käthe looked up she noticed clock. "It's half past, look. We need to go."

"Yes, yes. Back to the man's world." Gerda grabbed her cloak and draped it over her shoulders.

Käthe took a while longer to button up her coat.

"There's no point waiting for a tram," said Gerda once they were outside. "It'll be full and so heavy it will go really slowly. And it'll keep stopping because it will have a feeble-minded conductress taking the fares."

"You don't mean that, surely?"

"Of course not. Well, not the bit about the conductress. We'll certainly be quicker walking, though."

It was always difficult to keep up with Gerda. She had such long legs and she was so athletic. Käthe always felt as if she were a little Poodle trotting at her side. She hadn't got the breath to talk and Gerda seemed preoccupied with something anyway.

As they got nearer to the university they started seeing more of the other students.

"Still so many men," muttered Gerda.

Yes, all old ones and very young ones. She and Gerda were still the only women though. "I guess we're not going to become respected scientists any time soon."

Gerda shook her head. "No."

It was so different from at Vati's factory. Well, if they could accept women there then they could accept them anywhere. Käthe knew at that very moment that she must now do all she could to make sure that women like her and Gerda – no, in fact, all women – should take their place up in the world. "Well we'll have to do something about that, won't we?"

Gerda grinned. "We sure will."

Chapter 15: the shy professor

The students kept on piling into the lecture room. It was almost full, Käthe was sure. Still they kept on coming. It was a very big room, though, and the other students were still managing to find spaces somehow. Soon they were sitting on the steps in the aisles. Several people also stood up at the back. It began to get really warm.

"I'm surprised there are this many left. I'd have thought they'd all be at the front by now." Gerda turned round to face the back of the room. "They're still pouring in."

Käthe tried to swallow the lump in her throat and she blinked to try to stop the tears that were forming in her eyes from falling. They'd still not heard anything of Leo and it was November now. He'd been reported missing in February.

"Sorry," said Gerda. "I didn't think. But they do say no news is good news, don't they?"

It was all right for Gerda. Her only brother was fit for service. He was going in a few days. He wasn't missing yet.

A hush descended on the lecture room. The side door that led to the podium opened and in walked Professor Gurwell and the man they had all come to see.

Professor Gurwell cleared his throat. "Good afternoon, ladies and gentlemen," he said. "It is my great pleasure to introduce you to Professor Einstein who will talk to you about his latest ideas on relativity. He has agreed to answer questions after his lecture."

He looked just like the photos Käthe had seen of him. She recognised his dark intense eyes and his flyaway hair. She hadn't realised, though, just how short he was. He looked quite nervous as well.

Soon Käthe was fascinated. Professor Einstein introduced the idea of the LASER. That meant Light Amplification by Stimulated Emission of Radiation. It was quite a difficult concept to understand.

"An excited atom in isolation can return to a lower energy state

86

by emitting photons," said Professor Einstein. "I call this spontaneous submission. Spontaneous submission sets the scale for radioactive interactions. Such as absorption and stimulated emission. Atoms will only absorb photons of the correct wavelength: the photon disappears and the atom goes to a higher energy state, setting the stage for spontaneous emission.

"In addition, as light passes through a substance, it could stimulate the emission of more light.

"Photons prefer to travel together in the same state. If one has a large collection of atoms containing a great deal of excess energy they will be ready to emit a photon randomly. Yet if a stray photon of the correct wavelength passes by, its presence will stimulate the atoms to release their photons early – and those photons will travel in the same direction with the identical frequency and phase as the original stray photon. A cascading effect ensues. As a crown of identical photons moves through the rest of the atoms, ever more photons will be emitted from the atoms to join them."

This was all incredibly exciting, this LASER idea. And all those movements he described. They were things you couldn't really see. Not even with a powerful microscope. Yet this man was finding other ways of proving that they existed.

He had stopped seeming nervous now as well. He was so fired up by what he described. So was she. She really must learn more from him.

Gradually, his lecture came to a close.

"Thank you for listening to what some may consider to be slightly crazy ideas of a relatively mad scientist," he said. "I have just one more thing to explain to you. I beg a little more of your patience."

He paused and took a deep breath. He seemed to gain eye contact with everyone.

Käthe swallowed hard and felt herself blush as he caught her eye. She wanted to look away but it might seem rude.

"My health has not been the best of late," he continued. "So I will from now on be taking a less active role here at the university. I shall, however, still carry on my research and I shall still publish papers."

A shocked murmur made its way through the audience. The professor had to wait until everyone quietened down.

"It's just that I will no longer give lectures like this to classrooms full of undergraduate students like yourselves. I beg for your understanding."

Most of the students, including Käthe and Gerda, started clapping.

Professor Einstein beamed at them. Then he held his hands up and indicated that they should quieten down and listen to one last message.

"I do however wish to supervise some doctorates. In all cases I would have a deputy supervisor who would do most of the work. Nevertheless, I would meet up with students occasionally and all of the work would have to be written off by me. Interested students should contact me via the usual channels. If there are too many of you I shall have to make some sort of decision based on merit.

"Naturally that will depend to some extent on your ability and to some extent on the recommendations of other faculty members. Of course, your proposal must be something that interests me.

"But there is one more thing." He looked around the room and seemed to get eye contact with most people. For several seconds he stared right into her eyes. "I'll be more inclined to take you on if you show some spirit." He chuckled, then he nodded. "I wish you all a good afternoon."

As he walked off the podium everyone in the room got to their feet and started clapping again.

Käthe knew what she must do. She should act on Vati's advice again: act first and apologise later.

Was this a good balance between using the usual channel and showing a bit of spirit? Who could tell? The worst that might happen is that he would say no or be terribly shocked. He might push her away. One thing was very clear to her though: she would never get a degree if she just sat back and didn't do anything. Yes. She must do this thing.

She got up on to her feet. "I'm going to speak to him," she muttered.

"Are you mad?" Gerda pulled at her skirt. Fortunately it was made of quite slippery material and Käthe managed to pull away. Thank goodness for her flat, comfortable boots.

One of the men whistled as she ran past. "Go, Lehrs."

If only. What about sports for women on a Wednesday afternoon whilst they were doing their military training?

She just about reached lower door the corridor in time to see Professor Einstein closing the door from the podium exit.

"Sir. Professor Einstein." She was really close to him now. It was now or never. Did she dare?

Two dark eyes stared at her. A smile played around the man's lips. "So, young lady. What can I do for you?"

"I would like to study relativity. I'd like to do a doctorate about time. And I'd like you to be my supervisor."

"I see. So tell me more about yourself, Fräulein…?"

"Lehrs. Käthe Lehrs."

"So, Fräulein Lehrs. Why do you want to study with me?"

Käthe felt herself blush. "It's fascinating, The new science is exciting. I want to learn more. I want to discover something for myself."

"And you're good at your studies?"

"I think so. Yes. Yes I am."

"You think so?"

"Well, I am. Only, you see, they won't let us take the degree exams."

"They won't let you take the exams?"

"No." This was looking useless. He would never take her on. "We do do all of the experiments."

"And they've worked well?"

"Yes. They have."

"That's good."

Professor Gurwell appeared behind Professor Einstein. "Ah, Fräulein Lehrs. I hope you're not taking up too much of Professor Einstein's time."

"No, she was telling me how good her laboratory practice is. Can you confirm this?"

"Well, yes I can. She and Fräulein Oppenheimer are really disciplined."

"Good, good," said Professor Einstein. "And it's true? They're not allowed to take exams and receive a degree?"

"I'm afraid so."

"Why is that?"

"Well, because they're women."

"Tch. A pity. A great pity. I would have been only too pleased to supervise this charming young lady. Will you see what can be done about this?"

"Er, yes." It was now Professor Gurwell's turn to blush bright red. "I'll see to it straight away."

The two professors scuttled away.

"You didn't?" Gerda's mouth was hanging open and her eyebrows were raised.

"I most certainly did."

"You are wicked." She linked her arm into Käthe's. "I think we need to go and celebrate."

AH Munich 1917

He stared at his reflection in the mirror. Now there was a fine German soldier. Surely they must think of him as German now? He'd fought bravely, hadn't he? That's why they'd given him the Iron Cross.

He'd recovered almost completely. There was just a little twinge now and then in his back.

It had been a bloody battle. There's never been anything like it as far as he could figure out. Those Brits were beasts. Gas all over the place. Barbed wire, smoke and mud everywhere. Those Crimea battles he used to re-enact looked very tame compared with this 20th century reality. He'd been there and been proud to be a part of it.

There was something not quite right about the way he looked. He was still too boyish and too thin. He needed hair on his face to make him look like a man. A toothbrush moustache might suit him. He would let it grow straight away.

Berlin 1917

Chapter 16: found

The Café Victoria was packed. It had been Gerda's idea to go there that afternoon.

"We won't be able to spend Christmas together," she'd said. "Family and what not." Her face had dropped then. "I suppose it won't be much of a Christmas for you, anyway. You don't still do Hanukah, do you?"

For goodness' sake. We have to carry on. There will be Christmas in our house. And no we don't do Hanukah anymore but our Jewish friends do invite us to it. What's wrong with that?

For once Gerda was dressed like a woman. She was wearing a skirt and a smart hat. She was actually incredibly pretty, Käthe realised.

Gerda straightened her hat. "So we'll do Saint Nicholas instead. I wonder whether they'll have Stollen?"

They didn't have Stollen, of course. It was much too early. There was, though, a pretty impressive array of cakes. Who could believe there was a war on?

Käthe actually felt a bit overwhelmed by it all. She picked a slice of baked Käsekuchen. She hadn't got the appetite for it, though, somehow. She pushed it around her plate.

"More coffee?" Gerda was holding the pot up, ready to pour.

The coffee was good. She knew that. She just didn't want any today, though. She had this really strange feeling that she should be at home. Butterflies danced lightly in her tummy. She must go home. She really must.

"I'm sorry. I can't do this. Will you pay and I'll settle up later?"

"But what's the matter? Are you ill or something?" Gerda was frowning and had gone a little pale.

"No. I don't know. I just feel too agitated to stay here. I'll see you tomorrow."

She gathered up her things and made her way to the door.

"Is there a problem with your cake?" asked one of the waitresses as she hurried out.

She shook her head. "No. It's fine. I just have to get home."

"I hope no one's ill."

"No. I don't know. I don't think so."

Then she was outside.

As she made her way as quickly as she could along the icy streets, she realised that Gerda probably thought she'd gone mad. It was illogical. Why did she have this compulsion to get home?

She must, though. She really must.

She didn't actually run. She just walked as fast as she could. She soon became very warm despite the December cold. Her coat was thick and the movement made her glow. She became breathless but pushed on forwards.

She really didn't understand where this feeling was coming from. She just knew something dramatic was going to happen today.

She arrived at last and tried to insert her key into the front door to the apartment. Her hands were shaking and it was a job to get the key to line up with the lock. This was so ridiculous. At last though it slid into place and she was able to open the door. Her heart was thumping now.

She couldn't believe her ears. Her mother and Imelda were singing in the kitchen. Christmas carols. They were singing Christmas carols and it was only St Nicholas. Only the first week of Advent. Yes, they'd lit the first candle on the Advent wreath the Sunday before, but hadn't Mutti said they would keep it all very quiet? "Because if Leo *is* still alive he's probably not in a very good place. And if he has indeed died we need to be respectful." And here they were, singing their heads off.

She made her way to the kitchen.

"Käthe, darling. We've got the most wonderful news." Her mother's face was covered in flour. "We're making Stollen and Wiener Kipferl."

Too early. It's much too early. Käthe's heart was beating even more violently now. What was so good about making cake and biscuits anyway?

"He's back. Leo's back." Mutti wiped her hands on her

pinafore and walked over to Käthe and embraced her. "Your brother is alive. And quite well."

Käthe felt slightly faint. Was she dreaming?

But Imelda was nodding her head vigorously. "Yes, Fräulein Lehrs. Your poor brother had lost his memory. But it's just come back."

Mutti's face suddenly became serious. "Just as well, really, I think. But he did remember eating a lot of pea soup. Just think, they fed those brave young men on nothing but pea soup." She sat down on one of the kitchen chairs and Käthe thought she was going to start crying.

She was having some trouble holding back the tears herself. "How did you find out?"

Imelda put down the bowl she'd been holding. "He came here this afternoon."

"Why?" How could he find his way here if he'd lost his memory?

Mutti clapped her hands together. "It was so extraordinary. I'd been agitated all afternoon. I felt really restless."

Käthe nodded. Just how she'd felt.

"Well, I just looked out of the window and there he was. Looking up at our apartment."

"You see, Fräulein Lehrs, seeing the apartment made him remember who he was. Then they rang the doorbell and came in."

"They?"

Mutti nodded. "He and a nice young man who was looking after him. He was astonished when he found out who Leo was. Your brother has done so well in this war. Apparently, there'd been a bit of a mix-up because he'd given his jacket to a wounded soldier. So, he had no papers on him when they found him." A shadow passed across Mutti's face. "Let's just hope he doesn't remember too much more."

"Where is he now?"

Mutti grinned. "He has a little office job in the city. We don't think he'll have to go back to the front."

Suddenly it seemed that making Christmas cake and biscuits

was the most natural thing in the world. "Can I help you with the baking?"

Mutti laughed. "That will be a first."

Imelda passed her an apron.

Käthe was exhausted by the time they'd finished making six Stollen and four dozen Wiener Kipferl. She'd managed to make a complete mess of her pinafore.

Imelda laughed. "Never mind, Fräulein Lehrs. That's the purpose of the pinafore, after all. To keep all of the spillages off your good clothes."

Mutti snorted when she saw Käthe's attempt at making biscuits. "My goodness. Käthe. Kipferl are supposed to be crescent-shaped. Yours look more like shoes for crippled horses. Do you have no domestic skills whatsoever?"

They'd all three laughed. It was odd though. She was so perfect and precise with her experiments. Surely there were a lot of similarities between cooking and chemistry? Why couldn't she cook and bake, then?

Vati came home early that evening and brought with him a bottle of the best Sekt he'd been able to find.

"It's a shame Leo can't enjoy this with us," she'd said. She surprised herself. For once she was just pleased about something to do with her older brother. She was glad he was all right.

"Oh, I expect he'll be able to visit us soon properly. Let's drink a toast to him." Vati had then poured out the Sekt and they'd raised their glasses to Oberleutnant Leopold Lehrs.

Rudi as usual had been laid back and pragmatic. "Now I can boast about my brave older brother whenever people ask why I've not been in the war. It will change the subject nicely."

It had been a lovely evening. Vati and Rudi insisted on trying the Kipferl.

"Quality control, you understand," Rudi had said. He also insisted on taking one from each batch. "To make sure you're keeping up standards." Mutti and Imelda had protested, though, that the Stollen shouldn't be touched until the following Sunday.

They'd talked and laughed until nearly midnight. Imelda had eaten at the family table and then sat with them in the drawing room.

Sleep would come easily, Käthe thought. She had almost drifted off when she woke suddenly with a start. No! If Leo was back she was no longer the scientist in the family. No. This wasn't fair. Oh, and it was such a nuisance that she felt that way. It was so wrong of her. She should only be glad that her brother was back. Darn!

Berlin 1918

Chapter 17: losing Christian

Käthe couldn't help it. She just had to keep looking at the letter she'd found in her student pigeon hole. She read it over and over again. It was from Albert Einstein himself. The best bit was right at the very end.

"I really can see how frustrating it is for you and Fräulein Oppenheimer. I share your frustration in fact. I am now doing my level best to persuade my colleagues here at the faculty that the two of you should be allowed to study in exactly the same way as the men do. Women are just as capable of understanding science as men. We need you more than ever as this war drags on."

And there was the great man's signature right at the end. She touched it and smiled to herself. Some people would pay a fortune to own this letter. If she ever fell on hard times... No, she would not part with this letter for the world.

This really called for a celebration. For once she would have been only too glad to go to the Victoria Café with Gerda except that Gerda was tucked up in bed at home with the 'flu. Perhaps she could entice Vati to leave the factory for an hour or if not, perhaps he would just let her go and get coffee and cake for them to share.

Yes, Vati would most certainly do. She stuffed the letter into her satchel and set off towards the factory.

She hardly noticed the walk, she was so lost in her thoughts about what it would be like if she and Gerda were allowed to study properly. Perhaps they would go on and make some amazing discovery. The two of them might continue to work together for years and years. Perhaps they would become famous.

Then she was there and walking into the main entrance.

"Good afternoon, Fräulein Lehrs." Young Angelika, the new receptionist seemed hardly to be able to look at her. She was normally such a friendly and funny girl, always ready to tell Käthe a joke.

"I'm here to see my father. Is he in his office?"

Angelika nodded. "I expect he'll be glad to see you." She turned back to her desk and stared at some papers.

This was all very odd. Very odd indeed.

Frau Drescher was in the little office in front of her father's when she got there. The poor woman looked tired. She was stooped wearily over her desk.

She jumped when Käthe spoke to her.

"Oh, Fräulein Lehrs. I'm so pleased you're here. He's taken the news so badly."

What did she mean? Had something else happened to Leo? Had Rudi been taken ill again? Mutti? "The news?"

"Oh, you've not heard? I thought…"

Käthe shook her head.

Frau Drescher sighed. "It's young Christian Bauer. He was killed in action yesterday."

Käthe's heart missed a beat and she began to feel dizzy.

No. Not Christian. She wouldn't be a scientist at all if it wasn't for Christian, would she? He'd persuaded her, hadn't he, that she should really try? And it was his suggestion about what to do that had got her into the university in the first place.

Frau Drescher put her handkerchief up to her mouth and waved towards the door. "Go on in. He'll be pleased to see you."

Käthe rushed into Vati's office. He was standing by the window, leaning his forehead on his arm that was propped up on the window frame. He was staring at nothing in particular. "Vati, what happened with Christian?"

Her father shook his head. "He didn't stand a chance. Had to go over the top. They fired at him."

"How could they?"

"Oh, Käthe, they were just doing their job. Christian and his friends would have had to do the same. These high-up men just give their commands – on both sides – and the young men have to carry them out. It's always the same in war. At least Leo came back to us." Anyway, what brings you here?"

It was? Why did it have to be like that? It was so unfair. "Oh, it's not important. I'm so sorry about Christian." Nothing mattered now in comparison to the horrid thing that had happened to Christian.

"So, am I. He was such a reliable worker and such a nice young man as well. Such a waste."

"What about his family?"

"There's just the mother. She's a widow. Christian was all she had."

"Oh dear."

"Right. I'm going to close the factory early. I'll get your mother to go and see Frau Bauer later in the week."

"I can go with her if you like."

"That would be nice. As you knew him a little."

Käthe nodded.

Her father took his coat and scarf off the coat stand and arranged with Frau Drescher to send everybody home. They set off back to their own apartment.

Mutti and Rudi picked up on their mood straight away. Mutti went pale as soon as she saw them and Rudi looked awkward.

"What on earth's happened?" said Mutti. "Not Leo again?"

Vati shook his head. "Young Christian Bauer. Killed yesterday."

Rudi shuffled awkwardly and looked at the floor.

Vati rubbed his shoulder. "It's not your fault you couldn't go and fight." He turned to Mutti. "You will go and see his mother?"

Käthe jumped out of her seat. "I'll come as well, Mutti."

Mutti nodded. "Of course." She smiled at Käthe. They'd been getting on a lot better since that day Leo came back and they'd made the Christmas goodies early.

"It's madness this, war." Rudi kicked the door frame. "And it's just mad to get killed now. They say it's going to end soon."

Mutti sighed. "Oh yes, men and their wars. But we should eat now. We'll need to be strong tomorrow. I expect it's been a shock for everyone at the factory. Käthe, will you go and tell Imelda we're ready?"

Käthe nodded.

She quickly found Imelda, offered to carry some of the food to the table and then the two of them made their way to the dining room. Her father wasn't there when they arrived.

"Where's Vati?" she asked.

"He's gone to bed" said Mutti. "He's exhausted."

"Oh." She exchanged a glance with Rudi. He raised his eyebrows and shook his head. It was not like their father to be tired or ill.

"Come on then," said Mutti pointing to the table.

There was black bread, cheese, roll mops and salad. All things she normally liked. It was a bit of a miserable meal time, though. Mutti just stared into space. Rudi hardly looked at her. None of them ate much.

Then Mutti sighed. "Well, if nobody wants any more I suppose we should clear this up. I expect Imelda will want to get home soon."

"Is Vati ill?" asked Käthe.

Mutti shrugged. "I hope not. I do hope not. It's this war, you know. It's eating away at him. He's worried about the factory, too."

"Why?"

"Well, he's lost all of his best workers and he's worried he won't be able to keep up the standards," said Rudi.

Mutti stood up and glared at Käthe. So much for them getting on better, then. "There are no financial worries. We'll still be able to pay for your studies." Her face had gone bright red. She picked up two of the dishes and marched out of the room.

"I didn't mean that," Käthe said almost to herself.

"Don't worry," said Rudi. "She's just concerned about Vati."

"It's just not like him is it?"

Rudi shook his head. He looked away from her as he gathered the rest of crockery from the table. Oh dear. He must be worried too.

It wasn't until she went to bed that night that Käthe remembered about the letter from Professor Einstein.

Chapter 18: gaining a degree

Käthe's back was aching. She'd been leaning over her work for hours. Yes, she'd heard Leo arrive. Mutti had said he had something important to discuss so he was staying for lunch on Sunday. So, it was going to be like old times, then. She liked it better on the whole now that it was just her, Mutti, Vati and Rudi.

So, what was this big mystery, then?

She could hear Mutti and Leo talking but not what they were saying. Then the drawing-room door opened and closed. She could go and join them but she couldn't be bothered. She'd rather get on with her work. This was more important.

She got up out of her chair, stretched, and sat back down again. She couldn't really concentrate, though. What was going on, then?

The tap came at the door a few seconds later. She didn't really have time to answer before Mutti came in. "I have news," said Mutti, and sat down on the small chair by the window. She sighed. "Your brother has decided he wants to pursue another line of study."

"Oh?"

"He wants to go for the spirit, not the science."

What on earth did that mean?

"I've told him we expect him to finish his studies."

Who was we? Vati, Mutti and Rudi? Was she included in the "we"?

"We think we can find him the money to start on his new venture."

Now that wasn't fair. That might mean if it did become possible for her to study science properly there wouldn't be any money left to pay for her.

Mutti sighed again. "At least it means he'll be earning sooner. So we can then spare some for you if your studies ever come to anything or you decide to get married."

Oh. "What about Rudi?"

"He's already taken care of."

Mutti got up from the chair and shrugged. "I'd better go and see that the lunch is on its way." She turned as she got to the door. "I guess that makes you our scientist now."

"Not Rudi?"

"He's a mathematician." She shut the door behind her.

Käthe took a deep breath. She stood up and looked at herself in the mirror. "Scientist in the family," she muttered. If only they would let her study properly for a degree.

"It's incredible," said Gerda. "They've grown a few brains at last."

"I'm really surprised," said Käthe. "All the men are back now."

"Well, not all of them, really."

No, of course not. They were lucky to have Leo. A lot of the young men hadn't come home and or had come back injured.

"So do you think it's because they haven't got enough men to do the work?"

"Perhaps." Gerda stretched her arms over her head and her legs out in front of her. She was dressed in men's clothing again. "Or maybe it's just because we do such a good job."

It surely couldn't be just that. She looked at the letter again. "It actually says 'in recognition for your services to science we are going to allow you to take the exam with those who are studying on the first degree programme.' "

"So there you are. You'll be able to study with your mad professor."

"We'll have to pass the exam first."

"Piece of cake – for you at least."

"I'm glad you think so."

"Come on. Talking of cake, we'd better go and celebrate. Chocolate cake should do the trick." Gerda hooked her arm through Käthe's and led her towards the door to the street.

"It's just a Vordiploma," said Käthe. "There's no need to fuss."

"It's what the Americans and the British call a Bachelor degree. It's a very good thing to have. So I will make a fuss." Mutti poured the tea and then cut a slice of the chocolate cake. "Worth a slice of cake at least."

"Yeah, sis, I'm proud of you."

"Why? Just because I'm a girl." She glowered at her younger brother.

"No." He frowned. "Because I know you worked hard. And I know you deserved this."

"It's no different from what you and Leo are doing. You're only being nice because you think we women can't do these things."

Rudi sighed. "Suit yourself. I'll leave you two ladies to it."

"Ah well," said Mutti. "All the more for us. What a shame Leo couldn't be here."

"Yes," muttered Käthe. "What a shame."

She was glad he hadn't come. She still had the feeling that he was a bit jealous that she still enjoyed science more than he did and that she'd actually got a higher mark than he'd got for this first part of her academic career.

"So when will you start work with Professor Einstein?"

"Soon. Very soon."

Now that was something to look forward to. She took another slice of cake. Yes, something to celebrate after all.

Chapter 19: losing a father

Käthe had forgotten her key. She rang the doorbell. Normally at this time Mutti chatted to Vati in the bedroom whilst he drank his tea. No one hurried to the door, though. Was this a good sign? Was he a bit better? Perhaps they'd gone out for a short walk? Where was Imelda or Schwester Adelberg, the young nurse who'd been helping to look after Vati? Rudi even? Surely someone was in?

Vati did try to get up every day but he'd really been quite ill since they'd had the news about Christian.

The doctor hadn't really given a very clear diagnosis. "It's a combination of things, Frau Lehrs," he'd said to Mutti. "His worry about this war has weakened him. The rickets have got worse. And now this chest infection…"

"That shouldn't kill a man, though, should it, Herr Doctor? He will recover won't he?" Mutti asked.

"I'm afraid I can't say. He's still quite young but you know this terrible war has taken its toll. It's made men even younger than him want to give up. I'm sorry I can't give you any better news."

It had been Mutti's birthday the day before and she's made a cheesecake but nobody had wanted to eat it. Maybe they would today?

She rang the doorbell again.

This time she heard footsteps coming along the hallway. The door opened. It was Schwester Adelberg.

"Oh. Fräulein Lehrs. I thought you might be someone come about the arrangements?"

"The arrangements?"

"Your father…"

Suddenly Mutti was standing behind Schwester Adelberg. She signalled that Käthe should come in. "Come straight into the drawing room," she said.

What was going on? Mutti's face looked grim. Rudi was standing by the mantelpiece. He was very pale. Was he ill again?

"Sit down," said Mutti. She sat down herself on her armchair.

Käthe sat on one of the chaise-longues.

"It's your father," began Mutti. The words seemed to stick in her throat.

"Vati died at four o'clock today," said Rudi.

The doorbell rang again.

Mutti took a deep breath and seemed to regain some composure. "That's probably them," she said.

Käthe felt sick. This couldn't be true could it? She was dreaming wasn't she? She would wake up any moment and find that Vati was well on the way to recovery. Surely.

Rudi came over to her and put a hand on her shoulder. "It was very quick and very peaceful. Mutti was with him."

She managed to find her voice somehow. "Do we know exactly why?"

Rudi shook his head. "I'm guessing, though, that he's probably always had a weak heart. It's almost as if he was broken-hearted. Leo going missing. Then Christian dying. There have been other young men in the factory as well. You know also that he thought all wars are a waste."

Käthe nodded. He did indeed. They killed people unnecessarily. But now he had died and he had been much too young to die as well.

She could hear men's voices in the hallway.

"Did you want to see him before they take him away?" asked Rudi.

Käthe shook her head. If she was honest, she was a little afraid of seeing a human corpse. They were going to take her Vati away, though, and she wasn't sure she could quite accept that.

"Leo might want to. I'll go and ask if they'll wait until he's here."

Käthe was glad to be left on her own for a while. She was having some difficulty taking all of this in. Why couldn't she wake up from this terrible dream?

No, that didn't happen. The nightmare continued.

She wasn't crying. Why wasn't she crying?

The voices in the hallway continued. Then she heard Leo

107

arrive. Finally the front door opened again and she guessed they were taking Vati off to the undertakers.

The door to the drawing room opened and in came Leo and Rudi.

"Mutti's staying in her room," said Leo.

She was staying in the room where their father had died just a short while before?

"She wants to feel close to him," said Rudi.

Käthe thought that maybe she understood that. She might like to go and sit in Vati's factory at the office. That's where she'd spent so many happy times with him.

"I suppose I should go and let them know at the factory," said Leo.

"We could phone, couldn't we?" asked Rudi.

"I don't know. I think it would be better to do it in person."

Käthe nodded. "I'd like to do it, actually."

"I think I should. As the eldest." Leo was frowning.

Now she felt the tears forming. But they weren't for Vati. They were because Leo was being bossy again.

"Why don't the three of us go?" said Rudi.

Leo shrugged. "All right. Let's go now."

At that moment the door opened and in walked Mutti.

"I've decided we'll have a hybrid funeral," she said. "Partly Jewish and partly Evangelical."

What?

Leo didn't seem to know what to say. Mutti was quiet. How could she be so calm? All Käthe wanted to do was scream and shout. She still didn't want it to be true.

It must be, though, because here they all were, dressed up in their funeral clothes.

Leo leant over and gave her a hug. He slapped Rudi's back. "What needs to be done?"

"Nothing. It's all in hand," said Mutti. "The shomer is with your father now. The carriages come at three."

"I'll go and sit with him for a while."

Mutti nodded.

Why were they going back to their old Jewish ways? Käthe just didn't understand that.

She didn't want to go into that room where Vati was in his coffin. She stayed in her room until she heard Leo and the shomer come out. Suddenly she was standing face to face with them in the hallway. The shomer was a young man, she realised. She'd always thought the men who did these ceremonies would be old and stuffy. But here was someone who looked just like Leo. Not like Rudi. Rudi didn't have that look of puzzled despair she guessed had something to do with them having both fought in the war. Had they been talking about it? Were they allowed to chat while they kept their vigil?

Oh, it was all nonsense anyway. That wasn't their father in there. That was just an empty shell.

Mutti appeared in the hallway. The shomer gasped. No wonder. She was wearing a pale yellow blouse with her black skirt and jacket and her hat had yellow feathers attached.

What did she think she was doing?

Mutti smiled. "Well, what's the matter? Your father would have hated us to wear dark colours all the time. And look. I've torn my coat anyway."

She handed Leo a large pair of cloth-cutting scissors.

Leo took them and made a slit in his jacket and then tore it with his hands. He handed the scissors to Käthe. She made a small nick in her black silk dress and tore it.

What a waste. Even so, it helped somehow.

They were ready to bury their father.

Käthe watched as they lowered the coffin into the ground.

"Are you sure you don't want to see him?" Frau Biel had asked. "It's wise to see that they have the right corpse in the coffin you know."

"Oh what a nonsense and a fuss," Mutti had said. "That's the last thing I'd want. It wouldn't be Ernst."

"But Frau Lehrs," Frau Biel had continued, "didn't you say he looked terrible as he died? All that bile. Didn't you want to see him at peace?"

"It wouldn't be him. Just an empty shell," Mutti had whispered.

She was right. Whatever was in that coffin wasn't actually her father.

And now it was all over. The ceremony hadn't taken long at all in the end. Dust to dust. Ashes to ashes. Each of them – Mutti, Leo, Käthe and Rudi – had thrown a handful of earth and a white rose into the grave. That was it. Over and done with. Gone.

The carriages set off back to the Lehrs home in Pariser Strasse and a few moments later Mutti was welcoming the guests who had come for the small cold lunch.

"I don't think they like your yellow blouse and the feather in your hat," said Leo to their mother.

"Well, they will just have to put up with it," she replied. She pointed to Leo's torn jacket. "And if they're going to make comments, perhaps they'll have something to say about that. Oh it's just so much nonsense. The Jewish way. The Christian way. How does anybody know what exactly is right? Tell me that."

Leo was staring at Mutti. It was for a moment as if they both recognised something, that only they understood. There was something mysterious going on between them. It was nothing to do with her.

Berlin 1920

Chapter 20: a fine young man?

"I'm sure you'll like Professor Edler," Professor Gurwell had said. "He's a new colleague, a fine young man."

So, this Professor Hans Edler was to be her supervisor. She wouldn't get to speak to Professor Einstein for weeks though Professor Gurwell had promised that both he and Professor Edler would pass on notes about her work and that Einstein would have to approve of everything.

Well, she'd better go and find him.

She'd dressed smartly today. She had on her new velvet skirt and a smart jacket. She'd even bought herself a brand new satchel. She couldn't carry that old ink-stained one about much longer. She must make a good impression.

"You should wear your new kitten-heels," Mutti had said.

"Absolutely not," said Käthe. She was not going to totter about like a flapper. She had to impress this man and make sure he knew that she was his equal. Well, perhaps not just yet but she would be soon enough.

She found his office at last. Typical. In the basement. Trust the powers that be to hide new staff down here until they'd proved themselves. The rooms weren't even numbered properly. It was so gloomy that even if the rooms all had numbers you wouldn't be able to read them. But here she was at last. She'd worked out which was his office just by counting.

She tentatively knocked on the door. There was no answer at first but she could hear someone shuffling papers. She knocked a little louder.

"Come in."

She pushed the door open and walked in.

Professor Edler was sitting at his desk. He didn't get up to shake her hand. He remained in his seat, just about half turned towards her. How rude. He sniffed and nodded and then turned away from her. "Ah, yes, one of our lady-scientists. How very fascinating. So you think you're capable of studying for a doctorate, do you?"

"I know I am."

"We'll see." He smirked and turned back to his desk and started writing something on a piece of paper. "Do sit down," he muttered. "You're making the room look untidy."

Really. The cheek of the man.

Käthe sat down on the chair next to his desk. He carried on scribbling. She couldn't see his face but she could see at least that he was well dressed. She stared down at his shiny brown leather shoes. His suit was quite new and it looked as if it was made of good quality material. His shirt was starched and very white.

Perhaps it was his first ever job and he'd just gone out and bought everything new. Well, he'd better know what he was doing.

"Sorry to keep you waiting, Fräulein Lehrs, but I must get this off in the midday post."

Obviously she wasn't as important as whatever he was doing there. He scribbled for a few more minutes, blotted the paper, folded it and put it in an envelope.

Then he looked up at her. "Well, Fräulein Lehrs, how can I be of assistance?"

His eyes seemed to be laughing. Käthe wasn't sure she liked that. She couldn't help but notice, however, that he had a very handsome face. Why was she even thinking about that?

"Well, I'm here to talk about my doctorate."

"Indeed." He sat back, stretched his legs out in front of him and folded his arms across his chest. "So, tell me. What do you want to discover?"

"I want find out all about relativity in time. How time can be different according to the way it's observed. Time travel may even be possible."

"Really?" The corners of his mouth were twitching and his eyes were sparkling. Was he laughing at her now? "And what sort of experiments would you do to investigate your ideas?"

Oh, she knew that answer to that question all right. But she wasn't going to sit there and let this horrid man make her feel small. She got up on to the feet and started pacing the room as she outlined all of her ideas. She had so many!

At one point she stopped as a book on the shelf caught her eye. It was a newer edition of the book about planets that she owned.

"Have you finished, Fräulein Lehrs, or are you just trying to get your breath back? I'll give you that. Whatever else you can certainly talk quickly."

"I've almost finished. I'd add of course some of the discussions that are currently taking place – and prove several of them to be nonsensical." She paused for breath again. "May I take a look at the book?" She pointed to the planet book.

"Be my guest." He took the book from her and carried it over to the table. "There. Help yourself."

She looked through a few pages. The photographic plates were even more startling than in her own edition.

"So beautiful," she whispered as she touched the images.

"Indeed." She felt as if he was looking at her. She turned towards him. She was right. Professor Edler was staring at her. He caught his breath. "Well, I think we should make a plan."

"All right. What do you suggest?"

He beckoned her over to his desk. He pushed all of his books and papers aside and spread out a large sheet of paper. He took his pencil and ruler and divided it into forty-eight squares. "These are the months of each of your four years' study. We can add other things as we think of them. Let's start at the end and work backwards."

Between them they filled in the names of the months and the year in each box. Soon they were filling in details in the boxes.

At times he would add an idea and sometimes she would. She still felt as though he was laughing at her. He repeated everything she said as if he didn't quite believe her. It was annoying. At least he was filling in the chart, though, so he must be taking her seriously really, mustn't he?

"There, now," he said after about an hour. "That should do. If we can hold ourselves to this programme of research you should do well. I shall pin this up on the wall and we can refer to it whenever we meet. Do you think you'll be able to do it?"

"Wait a minute." She needed to take this in. It was a little frightening really. "I ought to keep a copy of this."

114

Professor Edler started rolling up the chart. "I'll get one of the secretaries to make you a copy and then I'll pin it on the wall later."

"Thank you, Professor Edler." She tried to mean it but she still couldn't get away from the idea that he wasn't quite treating her seriously. She could just imagine him in the senior common room telling his colleagues about "one of these funny little lady-scientists who has ideas above her station" and that he would write to Professor Einstein and tell him it would all be a waste of time.

"My pleasure. I suppose this was quite a pleasant way to spend an afternoon. With a lovely young lady who is pretty and may be intelligent as well. So much nicer than just poring over the fusty old books." His eyes were really shining brightly when he said that. The corner of his mouth was still twitching though, as if he wanted to laugh. Now he must really be teasing her but he seemed to be admiring her as well.

Käthe felt her cheeks going red. This was not what she wanted. She wanted him to ignore the fact that she was a woman. The question shouldn't even arise. She didn't want him to make concessions for her.

She suddenly had this vision of herself in the future. Her research would make her into a professor and she in turn would supervise young women so that they could study science without any of those silly questions about the difference between women and men arising. No, she did not want him to refrain from the type of jokes that the men shared, nor did she want him or any of them lifting heavy objects for her or thinking that she shouldn't bother her pretty little head.

He was looking at her again now and that silly little smile still threatening to erupt. She just had to get away.

"I'd better go now, Professor Edler. I've taken up a lot of your time."

He shrugged. "It's just part of my work. Just one more thing before you rush off." He put his hand on Käthe's arm. She wished he hadn't done. It felt a bit intrusive and a little patronising. Actually, though, it also felt rather nice. Bother that thought. "Shall we meet each Thursday at this time, to discuss your progress – if there is any?" His pupils were huge and his eyes were smiling now as well.

She had to look away. "Yes, good. That will be fine."

She turned towards the door.

"So, see you next Thursday," he called after her as she made through the door.

She closed the door behind her. Her heart was thumping. What was that about?

Chapter 21: an irritating professor

"So what's he like, this Professor Hans Edler?" Gerda had dragged Käthe to the Victoria Café yet again. It was a time to celebrate. She had a PhD supervisor. She was going to work with Einstein. Why shouldn't she celebrate? That had been Gerda's argument.

It seemed that the slightest little excuse got people buying cake and coffee. Mutti and Gerda were as bad as each other. It was getting a little irritating.

"Well. Are you going to tell me or not?"

Käthe sighed. "He's young. He's arrogant. He doesn't think women can be scientists."

"Huh! Well, you'll have to make him change his mind about that."

"Naturally."

"Come on, Käthe. There's something else you're not telling me."

Käthe shrugged. "He has excellent taste in clothing. He's obviously earning a lot. He has interesting eyes."

"Aha! You're in love with him."

"I am not."

"Käthe wants a beau. Käthe wants a beau."

"I do not!" Käthe could feel her cheeks burning.

"You so do! And you do know that once you go down that path you'll never be a scientist."

"I'm not listening to this." She stood up, pushed her chair in and made her way to the door.

"Leaving your coffee and cake again, Käthe Lehrs? Shame on you! Never mind. All the more for me," Gerda called as Käthe made her way through the door.

Käthe was sure everyone was staring at her.

She walked as quickly as she could back to the faculty. She was soon out of breath. She'd got too much to think about. She hadn't got time for these jollies. Why couldn't men accept that women were as good as them? They were possibly even better, weren't they? Why did she have to have Professor Hans Edler as a supervisor? He was a misogynist.

She walked faster and faster. She almost ran up the steps. Thank goodness skirts were shorter these days.

She must do something positive now. What, though? Go to the library perhaps? Read some more journal articles. In the lecture she'd attended on starting doctoral studies, the lecturer had told them that they must read widely around their subject before they started. Right then. She would go and do that. It was on the list anyway.

She turned towards the staircase that led up to the library. She'd been too busy thinking to look quite at where she was going. She bumped into someone. Papers flew up into the air. Her satchel dropped to the floor and she heard the too familiar sound of an ink bottle breaking Not again! That satchel was less than a month old.

She was about to harangue the person who'd bumped into her for not looking where they were going but she remembered it she'd been the one who'd failed to be careful.

"Oh dear," said a voice she recognised. "You seem to have a spillage."

Professor Hans Edler was pointing at a patch of spreading ink on her almost brand new satchel.

"I'm sorry," she managed to mutter.

"No harm done, except to your satchel." He held out a hand to her. She tried to resist taking it. She could get up on her own. He shook the hand at her and nodded his head slightly. Those eyes again. She wished they wouldn't tease her so. She took his hand. She could hardly breathe she felt so uncomfortable. She wished he would let her hand go. He did once she was on her feet.

He chuckled as he looked down at the papers strewn across the floor. "What a mess."

She bent down and helped him to pick them up.

"Thank you," he said, as she handed him the last few. "Come on. Empty your satchel. I'll give it to one of our friends in Chemistry and see if they have any ideas of how to get rid of the stain."

That was all very well but it left Käthe with a pile of books and papers she couldn't carry.

"Look. Take my briefcase and I'll get some of these monkeys to help me transport this lot back to my room. I have a spare one at home. I was probably carrying too much anyway."

He detained a couple of the young undergraduates and piled them up with the books and papers that had been in his briefcase and the ones that he'd dropped on the floor. "It's all right, Fräulein Lehrs. You can return the briefcase when you come for your next supervision." He turned and made his way down the hallway.

Käthe didn't know what to think or how to feel. She stood on the spot for several minutes after he'd disappeared. Then she slowly made her way to the library.

She didn't get much done that afternoon.

She wished she understood what was going on there. It was peculiar. It still irritated her that he'd seemed so dismissive. She just wanted to get on with her work but she wasn't sure that Hans Edler was the one to help her with that effectively. And she couldn't stop thinking about him.

The week went by slowly. Käthe couldn't work out whether she was looking forward to another meeting with her supervisor or not. She wanted to get on with her work, of course she did. But she found that man so disturbing.

Thursday came round and there she was knocking on Professor Edler's door again. She held her breath, half hoping he wouldn't be there.

"Come in!"

Her heart was thumping as she opened the door.

"Ah, Fräulein Lehrs. What a pleasure."

She couldn't quite bring herself to look at him. "I've brought along my notes," she said as she started unpacking the briefcase. "And don't let me forget to give you back your case."

"Indeed. And I have some good news." He got up out of his seat. "The satchel has been cleaned. It's almost as good as new."

He opened a cupboard and took out her satchel. "I'm afraid that part of the case will never shine up quite like it did before." He pointed to a dull patch. "But at least from a distance it will look fine."

"Thank you," she managed to whisper.

"So, then, what do you have for me?" That silly smile was at the edge of his lips again. Drat the man! Would he not take her seriously?

Käthe took a deep breath and laid her notes out on Professor Edler's desk. She talked about them, pointing out certain diagrams. She was soon so absorbed in what she was saying that she forgot to be put off by him just being there. Now, it was all about science.

She finally stopped. She looked at the clock on the wall. She had been talking for over forty minutes.

Hans Edler was nodding his head and had his hand over his mouth as he looked down at her work. "Most impressive. Most impressive," he mumbled. He started to gather up the papers. "Let me look at these in detail and I'll give you a few more ideas for next week. Is there much more you want to read?"

"About the same again."

"Good. Then that might conclude the literature review." He flicked though the papers and nodded several times, muttering something to himself that she couldn't understand.

"Good," he said again finally. He looked up at her. His eyes were sparkling. "Do you think we might go and have cake and coffee?"

What was he asking her? Had she heard right? Why was everyone so obsessed with cake?

Darn. Käthe felt her cheeks go red again. She looked away.

Why was he looking at her that way?

"I don't think I can," she said. "I don't have time."

She made her way towards the door.

"What a shame," muttered Hans Edler.

She went through the doorway and shut the door without saying goodbye. Her heart was bouncing in her chest as she made her way up the stairs.

Chapter 22: flirtations

"Why do you stare at that staircase every time we go past?" asked Gerda. "There's nothing down there."

Oh but there is. That is where Hans Edler has his office.

She lingered as well near the stairs that led up to the library. Would he appear there again and could she once more send his books flying? Why hadn't she gone for coffee with him? Oh, what was she thinking.

It didn't happen, anyway.

Once she did manage to see him across the crowded refectory. He was sitting on the staff high table, of course. She dreamt that one day she could be up there with him, a fellow academic, discussing with him some aspects of the new physics.

"You're staring at that professor of yours." Gerda nudged her. "Ah. Told you. You're in love with him."

"No I'm not." Käthe's cheeks grew hot.

"See, you're blushing."

Why was this happening? It was such a nuisance. It wouldn't stop, though.

And she didn't bump into him again. She was just going to have to wait until her next supervision.

She saw him again a few days later. He was walking along the street in front of the faculty. A young woman, possibly a couple of years older than her, was hanging on to his arm.

Who was she? What was he doing with her? She surely wasn't another student, was she? Weren't she and Gerda the only two females? Anyway, this woman wasn't dressed right for studying. Much too glamorous and no sign of any satchel or briefcase for carrying books and papers. His fiancée then? Wife? Sister? They seemed quite intimate.

It stung her that he was showing so much attention to another female. He should be proud of her, and showing her off – as his very clever student, of course, nothing else.

Then she did something she knew was terrible. She started to follow them.

They made their way along the street and then turned into an alleyway that Käthe had never really noticed before. They were chatting away and the woman kept laughing loudly.

Well, who would have thought he would be so witty? He was obviously saying something amusing, though.

A few metres into the alleyway they turned into a doorway. Käthe walked up to it slowly and looked into the window. It was a café, by the looks of it. A Turkish café, it said. Very nice for them, she was sure. Now she'd better get on. There was nothing more to be found out here.

Then Hans Edler saw her. He waved that she should go in.

Oh no. What had she done? She had to go in, though. Otherwise what could she say next time she saw him?

He stood up and shook Käthe's hand. "Adele, this is the talented student I told you about. Fräulein Lehrs, please meet Adele Edler, my cousin's wife."

Adele Edler smiled at her and held out her hand. "I'm very pleased to meet you. Hans has told me so much about you."

Yes, he probably had. All about her and the satchel incident, no doubt. And about how stupid she was for wanting to be a scientist. Could they have been laughing about her? She wished she could just disappear. Even if this glamorous young woman was just his cousin-in-law, she was outshining Käthe in so many ways. That very smart jacket and matching skirt, the hair that was sophisticated and tidy, the smart hat and was that rouge on her cheeks and lipstick on her lips?

"Come and join us for coffee and cake," said Professor Edler. "We are celebrating my cousin's promotion. Adele came to fetch me because he's too busy to take time off. So, you must help us to mark the occasion." He pulled up a chair to their table.

There was no way she could say no this time.

"This café's a particular favourite of mine," said Professor Edler. "You might have met it sooner if you'd agreed to come here with me last week."

The café was really different from the sort of places that Mutti liked to go to. It was smaller and had more dark corners. It was quieter.

Hans Edler smiled at her. "Well, what do you think?"

Käthe nodded. "I like it," she mumbled, though she wasn't really sure.

They were sitting in a small, dark alcove. There was a thick green velvet tablecloth on the table and a small white linen one over that.

"The coffee is Turkish here," said Professor Edler. "Have you tried that before?"

Käthe shook her head.

"It's really quite different. Stronger and sweeter. They make it with rose water."

A waiter arrived with the coffee pot and poured some into their cups. Käthe couldn't believe how tiny the cups were. She smiled at Adele Edler. "Why are the cups so small?"

"You'll understand when you take a sip."

She took a mouthful of the coffee. Yes, it was sweet and strong. It made her head spin. "It's so… So…"

Hans Edler nodded. "Difficult to put into words, isn't it? Some say it's an aphrodisiac and a cure for infertility." He was looking at her very intently. There was a mischievous gleam in his eye.

"I wouldn't know about that," said Käthe looking away. But yes, it was certainly doing something.

"Now you must also try this." He offered her a piece of the Turkish Delight that the waiter had brought along with the coffee. "It's quite unlike what you can buy in the German shops."

Käthe had only ever seen the pink sort before. She took a piece of the green. It tasted a little of mint.

"Tell us all about yourself," said Adele Edler. "And about your family."

So Käthe told them all about Rudi and his illness, Vati dying so young, Leo having been missing in the Great War and Mutti being such a fan of high society. And of course about her own determination to be a great scientist.

"Quite a colourful life, then," said Adele.

Was it? She wouldn't have said so. "So tell me about yours."

Adele waved her hand as if she was batting a fly away. "Totally boring. You should ask Hans about his."

Professor Edler shrugged. "Not a lot to tell. All a bit dull really, I'd have said. I suppose the most interesting is that I had some very large pockets sewn into my school jacket."

"Why?"

"So that I could hide all of my notes in them during exams, of course."

"You cheated?"

He looked away and shrugged. Then he chuckled. "What do you think?"

"Did you cheat your way into university as well?" She ought to be annoyed but she was actually really fascinated.

"Of course not. What do you think I'm like?"

She wanted to be shocked but she couldn't help giggling.

"Take no notice of him, Fräulein Lehrs. It's just probably one of his tall stories. Or wishful thinking." She tapped him lightly with her gloves. "Behave." She turned to Käthe. "I'm afraid I must leave you both now. I must go and prepare to meet that husband of mine for dinner."

What on earth had she got to do to get ready for dinner? Perhaps put on an evening gown but that was about it. She already looked perfectly groomed and actually very beautiful as well.

As soon as she they had waved and she had disappeared from view, Professor Edler leaned forward across the table. "Listen. I've just remembered. There is something I wanted to give you. Will you be really annoyed if I asked you to come with me to my office?" His eye were really sparkling again. The corners of his mouth were turned up slightly in a suggestion of a smile.

"I suppose not. Why would I be? If it's important? What is it?" Something about this didn't seem quite right. Surely if it was that important he would have sent a message via the internal mail, wouldn't he?

"Please don't be annoyed. It really is important."

"What's it about?"

"You'll see."

This was a bit of a mystery. She couldn't help feeling intrigued, though.

Hans Edler signalled to the waiter that he wanted the bill.

Käthe could hardly keep up with Professor Edler as they hurried along the street back towards the university and then the along the paths that led to the building that housed his office. She had to stop a couple of times to catch her breath. She almost tripped as they hurried down the stairs.

"Is it really urgent?" she asked.

He didn't reply.

"At last," he said after he'd fumbled with his key until he eventually slotted in firmly into the lock and managed to open the door. She followed him in. He shut the door. He put his hands on her shoulders. He cupped her face, pulled her towards him and stared at her for several seconds. Then he kissed her firmly on the lips.

Now, that was a surprise.

She found herself kissing him back, though, and then she didn't want to stop. He tasted of the coffee and the Turkish Delight. It made her dizzy and excited. Darn. It looked as if Gerda had been right. Eventually though, he pushed her away gently. He sighed. "Oh Käthe. Fräulein Lehrs. This shouldn't be. But I've wanted to do this since I first set eyes on you."

"I... I don't mind."

He sighed again. "But a lecturer can never court his student."

"Why not?"

He shook his head. "Because it's not allowed."

"That's stupid. Having a beau wouldn't stop me being a good scientist and a good student."

"I know but..."

"Then we'll just have to keep it secret."

He nodded. "We will." He pulled her towards him again and kissed her more slowly and gently this time.

By the time she left his study it was completely dark.

Berlin 1921

Chapter 23: changes

"Hans, I have to go." Käthe pulled away from him and started buttoning up her blouse. It always ended up like this when she visited him in his office. This time it wasn't a tutorial, though. They'd found excuse after excuse to see each other every day.

"Just as well I suppose or I might not be responsible for my actions."

She giggled. He was right. This could all get out of control. He'd pushed her against the wall earlier and leant on her. She'd felt his erection and she'd wanted him inside her. Oh, there ought to be something that women could do to stop them getting babies. It would be so handy if there were some little pill they could take to prevent ovulation. She'd touched the hard lump and he'd groaned. She couldn't tell if anything had happened because his trousers and underwear were in the way. Probably not because the erection was still there. She longed to touch his naked penis but that wasn't to be. Not yet, anyway.

Did he know that she understood about all of this? It was just biology, wasn't it?

"Just one more kiss." He kissed the top of her head and then titled her face towards him and kissed her on the lips again.

"I really have to go now. Do I look all right?"

"As beautiful as ever. What's going on today?"

"Something my older brother wants to tell us."

Hans nodded and sighed. "Families, eh?"

"Yes." Not that she had much time at all for them. What with seeing Hans now at least once a day and the work she was doing on her project, she was never at home.

He helped her on with her coat and handed her the flowers he'd bought her earlier. "I'll see you tomorrow. Come early."

That was one thing about him having this isolated little room in the basement: they were left in peace. "I will." She blew him a kiss as she hurried out of the door and up the stairs.

*   *   *

Käthe looked at the big clock at the front to the institution. Already quarter to one and Mutti had said that lunch would be at one o'clock sharp. She'd better get a move on. It wasn't easy as she had her best Sunday shoes on. She'd made some excuse up about attending a reception and now she was going to have to report that it had overrun.

She walked as fast as she could but the leaves on the pavements were a little damp and it was quite slippery. Soon, anyway, she had a stitch in her side. Mutti was going to curse her, that was for sure.

She guessed it was about ten past when she arrived at the apartment. She could smell the vinegary tartness of the Sauerbraten cooking as soon as she opened the door. There was no definite indication that the others were already at the table, though.

She took off her coat and went to the kitchen to fetch a vase of water for the flowers. There was no one to be seen. Not even Imelda. Perhaps she was setting the table.

"I'm back," she called. No one replied.

She made her way to her room. She put the flowers on the dresser and slipped her shoes off. They were really pinching now. At least she had a bit of time to day dream about Hans. Did he love her? Did she love him? Or was this just some sort of animal lust? All she knew was that she found it so exciting being with him. And she couldn't stop thinking about him.

She took one of the big yellow flowers out of the bouquet. She didn't know what it was called but it had plenty of petals. She started plucking them off one at a time. *He loves me.* Pluck. *He loves me not.* Pluck. Soon half of the poor flower's petals were strewn over the floor.

She saw Rudi walk past her open doorway. He nodded as he saw her. Then she heard Mutti and Leo come into the hallway.

"Rudi, Ernst, I think your sister is in love, but she won't say with whom."

What? How could she know?

"Ernst? Mother, you're getting your names mixed up," said Rudi.

"She isn't, actually," said Leo. "I've decided to take on Vati's name. I want to be known as Ernst from now on."

128

This was ridiculous. She jumped up off the bed and rushed out into the hall. "Why?"

"Why not?" Mutti replied. "Your father was a great man. It will be good if Ernst carries on his name."

Yes, Vati had been a great man and it still made her sad to remember him. But why, why, why was Leo doing this? Why did he want to do this strange thing?

Lunch was awkward. Ernst glared at her every time she called him Leo. Mutti was very matter of fact about it but actually probably called him Ernst more often than she needed to. Every time Rudi said anything to him he paused at the end of the sentence, took a deep breath, giggled and very deliberately added, "Ernst". The name was beginning to sound ridiculous. That wasn't so nice. It didn't seem too respectful of Vati.

Imelda came to clear the dishes.

"The Sauerbraten was glorious, thank you, Imelda. Which is more than I can say about the behaviour of my so-called grown-up children." She glared at the three of them.

"Yes it was," said Ernst.

"Thank you Master Leo." Imelda blushed. "I mean Master Ernst. Or rather Ober…"

"Just call me Ernst. We'll all get used to it soon, I expect."

"I do hope so." Mutti stood up from the table. "Imelda, we'll take the desert with coffee later. I'm going to have a lie down." She looked from Ernst to Rudi. "You two might talk to your sister. About that matter we discussed earlier."

I am here, mother. Oh how was she going to get out of this one?

No one said anything until Mutti was right out of the room.

"Well then," said Ernst. "Is it true? What Mutti suspects? That you're in love?"

"What on earth would you know about that?" She couldn't imagine her older brother with a girl. He hardly knew how to speak to her and Mutti. And she just couldn't see him almost getting out of control like Hans did. He was so serious, so careful and so well-behaved. Ernst was a good name for him really. If only it hadn't been Vati's who hadn't been at all serious.

She shrugged. "These things happen, don't they?"

"Well, you just be careful." He poked her shoulder with his index finger.

"That hurts."

"Good. I mean it. I know what they're like. These virile young men with not enough women around them."

"Takes one to know one." Except he wasn't of course. No way. In fact she'd even begun to wonder if he might be one of these degenerates she'd read about. Why did they call them that? Presumably they couldn't help being more interested in other men than in women, could they?

"I'd never disrespect a woman."

No, you're far too cold to even think about a woman. "No? You don't show me – or Gerda – a lot of respect."

"That woman's a nightmare. And you're going the same way."

"Thank you! You're just jealous because I'm studying under Einstein." Tears were beginning to prick at her eyes. This was so unfair. Why couldn't she tell them about Hans? He wasn't one of those silly little sex-hungry undergrads. He was a real man. With needs. That she wanted to satisfy if only the world would let her.

"I can assure you I'm not." Ernst now had his arm across his chest. "I can't wait to get away from all of this science. I really can't understand why you're so enamoured of it."

"That's so unfair. I love it and yet I've had to fight to be allowed to do it. Why should I give it up just because I've got a beau? I'm not saying I have, mind. But you wouldn't have to if you were walking out with a young lady."

"Anyway," said Rudi, "what were you doing counting petals?"

"Just a silly game." Why had he had to see that?

"And who gave you the flowers anyway?" Ernst was almost shouting now.

"Oh, they just came from the reception." Käthe felt her cheeks burning. She hated having to lie. But really. Was it actually any of their business?

Ernst sighed. "Just be careful."

"Yeah. And stop being so moody," Rudi added.

Her two brothers made their way out of the room and left her in peace at last.

Oh why did life have to be so complicated?

Chapter 24: secrets

Käthe was feeling more and more frustrated. Hans was being a good supervisor and a good lover but all of this secrecy was becoming extremely annoying.

They were sitting again in the little Turkish café. Neither of them ever gave anything away.

"That really was a very good analysis," said Hans. "And you're sure that you've everything you need for next week's experiment?"

"Doubly sure. Triply sure." It was usually quite fun when they talked like this as if they didn't know each other intimately whereas they both could hardly wait to get back to his office. She's always found it quite amusing that they'd talk seriously about her work in his study, then come over here to the café, where there'd be a lot of small talk with a lot of double-entendres, and then they'd rush back to the study where they would just fall into each other's arms.

Today, though it was all getting on her nerves. Why couldn't they show each other affection in public? Why did they bother with this routine? Why couldn't they just get on to the love-making as soon as the scientific discussion was over? She knew the answer actually. The cleaners. They came in at this time and they daren't go back to his office until they'd finished.

The coffee seemed to be a long time coming. She stretched her leg under the table, slipped her foot out of her shoe and pushed it up inside his trouser leg.

"Käthe," he hissed. "Somebody might see you."

She looked around the café. There was nobody to be seen and even the waiting staff were at the far end of the building. "Who? Anyway, they're more likely to hear you."

"Just don't do that." He looked round then leant over towards her and kissed her on the lips quickly. "It's so frustrating."

"Why don't we go back now? Forget the coffee."

"The cleaners."

How predictable. "They're taking forever, though."

At that very moment the coffee arrived. Hans took out his

wallet. "I'll settle up now. We're in a hurry today. No pastries this time."

They gulped down their coffee and made their usual dash to Hans's study.

This is a bit more like it.

They arrived breathless. Käthe slipped her jacket off straight away and opened the top two buttons of her blouse. "I want to feel your skin next to mine," she murmured.

"I want to sleep with you. Come inside you. Make love to your properly."

"Why don't we then?"

"You know we can't."

Couldn't they? Already she could feel his erection harder than ever, rubbing against her leg. Surely he would burst any second now and something was rising in her as she felt his tongue in her mouth and his hand on her exposed breast. Oh, she wanted him inside her too.

Then came the knock at the door, followed by a key rattling in the lock.

"Do something," Käthe hissed as she tried to tidy up her clothing.

"Can you leave the room today?" Hans managed to call out. His voice was thick and husky. "I'm in the middle of something and I can't stop now."

Käthe wanted to giggle. That was all true enough.

"Very well," replied a man's voice. "I'll do twice as much tomorrow."

The man went away.

"Now where were we?" Hans leant forward to take her in his arms.

The bulge had gone from his trousers Käthe noticed. The mood had been broken. It was really intolerable, the way they had to be so secretive all of the time. She pulled away from him. "I think we need to talk."

"Have I done something wrong?"

"It's not you. It's this situation. I don't want to stop being a scientist."

"I wouldn't dare ask you to."

"But we can't do this and let me carry on. You're my teacher."

"I can get you another supervisor. Or I can get another job." He was looking at her intensely now.

"You'd do that for me?"

"Of course I would. I love you."

Käthe's heart started beating wildly. He'd said the love word. She loved him too, didn't she? But she wasn't going to say anything. Not just yet. He held out his hand to her.

"Come on."

He pulled her gently to the floor. He undid her buttons again and stroked her breast. Then he lifted himself up so that he was lying on top of her. She could feel that his erection had returned. Oh, she wanted him again, so much. She didn't care whether it was love or lust. She pulled at the buttons on his trousers and found his penis. She touched it tentatively at first then picked up his rhythm as he moved up and down in her hand. He pulled up her skirt and slid his hand inside her drawers, touching her where she hardly dared touch herself. His fingers found their way into her. Soon they were rocking together. Something was bursting inside her. Just as she thought she could bear no more there was an absolute explosion and waves of release just at the split second that he ejaculated. It was sticky mess that soiled his trousers and her skirt but she didn't care.

"I'm sorry," he mumbled. "But thank you for that. Are you all right?"

"I'm fine." She really was. She was sure now that she loved him and she would tell him so soon.

Fortunately there was a wash basin and a towel and soap in the study.

"I really will make it right for you, you know," said Hans as they cleaned themselves up.

"I do want to carry on with my studies but I want to be able to stand proudly by your side."

"And so you shall."

"You promise?"

"I promise."

"How will you manage to make that happen?"

"I could go into industry."

"And abandon science?" That sounded to her almost as bad as if she had to give him up for science or science up for him.

Hans shrugged. "I've had a lot of fun. But I actually believe it can be as interesting applying what you know to invent new things to help society."

Maybe. "All right then. Do it. But only if you're sure."

"Okay. I will. It won't happen overnight, though. So we'll still have to be secretive for a while."

"I quite like secretive, really." *As long as there's a time limit.*

"You little tease." He went to grab her.

"Ah. You've got to make some progress first. And anyway, I need to get going." She put on her hat and coat, kissed him on the nose and made her way out of his study.

Berlin 1922

Chapter 25: a visit to the Tiergarten

Käthe's stomach was turning summersaults. What could he want? They rarely met on a Sunday and never outside.

The note had arrived the night before, just after supper. She was sure he'd delivered it himself. She'd heard the front door rattle. He hadn't put it in the mail box. He'd slid it under the door. She'd looked out of the window and seen a tall figure that was surely him get into a cab. He hadn't looked back, though, so she couldn't be absolutely sure.

It was a good job she'd found it herself. Could she trust Rudi not to read it? If nothing else Mutti and Imelda would have been curious.

She'd read it over and over.

Darling Käthe,

Please come and meet me at the café in the Tiergarten tomorrow at 11.00 a.m. The one by the lake. I have some exciting news. And there is something I want to ask you.

I can't wait to see you, to hold you in my arms... Yes, even in the Tiergarten!

All my love,

Hans.

She kissed and sniffed it, trying to take in the very essence of him.

What was he going to tell her? And what could that question be? A small thrill of excitement ran through her every time she thought of it. Meeting him in public, and not just as a student, would really be something. She was trying to keep calm, though. She really was. Of course, it had been impossible to eat breakfast.

Now it was time to go. She could put it off no longer.

"I'm not going to church today," she managed to say at last. "I'm going for a walk."

Mutti frowned. "But it's so cold, Käthe, and so slippery underfoot. It may snow again. I mean, we don't mind if you don't

137

want to go to church. But for goodness sake, stay in and keep warm."

"No. I need some fresh air. I can't bear to stay in a moment longer." She got up from the dining table and left the room.

She took a while to check her appearance in the hall. She looked a little pale, so she pinched her cheeks to make them look red. She knew she would have to wrap up warm but she must make sure she didn't look frumpy. Just how could you make a warm hat and scarf look elegant? She would have to wear her comfortable boots. She glanced at the hall clock. Twenty to, already. She would have to do.

She didn't know whether she could bear the excitement.

She hurried out of the apartment, slamming the door behind her.

She walked first towards the Kurfürtsendam and then she turned into Lietzenburgerstrasse. Walking so quickly stopped her noticing the cold.

She guessed her cheeks were really rosy now.

She ducked into one of the side streets that lead directly to the Kurfürstenstrasse. Perhaps with it being this cold there would not be too many people there. Would that make it better or worse?

A few moments later she arrived at the Tiergarten. She made her way along the tree-lined alleys. She was heading towards the café near the lake. She arrived at the entrance and went in.

Ah. There he was. He stood up and kissed her on the cheek. He was actually kissing her in public – on a Sunday! What had changed? She had a quick look round the room. There were only a few other customers.

"So what did you want to tell me?"

Hans waved at the seat. Oh, God, he did look handsome. What a pity there weren't more people to see her out and about being courted by this lovely man. "I'll tell you once you've sat down."

At that moment a waitress arrived. He turned to Käthe. "Coffee?"

She nodded.

"Anything to eat?"

She shook her head. She was still too nervous to eat. She wasn't even sure she'd be able to swallow the coffee.

"Okay." He turned back to the waitress. "So, coffee for two, and two soft white rolls with butter and jam."

"Oh, Käthe!" He grinned and touched her cheek. "I have such a lot to tell you."

"Tell me then!"

"Wait until she's brought the coffee."

Käthe sighed. "You're teasing me."

"I am. You're so delicious when you're annoyed. I could eat you all up."

She felt his foot rubbing her leg. She wanted him so much now it almost made her feel sick. She wanted to feel his skin next to hers again.

The coffee arrived. They watched in silence as the waitress poured them two cups.

As soon as she had walked away Käthe grabbed Hans's arm. "So, tell me."

He grinned again. "I'm going to give up lecturing."

"But you love it. I don't see why you should have to, just so that we can be together."

"I've applied for a job with an engineering firm."

"Which one? Where?"

"I don't want to say. That might jinx it."

"Teasing again!"

"And if I get the job, there will be nothing wrong with me doing this." He took her hand across the table. "Or whispering all sorts of nonsense to you like this." He moved his head so that it was almost touching hers.

She pulled away. "Drink your coffee before it gets cold."

Hans laughed. "Yes, I will. It's good coffee. Try it."

She took a sip. It was just the right temperature now. He was right. It was good. He wouldn't talk any more about this job even though she quizzed him thoroughly about it. He just kept on talking about the delights of living in Berlin and that he was going to miss them.

139

"Shall we order some more?" he said as he finished his rolls and the last of the coffee. "Would you like something to eat now?"

"Maybe a biscuit."

He signalled for the waitress and gave their order.

He pushed his hand under the table and squeezed her thigh. "I do love you, you know."

"I love you too." There, she'd said it.

He looked so pleased she thought he was going to cry. How embarrassing! She'd better change the subject quickly. "So this question?" She felt herself go red. She was certain she knew what it was and she wasn't sure she wanted to answer it. Not just now anyway. She wished she hadn't asked.

The waitress came back just at the right moment. They watched as she poured the coffees. Käthe was hoping Hans had forgotten what she'd just said when there was a bit of a kafuffle. One of the other waitresses had spilt some coffee and was ushering her customer to a new table. Hans turned round to see what was happening but Käthe looked up at the mirror that ran around the walls just above the dado rail. Her mother was staring back at her.

"Mutti!" she called. "What are you doing here?"

Mutti turned to face them then walked over to her. "I... er... I just wanted to see what you were up to."

"Mutti! Don't you trust me?" She was being impossible again.

"Well, aren't you going to introduce us?" Mutti looked from her to Hans.

She would just have to, she supposed. "Mutti, this is Professor Hans Edler. Hans, this is my mother, Clara Lehrs."

"I'm very pleased to meet you, Frau Lehrs," said Hans, offering his hand to Mutti. "Why don't you join us?"

Mutti took his hand and nodded. As she sat down at the table, the waitress appeared with another tray laden with a coffee pot and fresh cups.

"So, tell me how you two met," Mutti said. She patted Käthe's arm. "Why have you been so secretive about this? I'm sure Professor Lehrs is a very respectable young man."

"I am one of Käthe's lecturers," said Hans. "If our friendship comes into the open, she will have to give up her studies. We're hoping that attitudes will change in due course."

He didn't say anything about the new job, though. Wasn't it real, then?

Käthe watched in amazement how Mutti and Hans jabbered away. On and on about the wonders of Berlin and the belle époque. It was almost as if she wasn't there.

After twenty minutes of being ignored she sighed.

Mutti turned to face her. "Yes, Käthe, I think we should get going."

What? Mutti was treating her like a child.

"Come on. Get your hat and coat on."

Really. So much for things being out in the open. And no chance of a real kiss from Hans.

The journey home wasn't easy. Mutti was almost too nice. She must be up to something.

"You're right, Käthe. It isn't fair that you should have to give up your studies just because you've fallen in love with your professor. Can't we have a word with the father of that friend of yours?"

"Mutti, they'll never listen. And if we tell them, they'll either sack him or make me leave."

"You know you didn't need to keep it from me, though. Yes, he's a little older than you but I think that's nice. He can look after you well. I don't mind his age at all."

Hmm. And if you hadn't have come along when you did we might have got somewhere with that.

"And he really is a charming young man."

Käthe couldn't help smiling. As if she didn't know that already.

They walked briskly. That at least helped to calm her frustration. Not quite completely though. She made a point of slamming the door as soon as they were through it. "I don't see why it matters. Why can't I walk out with Professor Lehrs and still carry on with my studies? It's barbaric. This is the twentieth century you know."

She rushed off to her room and slumped down on the bed. It was all so annoying. Tears pricked at her eyes. She tried to imagine being in Hans's arms. That was getting her nowhere though.

She tried to read but couldn't concentrate.

There was a tap at the door.

"Come in," she mumbled reluctantly.

Mutti put her head around the door. "I'm going to invite your Professor Edler to dinner. I feel I need to get to know him better."

That was it. Then she was gone.

Well then. Would that help or make it worse?

Chapter 26: the proposal

"So, then, how's it going with the famous Hans? With Herr Professor Edler? Are you being a good little student and getting on with your research or are all these daily visits about something else?" Gerda was grinning.

Damn the woman. How did she know? Käthe was glad she was bending down and putting the measuring equipment back in the lab cupboard. Her cheeks were burning again. Why did she have to blush so easily? "I can't think what you mean."

Gerda touched her shoulder lightly. "Sweetheart, you know exactly what I mean. I can tell, you know."

Käthe got up and looked straight into her friend's eyes. She shook her head. "How can you know? How can you possibly know?"

"You have a glow about you. Have you actually...?"

It was no good. She just couldn't deny it. Gerda was just too clever. She sighed. "Not quite. Too dangerous."

"How frustrating."

Well it was all right really. Now they knew how to make each other climax without there being any danger of a baby. But yes, she wanted the whole experience and sooner rather than later. If only Mutti hadn't turned up when she did at the Tiergarten. She might have a ring on her finger by now and a wedding date fixed. That would also mean a date fixed when she could finally feel him inside her properly. "He almost proposed, you know."

"Do you think he will?"

"Mutti's invited him to dinner next week."

Gerda nodded. "Then what you need is a beautiful dress. Shall we go shopping?"

That did seem like a nice idea. Käthe suddenly felt guilty though. They were always talking about her and never about Gerda. "So what about you? Isn't there anyone on the horizon for you?"

Gerda laughed. "You don't know?" She stared hard at Käthe

143

and shook her head. "I'm not interested in men. I wish you weren't." She placed her hands on Käthe's shoulders, leant forward and kissed her briefly and gently on the lips.

What was happening? This wasn't just a friend's kiss for all that it had been gentle and short. She's felt Gerda's body tremble as it had lightly nudged into hers and she could see that her friend was shaking slightly as she pulled away.

The kiss wasn't unpleasant even if it surprised her. And no, she hadn't realised. She had heard there were women like that, though. She had suspected as well, hadn't she, that Ernst was more interested in other men than in women? All of that was supposed to be degenerate. Poor Ernst. Poor Gerda.

Gerda smiled. "Don't look so alarmed. I'm not going to make you feel uncomfortable. I'm really jealous of Hans and I hope he'll love you as much as I do. But anyway." She squeezed Käthe's arm. "Put on your hat and coat on and let's go and choose that dress."

"Oh, I don't know." Käthe looked at the pile of frocks draped over the chaise-longue in the changing room. "They're all lovely but they're not really me. I don't do dresses."

"But you have to seduce this man."

"I don't need a dress for that." She had a flash-back of one of their meetings in his study. A scruffy satchel, some immaculately-written notes and her lecturing him about her research seemed to do the trick. That and the sweet coffee and Turkish delights. What did she need a dress for?

"I don't mean to make him all lusty. I mean to make him realise that you would be a wonderful asset as a wife." Gerda frowned at the dress she was holding up. "Well, not this one anyway. It's too green."

Yes it was rather a bold colour and the pink shields looked slightly ridiculous. Käthe liked the shape, though.

Gerda looked critically at the one she was wearing again. It was pink and was almost the same shape as the green one. Gerda shook her head. "It's a bit too short, even for you and the naughty Hans."

She rummaged through the other dresses. There was another pink one that was even shorter. "Ridiculous," she muttered. "Not the black either. You're not going to a cocktail party. The two with jackets might be all right for your mother but not for you. That gold one with silver lace and its stupid tie at the front will make you look as if you're walking with a great big cock between your legs. Here, try this one again." She handed Käthe the one that was almost white with a hint of gold and had some darker golden diagonals on the skirt.

Käthe pulled on the dress and then stared at her reflection in the mirror. Could she really look that glamorous?

"You know it's very clever. Modest in many ways. It doesn't show any cleavage and it does flatten your chest, the modern way. Look, the longer panels come almost down to your ankles but the shorter ones almost show your knees. He won't be able to resist. Do a twirl."

Käthe did as she was told.

"It's perfect. Now for the right shoes."

She just hoped Mutti wouldn't be too shocked. Hopefully she would be relieved to have got rid of so much cash in one go. Money was mad at the moment. You had to spend it the minute you got it; it became totally worthless within hours.

Three days later Käthe was staring at herself in a mirror again, this time in her own bedroom. She still couldn't believe what she saw. Now that she had her make-up right, her hair trimmed into a modern bob and the smart strappy heels she looked so much older and more sophisticated. Would that be what Hans wanted, though? And was this really what she wanted? To become his wife? Would she really be able to carry on with her science? Which was the more important if she did have to choose? And more immediately, what would Mutti make of this dress?

The knock came at the door. Käthe hesitated to open it. There was another knock. She would have to face her mother. She walked over to the door slowly and opened it. Her mother rushed into the room.

Käthe held her arms up so that the sleeves floated down. "What do you think?" She watched her mother look down over the low waistline and then to the soft bias-cut panels. Then Mutti looked up again straight into Käthe's eyes. "You look lovely, dear. Would you like to borrow my pearls?"

Käthe couldn't believe her ears. "May I? Oh thank you, Mutti." She embraced her mother and kissed her on the cheek. "I thought you were going to be terribly old-fashioned and tell me it was too short."

Mutti shook her head and scuttled out of the room.

Käthe couldn't help smiling at her reflection in the mirror. And oh, yes. The pearls would make her look even more grown up.

A few moments later, Mutti came back with necklace. She gently fastened it around Käthe's neck. "There. They go really well with your dress."

The doorbell chimed.

"Come on," said Mutti. "Let's go and welcome him together."

This was it then. Better get on with it.

The meal ought to have been very pleasant. Imelda had made one of her famous Sauerbratens. The pork was delicious. They ate a lot of pork now. Käthe always wondered whether it was an act of defiance. Never mind. The roast potatoes were crisp and light and the vegetables were just right – neither too crunchy nor too soggy. But when was he going to say something?

He and Mutti chatted away again, just as if she wasn't there. Of all things he was telling her about his research. As if Mutti would understand. And did this mean there was no chance of him getting a job with an engineering firm? He seemed a little too interested in his own studies. Every time she went to say something, either he or Mutti would interrupt. Was it Mutti who made this happen? It was just like meal times with Ernst and Rudi. Oh, she did miss Vati. What would Vati have made of Hans? He would have approved, surely?

The dessert was Apfelstrudel.

"That was absolutely delicious," said Hans as he finished his second helping.

"I made it myself." Mutti's face was pink and her eyes were all sparkly.

Her mother was flirting with him. For goodness sake, Mutti.

"Wonderful!" Hans looked straight at Käthe. His eyes were sparkly too. That was the way he looked when he was about to make love to her. Not that there was any chance of that happening here and now. He wiped his mouth with his napkin. "I do hope Käthe has inherited some of her mother's culinary prowess."

Käthe's heart began to beat wildly. Was this it? Was it coming now?

No. A discussion of how various mothers and grandmothers made Apfelstrudel ensued. Oh yes. You had to be able to read a newspaper through the spread out strudel dough. Everybody knew that, didn't they? Käthe began to waggle her foot impatiently. She caught Hans's ankle. He frowned.

Imelda came and cleared the table.

"Can I offer you some tea or coffee? Or a Schnapps, Professor Edler?" asked Mutti.

Hans shook his head. "Thank you for such a lovely meal, Frau Lehrs. And now there is something I'd like to discuss with both of you."

"Oh?" said Käthe. Her heart started bumping again.

"I'm giving up my post at the university. I've been offered a position with Siemens. It will mean I need to move to Jena." He looked directly at Käthe. "Our relationship can come out into the open now."

"But Jena…?"

"Please let me finish." He turned towards Mutti. "Frau Lehrs, may I ask for your daughter's hand in marriage?"

"Of course," said Mutti. She made eye contact with Käthe and nodded her head slightly.

Käthe went to say something. She wanted to say she'd known all along what he'd wanted to ask and of course the answer was yes but Hans put his fingers on her lips, stood up from the table and got down on his knees. He took her hand. "Käthe Lehrs, will you marry me? You can continue your studies in Jena. You may come back to Berlin if you wish. I am even happy for you to visit Professor Einstein in Switzerland. But please be my wife."

Mutti was holding her breath. Käthe felt her cheeks begin to burn. Poor Hans. He looked so pale. She couldn't hold the tears back. How could he possibly think that she would refuse him? With an offer like that? "Yes," she whispered. "Of course. Yes."

"I think we should open a bottle of Sekt," said Mutti, getting up from the table. "And welcome to the family, Hans."

It was late by the time Hans left. Mutti had allowed Imelda to go off duty so she and Käthe were washing the dishes in the kitchen.

"You do understand, don't you, what happens when a man and his wife lie together?" said Mutti. She looked away from Käthe and blushed.

Don't even go there, Mutti, thought Käthe but she couldn't resist embarrassing her mother even more. "Oh you mean that he gets an erection when we touch and that then he puts his penis into my vagina and when he climaxes his sperm goes into me? And that's what makes babies? Mother, what do you think? I'm a scientist. Of course I know these things. In fact, I've even noticed his erection when he's held me close a couple of times."

Mutti bent further over the sink.

Oh goodness. Mutti and Vati. Just imagine. It must have happened of course. She knew that. Well, Mutti had brought the subject up. She may as well make the most of it. "I've even read that a woman can get a climax as well," she said as loudly as she could. "An orgasm. Have you ever experienced that, Mutti? With Vati? Oh no. Don't tell me. It doesn't bear thinking about. You and Vati."

Mutti sighed and then turned to face her. "Good, then. I suppose we'd better get our heads together about the wedding plans."

148

"Oh, yes please. The sooner the better. I can't wait for Hans to make love to me properly."

Yes, indeed. And there would be another nice dress, wouldn't there, surely?

Berlin 1923

Chapter 27: a married woman

Mutti removed the dress carefully from its tissue and hung it up on the stand. It was exquisite. So much like the one she had worn the day Hans had proposed: low-waisted, soft and floaty and quite short – coming just below the knee. It had that same golden shimmer about it too.

"I don't want pure white," Käthe had insisted. "I'm not all innocent and virginal. I want something modern."

She could tell her mother must be wondering about just how far she and Hans had gone. *No, don't worry Mutti. I'm still a virgin. Technically.*

She touched the dress and for a moment imagined Hans touching her in it. It was lovely, anyway, even if a little unconventional and not at all pure white. The train that would flow behind her and the veil that would drape over her head and shoulders at least made it seem like a wedding dress. She wondered how it would compare with what the bride of the young British prince would wear. Prince Albert was due to marry Lady Elizabeth Bowes-Lyon just a few days before her own wedding.

The dressmaker, Frau Schachner, would bring the veil along when she came to fit the dress later that evening. And Mutti wanted to discuss the question of payment again.

Frau Schachner had been very kind. "Don't worry," she said. "The government will have to do something soon. Once they have found a solution we can settle this."

It wasn't too bad for her, her brothers and Mutti. Mutti received a pension from the firm. It wasn't fixed and followed the rate of inflation. But she never actually took the money in notes or coins – except for just enough for the house-keeping. She used most of her income as credit. Frau Schachner was relatively fortunate too. Her son was one of these rich young men who was playing the system and gaining good dividends on his shares. He looked after his mother. She, in turn, was able to offer her clients credit.

Mutti had suggested she might want to take one of the oil paintings or even Vati's gold watch as payment.

151

"No," Frau Schachner had insisted. "We'll wait until there is real money again. This dress has been about a month's work. We'll decide at the time when they fix the new money exactly how much a month of my time is worth."

It was all very sensible. Would Hans's money be all right? Would they be able to cope with this having to spend his salary as soon as he got it? Oh, she thought she might be quite good at that, actually.

"Okay, little sis. You ready to go then?" Ernst was being uncharacteristically charming. He offered his arm to Käthe. She was at least glad of a prop. She was feeling incredibly nervous. What if he didn't turn up? What if her marriage vows got stuck in her throat? And underneath it all this incredible excitement. If all went well it would be soon. They could finally be together properly as a man and a woman.

They stepped into the carriage. Soon they were on their way. She thought about that other wedding that had taken place this week. Lady Bowes-Lyon had made a grand gesture and laid her bouquet on the Tomb of the Unknown Warrior. She squeezed Ernst's arm as she remembered the time when he'd gone missing. He squeezed hers back. They smiled tentatively at each other.

Well, she didn't think she could make any grand gesture. Perhaps it was enough that they were marrying just in a registry office. That way no one could be offended. Not their Jewish friends and relations, nor their new Evangelical ones, nor Hans's Catholic connections. Most importantly, it suited her and Hans. They didn't need any sort of church or synagogue. No religion for them. They were scientists and proud of it.

Oh, but the anticipation was killing her.

Had Elizabeth Bowes-Lyon had such wicked thoughts? Or was she all white and virginal as her dress suggested? Had the young Duke of York touched her in that forbidden place? Probably by now if not before. Would it be easier or harder for a royal couple to sneak around like she and Hans did? Did they even love each other or at least lust after each other or was this just a marriage of convenience?

She was glad she wasn't royalty.

The carriage stopped.

"Ready?" asked Ernst.

She nodded.

"You've been very quiet? You're sure about all of this?"

"It's all fine. I've just been thinking about a few things."

He was there, handsome as ever, straight-backed and looking more royal than Prince Albert. He turned to face her. She didn't think she could breathe. She had to lean more heavily on Ernst as she walked towards the front of the room.

Mutti was frowning slightly.

Don't worry so much, Mutti. I'm just oversexed.

Ernst gave her hand to Hans. She could hardly bear the thrill of tingles that ran through her body as their hands touched. She wondered whether he had an erection. Her eyes wondered down but it was impossible to tell. As she looked back up at him he smiled faintly and just about nodded. His eyes sparkled. He'd understood exactly what she'd been thinking.

The service was a little dull. It was mainly about checking their names and making sure that no one objected to the wedding. They then had to confirm that they both willingly entered into the marriage. They both gave their Jawort. The dull little civil servant gave them words of advice. "Never go to bed angry," he said. "Don't let the sun set on an argument. Remember to talk."

It wasn't the talking that she was worried about.

At last it was time to place the ring on her left hand.

"I now declare you man and wife," said the dull little man. "You may kiss the bride."

Everyone cheered. Hans leant forward and kissed her. Oh the taste of him. She melted into his kiss and the room and its occupants disappeared. Only for a few seconds, however.

He touched her shoulder lightly. "Soon," he whispered.

There was a lot of Sekt at the reception. The bubbles calmed her and excited her at the same time. She was careful not to drink too much. *I must stay sober or I might say something outrageous.*

Hans kept disappearing. He was doing the right thing, she noticed. He was entertaining their guests. She must do likewise. She made herself as amenable as possible to everyone who spoke to her.

"What a lovely dress," said Hans's mother.

"We have a very good dressmaker. I could recommend her to you… Frau… what should I…?

"Call me Clara. It's my name. Yes, do ask her to come and visit me."

"You know, your mother's been talking about this wedding for weeks," said one of Mutti's Kaffeeklatsch friends. "So clever how she's handled the money. And what a lovely young man you've caught for yourself."

"He is, isn't he?" And he's all mine. She glimpsed Hans across the room. Oh yes. He was a good catch all right.

"You look so beautiful," Gerda said. "I'm so proud of you and I hope you'll be happy." There were tears in her eyes. "Don't you ever let him make you unhappy and if he does. you know where to find me."

Käthe squeezed her friend's hand. "I won't and I do."

"Hey, Sis, how's it going?" Rudi tapped her on the back. "Good show today."

"Yes, wasn't it?" *And something even more spectacular will happen soon.*

A rather formal-looking gentleman shook her hand. "I gather you're a bit of a scientist and that young nephew of mine intends to let you carry on studying?"

Oh, here we go. "Yes that's right." She tried to remain pleasant.

"Well, I'm very glad to hear it. Get more women into thinking jobs, I say. They are the brains. Let we men be the brawn." Now that was a surprise.

Someone tapped her elbow. "It's time, Fräulein Lehrs… I mean Frau Edler."

Käthe turned to see Imelda standing at her side.

"Frau Lehrs says you should be getting into your going away outfit now and she's sent me to help you."

It was delightfully quiet in the small room where she changed.

"There now," said Imelda. "Don't you look a treat."

The green suited her, there was no doubt about it. She loved the way the bands crossed the skirt and made it swing. The shoes matched exactly and gave her legs a good shape. The fox fur would keep her warm if the train was draughty. The gloves and bag matched it as well. Mutti had lent her the pearls again. Yes, it would most certainly do.

There was knock at the door. Hans. She would recognise his knock anywhere.

"Come in," she cried.

Not long now. Not very long at all.

At last they were alone together. They had booked a private compartment on the train. As soon as they'd finished waving to their guests and they started leaving the station, Hans pulled down the blind.

Suddenly she felt shy and awkward. Was it going to happen here? Would it be difficult with her new clothing? She didn't want to mess that up anyway. She must look respectable when they arrived at the hotel.

He gestured that she should sit down. He pulled her into an embrace. Soon he was kissing her. She pushed her tongue into his mouth and her hand strayed down towards his crotch. She giggled as she felt his erection.

There was a knock at the door. They had to tidy their clothing quickly. It was the ticket collector.

Then it was the border control officer.

Next came the waiter taking orders for dinner.

Another border control officer.

There were a few cuddles. His hand found its way into her blouse and she gasped in delight as he fondled her nipples. But they were interrupted time and time again.

"I fear we must wait, my love. But perhaps it will be all the lovelier in that splendid hotel I've booked. Let's admire the scenery."

He flicked up both blinds.

Käthe turned away from him and closed her eyes. Being awake was just too frustrating.

The sun was streaming in through the French windows when Käthe awoke the next morning. Oh she felt so smug. Now she could really say she was a married woman. A virgin no longer. Hans was still asleep. Poor darling. He deserved it. He had worked so hard last night.

She got out of bed, pulled on her dressing gown and tiptoed over to the window. She opened the curtain slightly. What a view. The lake was enormous. She would enjoy sitting on that balcony this afternoon. Perhaps they could have their lunch brought to the room and eat out there.

She was a little bit sore but she didn't mind. Well they had done it three times. Three times, mind you. No wonder Hans was still asleep. The first time it had hurt and there had been a bit of blood but it hadn't stopped her having an orgasm. That was such an inadequate word for that incredible explosive feeling.

It had been embarrassing when the concierge had whispered something to Hans about there being fresh linen in the cupboard in the room if they needed it. She'd been mortified when they'd had to get up and change the sheets.

Hans had been kind. "It's perfectly normal. You really mustn't worry. We are in the honeymoon suite. It's expected."

They got back into bed. He chuckled. "The only trouble is, I'd really like to do it all over again."

"Well let's do it then."

"Really? You're not too sore?"

She shook her head.

"You wonderful woman." And the whole thing had started again with a long drawn-out kiss.

Then they'd sat and talked for a while then until one thing led to another. Poor Hans had fallen asleep straight away after that third time. Seconds later she was having the loveliest of dreams.

Hans woke up. "Hey what are you doing over there?"

"I'm just admiring the view."

"It can't be as good as the one I've got from here."

She scurried back to the bed and slipped in beside him. She passed her hand nonchalantly over his penis and a thrill ran through her when she found that it was hard. Very hard indeed. He lightly touched her between her thighs. "Shouldn't we bathe first?"

She shook her head. She could still just about smell his cologne from yesterday. There was also a slight sweaty, manly smell that she really liked. "Do I stink or something?"

"No. Not all. You just smell very desirable. Very desirable indeed." He leant over and kissed her firmly.

She wondered whether they would be up in time for breakfast.

AH Munich 1923

It was a triumph. They'd done it. He held the bright red flag proudly. The swastika, a bit like a cogged wheel, showed how they would march forward in progress. They would be like a machine, mowing down the chaff.

They'd burst in, he and his faithful storm troopers. Kahr had winced like an old lady when he'd pointed the gun at his face. Yes, he would do what they said, yes there must be an end to the silly money. Why should a loaf of bread, already expensive at 250 marks, now cost 200 billion?

Three thousand people they reckoned. Three thousand had followed him along the streets.

He had said he'd be great one day, hadn't he? Well, watch out. Here it came.

Watch out here they came. The police were coming for them. No matter, it was just a minor setback after all.

Jena 1924

Chapter 28: a bored woman

"I wish you weren't going away again." Käthe scowled at Hans. "You're never here."

"Darling, you know I had to take this job so that you could carry on with your studies. I'm afraid the travel is part of it. You've got enough to do, haven't you?"

Käthe shrugged. She wasn't enjoying her university course anymore. She missed Gerda. And now, when she wasn't studying, she was just a housewife. She almost longed for her cramped little desk in Vati's factory but all the men were back now and the women had had to give up their jobs. That had been in Berlin anyway and she was in Jena now. Jena seemed to be behind the times.

She hadn't heard from Professor Einstein for weeks or was it even months? Even relativity had become relatively uninteresting. Yet she couldn't let Hans know this. He'd given up his academic career so that she could carry on with hers.

She'd better try another tactic. She put on her best sad face. "I'll miss you though." She embraced him and pecked him on the cheek.

His body stiffened and he pulled away from her. What was that about?

"Look, I must get going. You'll have a nice time with Rudi, won't you? Tell him he can use the car as much as he likes."

Then he was off into the waiting taxi. He hardly waved to her as it set off. Well, that was that then. Still, she was looking forward to seeing her brother.

"You know this is a pretty smart machine," said Rudi as they came to a halt outside the café where they were going to have coffee and cake. "It drives so smoothly and it's very light to handle. Fantastic engineering."

"Hans is hardly here to use it, though. It seems such a waste."

"Well, I'd certainly use it all the time if it were mine. Do you think he'd sell it to me?"

"No. And anyway you can't afford it."

"I could ask Mutti to pay."

"You wouldn't."

He was much too proud for that, she knew. He always liked to pay his own way even though Mutti could afford to give him much more.

"True enough. But does it just sit there all the time when Hans is away?"

"Not really. Herr Brandt next door drives me to places sometimes and then he can use the car for himself. Hans lets him." She closed her eyes and shuddered. She didn't like being driven by Herr Brandt. He was always making rather suggestive remarks and sometimes touched her inappropriately.

Fortunately Rudi didn't notice her reaction. He was still playing with some of the controls. Then he suddenly hit the dashboard. "I know what, sis. You should learn to drive."

"You're joking, aren't you?"

"No. Come on. It's quiet here. Let me show you. The coffee and cake can wait."

Käthe's stomach flipped. But yes, this was an exciting thing to do. "All right."

They changed places.

"Starting her's actually harder than driving her," said Rudi. He showed her how to use the starting crank and then how to get the throttle right so that the car ran smoothly.

Käthe found the right point quite quickly.

"You're a natural," said Rudi. "Now, foot pedals. Right foot for the accelerator and the brake. Quite straightforward. Left for clutch. You use that for changing gears. Yes, put her into gear and let the clutch out gently."

It was simple really. The car hiccupped a little at first and then started going along quite smoothly. She found steering really easy.

"Good. Good," said Rudi. "You're picking this up really quickly."

She enjoyed it and even managed to turn a couple of corners quite easily, changing down the gears and then back up.

"I always stalled the car the first few times I did that," said Rudi. "You're doing great."

Half an hour and a few kilometres later they did go and have their cake and coffee.

"So what do you think of driving then, sis?" said Rudi as they finished their cake.

"Love it. Can I drive back home?"

Rudi threw back his head and roared. When he'd calmed down he shrugged and grinned. "If you insist. Not too fast, mind. There might be more policemen around when we get into town."

Good.

Herr Brandt was standing in front of his house when they got back. What on earth was he doing, Käthe wondered. It was almost dark now. He touched his hat as they got out of the car, nodded and then walked into the house.

What would he have made of that, then?

She and Rudi went out several more times in the car over the next few days. She drove most of the time. By the time Rudi was ready to go home she was really quite competent.

"You should think about getting a license," said Rudi. "Then you could be completely independent when Hans is away."

She wasn't sure, though. What would Hans think? Would he want his wife to be all independent? He seemed to like her being the little German housewife these days. Then what if it broke down while she was out somewhere? She wouldn't know what to do.

On the day Rudi's visit came to an end, Herr Brandt was leaning over the garden gate again when she was waving goodbye.

"It's not right, you know," he said after Rudi's taxi had disappeared. "Women shouldn't learn to drive. They wouldn't even be able to change a wheel if they got a puncture. They should leave it to the men."

That probably wasn't all that he was bothered about. He was probably quite worried that if she got her license he wouldn't be able to use the car so much. Nor touch her thigh when he was driving. "Well, you're entitled to your opinion, Herr Brandt. I'm afraid I don't agree with you."

She went into the house and slammed the door behind her.

The cheek of that man. Getting her license would be a very good way of getting back at him. For all of those rude remarks he'd made over the months, for all of the times he'd put his horrible hands on her and for the way he'd always looked down at her because she was a woman. Hans would just have to put up with it.

She went to the phone and after an hour she had all the details she needed. It wasn't all that straight forward. She was sure her actual driving was competent enough now but she must keep that level of competency up. She also had to learn something about basic car mechanics. At least then, if she could only pass her test if she understood that, she wouldn't need to be too afraid about breaking down.

Time to talk to Herr Brandt again.

"You see, Herr Brandt, it will be impossible for me to concentrate if you squeeze my thigh whilst I'm driving, or if you make any of your unreasonable remarks about how incompetent and silly women are. We are most certainly not."

Herr Brandt was frowning and his face had gone very red. He did look uncomfortable. She was enjoying this. Still, she ought to be a bit nicer to him really. You get more with sugar than with vinegar. Wasn't that what Mutti always said?

"I'm sure we'll be perfectly happy to lend you the car now and then still."

Herr Brandt raised one eyebrow and nodded.

Now that was enough of being nice.

"But if you don't agree to help me, I shall be obliged to tell my husband about your behaviour. Do you understand?"

Herr Brandt nodded again.

"Good. Can we start tomorrow?"

Chapter 29: more changes

Berlin, 24 February 1924

Dear Käthe,

I have some very big news. I have decided I will take up Ernst's offer of being the housekeeper at the institute in Jena. I was really impressed by his friend Doktor Albrecht Strohschein when he visited me in Berlin. Also on my recent visit to Stuttgart I met one of the youngsters they look after there. A very impressive young man, despite his obvious intellectual difficulties, who seems to know and understand a lot about angels. Yes, that's right. Angels. I don't believe in them and I'm sure you don't, but he was most impressive and almost persuaded me.

I'm ready for a change, anyway, and it really is time I made myself useful. I did tell Ernst there are some very important conditions, however:

When you start having children I shall be allowed to take time off to be present at the birth and time to visit when they are very little. (And won't it be handy that I'll be living closer to you?) No sign yet? You do want children, don't you? There isn't a problem, is there?

You and Hans will be allowed to visit as often as you please.

If anything happens to Rudi I shall be given leave straightaway to return to Berlin or to go to wherever he is at the time.

Ernst will visit me often there.

I shall be allowed to pay for young Kurt (that's the youngster I told you about) and Sister Greta (his special carer) to come to Jena.

I shall not be expected, yet, to take on the whole of Steiner's belief system. I admire what he does with young people, but I can't quite agree with him on other matters. I am quite willing to learn, however. I do find it a little tricky.

There. Now I'm sure Ernst will want to celebrate this. I hope you and Rudi will also see it positively.

I'll now have plenty to do. I must rent out the apartment, get rid of a lot of personal belongings and inform all my friends and associates. I'll probably need different clothes for this type of work. Most importantly, I must try and find a new position for Imelda. I suppose she might come to Jena too, if there is a need for people with her skills, though she may not want to leave Berlin.

I've invited Ernst to Berlin soon so that we can make detailed plans and I've told him I'd also be willing to visit him in Stuttgart.

I really look forward to catching up with you and Hans again when I come up to Jena.

I hope to hear from you soon and I hope you will be behind me in this new venture.

Your loving mother,
Clara Lehrs.

Käthe reread the letter several times. Why was Mutti being so nosy? It was nothing to do with her about whether she and Hans had children or not. Was there anything wrong? Not what Mutti was thinking. There was something wrong though. There would be no question of them having a baby yet. There were certain things you had to do to make that happen and Hans was so tired and irritable at the moment that there was never any chance.

Then there was all the business about Steiner. She didn't mind her mother working so much – she thought it would do her good. She couldn't imagine why she would want to work with these difficult children but that had to be her choice. This strange religion, though? Was it even remotely like Christianity? She could just about stomach that but couldn't actually believe that Christ was the son of God. She wasn't sure if there was a god. At least, though, Christ had said some pretty sensible things in his sermons. This Steiner stuff all seemed a bit peculiar.

165

It was dark when Hans came home and she was still sitting in the armchair without the light on.

"It's bit gloomy in here, isn't it?" Hans flicked on the light. "Is there something wrong?"

"Oh, it's just a letter I had from Mutti." She folded it back up and put it back in the envelope. There was some content she didn't want him seeing. "She's thinking of coming to live in Jena."

"That's good, isn't it? She'll be on hand when we start a family."

Ah, so he was expecting that to happen?

"It's just this crazy Steiner stuff."

"Oh, they're harmless enough. No worse than any other religion. And they do some good things, I've heard." He kissed the top of her head.

So, he does still care for me. She grabbed his hand and pulled him towards her but then felt his body stiffen and he pulled back. *Or maybe not.*

"Don't worry. It'll be good. I'll go up and change now." Then he was gone.

They ate dinner in silence that evening. Käthe still couldn't stop thinking about the letter. Hans must be thinking about whatever it was he was always thinking about. He was always deep in thought these days.

He did say something at the end of the meal, though. In fact, he stood up and he looked as if he was about to make a very formal speech. "It will be all right, you know. You really might be glad to have your mother around soon. Why don't you go and write her a nice encouraging letter? Now, if you'll excuse me, I must go and work in my study."

He didn't kiss her as he left the room.

What was he saying? Was that some sort of warning? Was her marriage failing? Yes, if that was the case, it might be good to have Mutti nearby.

She didn't want to think too much about what he might mean. She would go and write that letter and try not to worry about it.

166

Jena, 29 February 1924

Dear Mutti,

I have to admit that your letter came as a bit of a shock at first. It's really odd to think of you starting to work at your age. But yes, I'm sure you'll make an excellent housekeeper. After all, you've kept house for us for many years and you've helped Vati with the social side of the business. What will happen to that now? Who is going to look after the factory when you come here?

Do you think it will be easy to let the apartment? I suppose people are keen to live in Berlin. Oh, it will feel odd not being able to come back home and see you. But it will be very nice having you nearby. Hans says so too.

Perhaps as well you'll be able to tell me a bit more about this new religion that Ernst has taken up. I really don't understand it. In fact, I can't really understand how any scientist can believe in that type of thing. I have heard, though, that Steiner does a lot of good. Especially with the type of children you'll be looking after. Hans says so too.

Hans is really busy and very tired at the moment. He has to be away from home a lot. But he sends his love and we both look forward to seeing you in your new home when you move nearer to us.

Your loving daughter,
Käthe.

She reread the letter a couple of times. It was a bit short, she knew, but that was all she could manage without giving too much away. Mutti would have to stop being so nosy about their personal life. Yes, it would have to do. She put it into an envelope and sealed it. She couldn't find a stamp. Never mind. She would have to post it tomorrow. A walk to the post office would do her good.

167

Chapter 30: a licensed woman

"So Frau Edler, you have answered the questions about the working of your vehicle very well. You have shown me that you can put water into the radiator, oil into oil reservoir and that you can put petrol in the petrol tank. All I need now is to see you drive."

That will be the easy bit, thought Käthe. She'd practised enough when Rudi had come to stay. Herr Brand had given her plenty of useful instruction in the end. She just hoped the temperamental Mercedes would start properly this time. She held her breath as she cranked the handle. She turned it once. No good. Then a second time. Almost. It spluttered a little. The third time it caught properly.

She jumped into the driving seat, pressed down the clutch, let it into gear, took off the handbrake and away she went.

Oh she loved this. She soon forgot that it was a test. The vehicle gathered speed and she knew she must keep an eye on it or she would be going much too fast. She thought she heard the man from the Dampfkesselüberwachungsverein tut to himself. This was definitely the way to travel though. Surely she would pass, wouldn't she? Surely this was just a formality?

"You can drive back to the centre, now, Frau Edler," the official said.

"It's left here, isn't it?"

The official sighed. "I do hope you will remember to take a road map with you whenever you travel if I decide to grant you a license."

"If?" She wished she hadn't said that. It must have sounded impertinent.

She didn't wait for his confirmation. If she had done it would be too late. Thank goodness she remembered to signal first.

Seconds later she pulled up in front of the test centre.

"Thank you, Frau Edler. You may turn off the engine now. Very careful driving indeed."

"Thank you." Was that it then? Was he going to give her the license?

"But tell me. Why does a well-to-do young woman like you, with an obviously successful husband, want to drive a motor car?"

What on earth had it got to do with him? "I just want to be independent and not have to rely on my husband too much. He's away from home a lot, you see."

"Very well. I'm happy to grant you the license." He took a form out of his briefcase and filled it in. "There," he said handing it to her. "Just promise me you won't drive too fast."

Käthe nodded her head enthusiastically.

Just before he closed the door he leant forward once more. "By the way, congratulations. You are the first lady to get a driving license in Jena."

He shut the door and he was off.

Käthe stared at the license. It wasn't much to look at. A plain-looking form with some illegible handwriting on it. Didn't she have to exchange it for something more permanent later on? Oh well, Hans would know. Still, she'd got it. That was the main thing. Now. If she set off straight away she'd get there in plenty of time to meet Hans's flight. She couldn't wait to see his face when he realised what she'd done.

She'd better get going straight away. It was already getting dark and she'd not driven at night before. She had no idea what it would be like driving with lights. At least she knew how to switch them on. She flicked them on and off. *That's one thing he didn't ask me to do.* They worked, evidently.

Road map, he'd said. She didn't need one of those, surely? How many times had she been to the airport? She knew the way really well. If she got lost she could always stop and ask.

She restarted the engine, got the car into gear and set off. It was easy at first. But as it grew darker the roads looked less familiar. The car started to cough and splutter a bit. Twice she had to get out and restart it.

I really need to take the spark plugs out and give them a good clean, she thought. But she wouldn't be able to see here and she might not get there in time to meet Hans if she stopped now. Best keep on. It would have been all right if she hadn't taken a wrong turn suddenly and found herself in the middle of a little village. There was no one on the street. She had to stop the car, get out and knock on one of the doors.

"I'm looking for the airport," she said to the elderly man who answered.

He chuckled. "Taking the short cut were you?"

"Short cut?"

"You've cut about fifteen kilometres off your journey by coming this way. Don't tell everybody though. We don't want all those cars and cabs coming through here. Just follow the road all the way, turn left at the end, then follow that road all the way until it meets the main road. You're just a kilometre away then."

"Thank you."

"Do you want some help getting that thing started again?"

"Thank you, but I'll manage."

The man nodded and watched as she cranked the engine again, climbed back in and set off once more. He was frowning as he shut the door.

Oh dear, he didn't approve? Too bad. It all seemed all right to her.

Twenty minutes later she arrived at the airport and was able to park next to the taxis right under one of the bright lamps. There were still another forty minutes until Hans's flight was due in. Good. That would give her time to have a look at the engine.

She undid the latch to the bonnet and folded the cover back. She took the spark plugs out one by one and held them up to the light to examine them.

"There you are, got you, you troublemaker," she whispered as she found a piece of debris in the third one. She cleaned it as best she could.

"Do you need some help, ma'am?" said a gruff voice next to her.

She turned to face one of the taxi drivers. "Well, if you've got something I can clean this with, that might help."

"I'll do it for you if you like, ma'am." He started taking a rag out of his pocket.

"That is so kind. It's making such a mess of my gloves." She looked at them. She would never get those marks out of the ivory leather.

She watched as the man cleaned the plug and put it back into the engine. "There you are, ma'am. She should go like the wind now." He grinned at her. "Now I never thought I'd see a lady like you driving a car like this, let alone taking it to pieces."

"Well, I've passed my test today. And you have to know how the mechanics work, don't you?"

"True enough."

"I'll have to remember to dress properly next time."

"I dare say. Though if you're meeting someone special…"

"My husband. I wanted to surprise him." As she said the words she realised that for the first time in a while she actually felt excited about seeing Hans again. Of course, this was partly to do with this big secret she'd got.

"I'm sure he'll be very glad to see you, ma'am." The taxi-driver touched his cap and turned to go back to his taxi.

"Thank you again," cried Käthe.

The man waved.

A plane was just coming into land. That must be it. Käthe hurried into the arrivals hall. He would be here any moment. Her heart started thumping. It wasn't because the old excitement had come back, though. No, she was just worried about what he was going to say. Of course he wasn't expecting her to be here. She'd have to make sure they didn't miss each other.

Fortunately it wasn't too crowded. The first few passengers were coming through just as she found her way to the barrier. Oh please let him be here soon so that they could get this over with.

Then he was there. As tall as ever and as usual looking down his nose slightly at the people around him. Oh, Hans. They're really all right, all of these people.

He'd seen her. She wished she could disappear. Had this been a bad idea, really? She lifted her arm and waved, then curled her fingers back up and dropped her hand to her side. She bit her lip.

He stopped and changed his suitcase over to the other hand. Was he frowning?

171

Then he set off again, walking purposefully towards her.

"So what are you doing here? What's all this about?" Yes, he was most certainly frowning.

"I've come to meet you in the car."

Hans tutted. "Why? Such a waste of time for you and Herr Brandt."

"Herr Brandt's not here."

"So, who drove the car?"

"I did."

Hans dropped his suitcase. "What do you mean, you did?"

"I've been learning to drive. Rudi and Herr Brandt have been teaching me. Look." She fumbled in her handbag and took out the license.

Hans took it from her and read it. "Today? You got your license today?"

"Yes."

"But how did you know you'd pass?"

"I didn't." She giggled and felt her cheeks go red. "But I did send Herr Brandt home. I was pretty sure I would."

"What have you done to your gloves?" His eyes were round as he stared at her hands.

"Oh, I was fiddling with the spark plugs. It was misfiring a bit."

He suddenly threw back his head and roared with laughter. "That's my feisty young woman back. God, Käthe, I love it when you behave like a man." He stopped and frowned. "But the license says 16.30. You must have driven in the dark. I'd have thought you would have driven over while it was still light."

Käthe nodded. "I couldn't, could I, if I didn't pass my test until half past four?"

"Well. Well." He was grinning again and there was a sparkle in his eyes that she'd not seen for some time.

"You really don't mind driving in the dark?" said Hans, as they walked out towards the car. "Only I'm really too tired to concentrate."

"Of course not. I got here all right, didn't I?"

"That's my girl."

Käthe felt pleased. He'd been so cold recently. Yes, he'd had to work hard for the firm. She'd understood that. But life had become so mundane. She was losing interest in science. The university at Jena was nowhere near as exciting as the one in Berlin. Perhaps it was just because her supervisor there was a stuffy old professor who actually seemed not to agree with Professor Einstein. Professor Einstein anyway was a little bit aloof. He didn't respond to her letters. She did know he was quite ill, though, so he was forgiven. She was gradually changing into her mother as well. All those coffee mornings and fine clothes. Well, she had to be a bit sociable in order to support Hans, didn't she?

There was also the matter of there being no sign of a baby yet. Mutti was always asking about that. Well, obviously, it wasn't going to happen unless you made love was it? That just didn't happen enough these days.

Still, learning to drive had been something and she was looking forward to impressing him by taking the shortcut.

It wasn't to be, however; within five minutes of getting into the car, before they'd even turned off the main road, Hans was fast asleep.

He awoke as they came to a stretch of road that went through some sharp bends and was bordered on both sides by woodland. He stared at her for several minutes then put his hand on her thigh.

That was distracting but she managed to keep the car under control. She almost liked it. Not like when Herr Brandt did the same thing.

"Such a competent young woman. I'm so proud of you, darling. I can't wait a moment longer. Take that turn on the right, there, into the woodland."

Jena 1925

Chapter 31: new life

Three days running now, this had happened. She'd wake up feeling really sick and only just about make it to the bathroom in time to be sick. Plus her breasts were really tender. And she hadn't had her period now for two months. Yes, she was sure: she was pregnant.

She was managing to keep it from Hans, though. She just didn't want to say anything until she was sure the pregnancy was viable. Mutti had had so many miscarriages she might be susceptible to them as well. In fact she was quite convinced it had already happened. Six months ago she had had a particularly heavy and painful period that had been about three weeks late. Mutti had made a fuss.

"You should go and see the doctor. I'm not sure this is just a period."

"Stop nagging, Mutti. I'll be fine." She'd thought at first that time that it was impossible.

She'd also wondered whether Hans might be having an affair. Their love-making had become so infrequent. She'd never found any evidence, however. Then as well she'd worked out that the last time they'd made love could have led to her being pregnant then. Then she'd gone and lost the baby.

It was different this time, though. It was just that this morning sickness was so annoying.

She retched for the third time and managed to vomit a little more.

There were footsteps on the stairs just as draught through the window made the door open.

"Käthe? What is it?"

Darn! Why did he have to see her looking like this? She closed her eyes and shook her head. Then she sighed. "I might be pregnant."

"Really?" He beamed.

"In fact, I must be."

He rushed over to her and took her in his arms. "That is fantastic, Käthe."

She shook her head again. "I didn't want to tell you until it was certain I could carry it. Anyway, I must smell of vomit. Go away."

"I don't care."

She told him all about Mutti's miscarriages.

"But medicine is so much more advanced now. They can look after you better. Anyway just because your mother miscarried doesn't mean you will. And because she did, all the more reason for you to see a doctor as soon as possible. Don't you agree?"

It did sound sensible. "All right. But go away now and let me get cleaned up. And we don't tell anybody else until at least sixteen weeks, right?"

He turned to go then suddenly turned back. "How many weeks?"

"Nine."

He frowned slightly as he calculated. Then his face lit up.

Käthe nodded. Oh yes, she must have conceived that night they made love in the back of the car on the way back from the airport. It had been rather romantic even if it had all been a little awkward at first. Since then, things had got better between her and Hans again. She was so glad she'd learnt to drive.

He touched her arm gently. "This baby really will be special."

Käthe sat impatiently in the waiting room of the Lauenstein institute where Mutti was now housekeeper. She didn't like this place very much and she worried about why her mother had been so easily persuaded by Ernst and his strange friend to take up work at her age and for such a puzzling organisation. Still, she had to admit, Mutti seemed to be doing well. That young girl who had opened the door to her and shown her in obviously had severe learning difficulties but she'd been well-mannered and had made every effort to make her feel comfortable. This place was immaculate as well. Mutti must have very good house-keeping skills. And it was good having her so close now that she was going to become a mother herself.

It was time to start telling the world and Mutti must be the first to know. Käthe stared down at the new shoes. They were so lovely with their little red bows and short but spindly heels. They were a little difficult to walk in if she was honest. Probably a pregnant woman shouldn't be wearing ones like these but she was determined not to become frumpy. Especially now that she had her Hans back. Yes she must let Mutti know. The poor woman had probably wondered what the matter was over Christmas when she'd merely pecked at her food. She was still having a lot of nausea then. It had stopped just three weeks ago and all of a sudden she felt better than ever and had tons of energy.

The door opened and Mutti came in. "Mutti, I'm going to have a baby. You're going to be an Oma." There. It was out in the open now.

She watched her mother's face change. She frowned, then stared, and then smiled.

"When?"

"August 15th. That's what the doctor said."

"I was quite worried at Christmas. You looked…"

"Chronic morning sickness. Kept throwing up. Couldn't eat. But that's all over now. I'm feeling good."

Now she knew that her eyes were bright, her cheeks were pink and her hair was beautifully shiny.

"So, Mutti, what do you think about becoming an Oma? Doesn't that make you feel old?"

Mutti shook her head. "Quite the opposite. It will make me young again. Having a little one in the family."

Käthe rolled her eyes. "I'd have thought you were quite used to having little ones around. You're surrounded by them." She gestured vaguely round the room.

"Yes, but my own flesh and blood. That's different. Is Hans pleased?"

Käthe nodded. "Yes. Yes, he's pleased. Of course, he's hoping for a boy."

"What about you?"

Käthe shrugged. "I don't mind. A son would be nice but it'll be more fun dressing up a girl."

"So, you and Hans…"

What was her mother trying to say? Oh, she could be so annoying sometimes.

"Mother! Not that it's any of your business, but since you're asking, yes, absolutely: we have a fantastic sex life, thank you very much."

Mutti blushed. There was an awkward silence. Then Mutti took a deep breath. "So, you're taking good care of yourself?"

"Of course I am. Mother, you know I understand all about biology. I'm eating plenty of nutritious food, getting plenty of rest and keeping nice and calm. I know what's good for the baby."

"You need to be careful though. It's still quite early days." Mutti seemed to be looking at Käthe's feet. "Don't you think...?"

"Oh for goodness sake, Mutti. I'm not going to end up looking like a frump just because I'm pregnant. I'm being careful. I said so. And do you know what? I'm getting quite used to my afternoon nap. It's delicious. I'm going to carry on after the baby's born. I'll take a nap when he does. Will you stop staring at my ankles?"

A car horn hooted.

"Oh, that's Hans. I'd better go. Love you, Mutti." She kissed her mother's cheek and rushed out of the room and through the hallway towards the front door. Her mother followed. Hans got out of the car and waved to Mutti.

"Good morning, Clara. Sorry we can't stop. I have to get her to her appointment with Doctor Rippel." He grinned. "It's wonderful isn't it?"

Mutti smiled and nodded.

Seconds later they were off, Käthe waving frantically. She was glad Mutti knew now.

"You're getting fatter." Hans stroked the bump that was now showing quite well.

The baby moved. "Stop it. That tickles. I'm not getting fat. It's just the baby. She's still quite small."

"She? How do you know it's a she? I thought we'd have a boy."

Käthe shrugged. "Just a feeling."

"I think we should have a boy."

"We can't choose."

"Well, if it is a boy, we should name him Ernst Leopold Rudolph after your brothers."

"No, Leopold first. Leo for short, just like Ernst was before he became Ernst."

Hans shrugged. "If you like." He stroked Käthe's belly again. "He'll be a fine boy."

"And if he's a girl?"

"Hmm. I don't know."

"What about Clara. With a C? After both of our mothers?"

"Yes a good idea. But what about Renata, spelt the Italian way not the German way?"

Käthe remembered the little Renata they'd met on their honeymoon. She was a sweet, little girl who said the funniest things and whose dark curls bounced when she laughed. They'd both said that if they ever had a little girl they hoped she would be just like Renata.

"Yes. Clara Renata or Renata Clara?" said Käthe.

"Renata Clara. The exotic name first. Though I'm sure it's going to be Leopold Ernst Rudolph."

The baby kicked again, making Hans's hand bounce. "He's so strong." said Hans. "He doesn't half kick hard!"

Käthe sighed, folded the letter up and put it back in the envelope. At least it was kinder than the one she'd had from the university. Even that one had been fair, though, if she was honest. Yes they were right. She had been neglecting her studies. It had been getting quite bad before she became pregnant. Then it became impossible, especially when she had been so very sick at the beginning. She had cancelled meetings with her supervisor month after month. And yes they'd been monthly, not weekly as they'd been with Hans. Nobody was excited at Jena.

What a horrible tone they'd used, though. "As you have shown no commitment to your course, as you have not communicated with us, you have produced very little work and you have not attended well, we have no alternative than to ask you to withdraw from the university. Fees must continue to be paid until the end of

179

this calendar month." Quite. Hans and Mutti were still paying her fees. What did it matter to them? She would have returned to her studies eventually. Perhaps after the baby was born.

Professor Einstein's letter was much kinder. She took it out of the envelope and reread it.

10 June 1925

Dear Frau Edler,

Oh how I wish I could call you Frau Doktor or even Frau Professor one day. Alas, it is not to be. The university will no longer support you in your studies.

I have to admit I think it is perhaps for the best at the moment. You are preoccupied with your family. Becoming a parent is a major life event and you should really give that all of your energy and concentration.

I'm sure you will be as admirable a parent as you have been a scientist. I'm sure you will produce a clever son or daughter who one day may also become a fine scientist but for now forget all about relativity. If you want your child to be intelligent read her fairy stories. I mean that most sincerely. I am not being flippant.

When you really have the time and space for science again, do come back to us.

I wish you and your family well.

Kind regards,

Albert Einstein.

Two big tears rolled down Käthe's cheeks. So she was to be a mundane little Hausfrau after all. She would make no great discoveries, nor work in a man's world. There would be no more experiments nor writing up papers. This felt like failure.

The baby kicked.

Käthe put her hand to her belly.

"You've got a lot to answer for," she whispered.

It was the most spectacular storm yet this summer. Black clouds rolled across the sky. Fork lightning tore it in half, lighting up the whole of the room then disappeared and plunged it into darkness. Not for long, though, for then there would be another explosion of blinding light.

Käthe felt a sharp pain in her back. She must have been sleeping funny. It was certainly getting very uncomfortable now. She was huge. Standing, sitting, lying down; nothing felt right.

The lightning flashed again. One elephant, two elephants, three elephants, she counted. Six. Six kilometres away.

Three more flashes of lightning and another sharp pain.

Another two minutes. Another pain. It couldn't be, could it? Weren't the pains supposed to be at the front? Not the back? It was three weeks too early anyway.

Oh, God, she needed to pee. She struggled to her feet. She wasn't going to make it. The warm liquid splashed on to the Persian rug. Oh, no, it would be ruined. And she also knew it wasn't pee.

"Help! Help" she cried.

Seconds later both Lotte and Hans ran into the room. Thank goodness Hans was at home today. "What is it?" he said.

"The baby's coming."

"It can't be."

"She is."

Lotte took charge. "I'll go and phone the midwife." She hurried out of the room.

"I want Mutti."

"I'll go and fetch her." Hans was pale and she could see that he was shaking.

There was another great flash and a loud clap of thunder almost at the same time. The house shook. She was sure it had been struck. A pain worse than all of the earlier ones tore through her body.

"Hurry!" she cried.

Hans seemed to spring to life. He rushed out of the room and seconds later the door slammed. She heard he car start. "Please drive carefully," she whispered. Another pain began.

AH Landsberg 1925

He smirked to himself as they let him out of the small prison in Landsberg. So much for five years. He'd been there just 264 days. It had been almost like a holiday apart from the lack of freedom.

He'd shown them what a moral upright young man he was. He'd been polite, always. He didn't smoke. He didn't drink. He'd even given up eating meat. People had sent fruit and flowers, wine and other alcoholic beverages, ham, sausage, cake, boxes of chocolates. He passed the alcohol and meat on to the guards. They'd let him hold forth to the other prisoners.

"You make damn good speeches, Adi," said one of his storm troopers. He didn't know the man's name.

They'd even called his cell on the second floor the Feldherrenhügel – the General's hill.

And all that time he'd worked on his grand plan.

The white Aryan race was the master race and must be preserved at all costs.

The Jews were particularly troublesome. They were parasites. They should be eliminated and this would be a bloody process. Germany would have to come under the control of the National Socialist Party. The military must expand. It didn't matter what the Versailles Treaty said. They had to get rid of the "impure" races.

They would need a dictator to do this.

He had written it all down. This was now a book waiting to be published. So, maybe he would be a famous writer instead of an artist. Or, what about dictator? Now then. Wouldn't that be something?

Jena 1925

Chapter 32: what's in a name?

"Again!" cried Käthe, her face screwing up in agony.

"Try not to push. Not yet," said Frau Wilderberg, the midwife. "You're not open enough."

"Damn those bloody men and their insatiable desires," shouted Käthe. "Castrate the devil. See how he'd like this much pain."

"Käthe!" said Mutti.

"Don't worry, madam," said Frau Wilderberg. "I've heard a lot worse, believe me. She'll be fine once we have the little one out."

Greta, the nurse who had come with Mutti from the Lauenstein, went bright pink but continued to hold Käthe's hand. "It will be all right," she said. "The baby will be here soon."

The doctor leant over her with his stethoscope. He put it to Käthe's enormous belly. "Mm," he said. "The heart beat is strong, if a little slow. But I think we should get this baby into the world as soon as possible."

"Excuse me," said Frau Wilderberg. "If you wouldn't mind looking away."

Mutti and the doctor turned their backs on Käthe. Greta looked to the ground.

Frau Wilderberg poked around in that part of Käthe that she would prefer nobody except her and Hans to touch. It hurt. She was just about to protest when the woman stopped and stood up straight.

"Right. Fully crowned. With the next pain, push as hard as you can."

Silence followed. Everyone waited for the next pain. They seemed to have stopped. Or was it just like the difference between observed and elapsed time again? Why was she thinking of science now of all times? Oh, this was biology and that was science as well.

Then there was another flash outside and a clap of thunder. Here they came again. More intense than ever. Käthe groaned.

"Push, push, push!" called the midwife.

Mutti and Greta held her either side.

"Good," said Doctor Rippel. "You're doing really well, Frau Edler."

"One more push," said Frau Wilderberg. "Push down, down, down. Don't strain your throat. Imagine you're constipated. That's it."

Käthe groaned once more. Something gave way.

"Baby's here," cried Frau Wilderberg. "Frau Edler, you have a little girl. She's tiny, though." She took up the child and wrapped it in one of the towels and handed it to Sister Greta. "Could you... ? I have to deliver the after-birth."

Why wasn't she crying? The baby's face looked blue. Wasn't she breathing? No. Please God don't let this happen.

The doctor put his hand on Käthe's abdomen. He nodded.

"My baby. I want to see my baby," said Käthe.

"All in good time," said Doctor Rippel, moving over to the table where Sister Greta was bending over the baby. He put the stethoscope on her chest. "Yes, a good heart beat and she's breathing but with a little difficulty. Let's see if we can clear this mucus from her."

Sister Greta worked away busily at her.

"That's right. Rub her tummy. Yes, she's pinking up nicely."

Thank goodness!

Suddenly the baby yelled.

Hans burst through the door. "Are they all right?"

"Yes, Professor Edler, for the moment yes. Your wife should make a full recovery. Your daughter is very small, however, and I fear a little underdeveloped."

"She has a soul, though," said Sister Greta. "And we must take care of that."

"If you are religious at all," said the doctor, "you might consider getting her christened. She seems quite strong but we don't know how well her vital organs will work at this degree of prematurity."

"I think we should," said Mutti turning to Hans. "We've got to get her a birth certificate anyway."

Hans nodded. "I'll go and see if I can rouse someone at the rectory."

"Let me hold her," said Käthe as soon as Hans had left. Religion wouldn't help them, of that she was sure. This little one might not live very long. She must make the most of her.

Sister Greta brought the baby over. The little girl immediately tried to put her mouth to Käthe's breast.

"That's a good sign," said the midwife. "Come on; let's see if we can get her to feed."

Sister Greta and Frau Wilderberg helped Käthe to get the baby latched on to her nipple and soon she was feeding away greedily.

"Well, there doesn't seem to be much wrong with her," said Sister Greta.

"Early days," said the midwife. "But it's a good sign at least."

"Have you thought about names?" asked Mutti.

"Yes. Renata, spelt the Italian way. Then Clara, as her second name, after you and Oma Edler."

Mutti blushed. She seemed pleased.

At least she'd done something right for once.

Just as the baby finished feeding, they heard the front door shut. Footsteps came up the stairs.

"I've found him," cried Hans, flinging the bedroom door open. "Father Brandt."

The two men entered the bedroom. Father Brandt was a strange-looking little man. He had long grey hair, scraped to the back of his neck and tied with a piece of string. His cassock was faded and grubby.

"Where is the child?" he asked.

Mutti screwed up her nose. Käthe felt nauseous. The man's breath smelt of alcohol. He seemed unsteady on his feet too.

Sister Greta took the baby off Käthe and walked over to the priest with her. Father Brandt took out a bottle of water. He held his hand over it and mumbled something Käthe found quite unintelligible. Then he turned to Hans. "How is the child to be named?"

"Renata Clara," Käthe called from the bed. "Isn't that right, Hans?"

"Yes, Renata Clara."

"Very well. Klara Renate."

"Renata Clara," said Mutti.

"Renata Clara," mumbled Father Brandt. He sprinkled some of the water from the bottle onto his fingers and made the sign of the cross on the baby's forehead. "In the name of the Father and of the Son and of the Holy Ghost, I name thee Klara Renate."

"Renata Clara." Hans glared at the priest.

"Clara Renata," Father Brandt whispered, once more making the sign of the cross on Renata's head.

Renata started screeching. Sister Greta tried to soothe her. "Hush, hush, little one. It's all over now. You can go back to your mama for a nice cuddle."

"I'll need to fill in the certificate," said Father Brandt.

"Come along to my study," said Hans.

"Remember, it's Clara with a 'C' and Renata spelt the Italian way," Käthe called after them.

"Yes, yes," answered Hans.

"I'll be on my way now," said Doctor Rippel. "You should all try and get some rest."

"I'll be going too," said Frau Wilderberg. "Call me if you need any more help." She handed Mutti a card and started packing away her things.

"I shall call round tomorrow soon after breakfast," said the doctor. "The next twenty-four hours are crucial for the baby. Do send for me in the meantime if you feel the need to, though it looks as if she's doing well."

Renata was clearly enjoying another feed.

"Greedy little pup," Käthe whispered, looking down at her baby.

A few minutes later the baby stopped feeding and fell asleep.

"I'm so tired as well," said Käthe.

"Then rest," said Mutti. "I'll sit here in the armchair until you're asleep."

"I'll leave you in peace," said Sister Greta. "But I'll stay overnight, if that's all right Frau Edler. Then I'm here if you need me."

Käthe nodded and yawned.

Sister Greta took the baby and put her into the cot they'd got ready. "Sleep little one," she whispered and then tiptoed out of the room.

Käthe's eyes closed and soon she was fast asleep.

When she woke sun was streaming through the window. The grandfather clock in the hallway struck seven. Goodness the doctor would be here again soon.

Mutti was bending over the cot and Renata was wide awake and sucking her fist. "Hello, little one," whispered Mutti.

There was a faint tap at the door and then it opened slowly. It was Sister Greta with a breakfast tray. She set it down on the small table near Käthe's bed and joined Mutti next to Renata's cot. "She's doing well, isn't she?"

Mutti nodded and smiled.

"Bring her over to me," mumbled Käthe.

"Have your breakfast first, darling," said Mutti.

"No, I want her now," said Käthe. "I'm her mother, after all."

Mutti brought the baby over and seconds later greedy little Renata was feeding again.

Suddenly there was a loud bang as a door was slammed shut. Hans ran into the bedroom holding a piece of paper. The birth certificate by the looks of it.

"Damn the man. Damn the drunken old fool," he cried.

"What's the problem?" Mutti asked.

"He's only gone and put Klara – with a 'K' and Renate spelt the German way. And he's put them the wrong way round. Klara Renate instead of Renata Clara."

Käthe felt as if she'd been thumped in the chest. Tears ran down her cheeks. She knew Mutti hated it if people spelt her name with a "K". She suspected Oma Edler would as well.

Jena 1927

Chapter 33: on the move again

"You're going to move to Stuttgart and you're going to build a house with Ernst?"

"Oh, don't worry, dear. Your inheritance is safe."

That's not what I'm worried about actually. No, it was this crazy religion that Mutti and Ernst were both getting more and more keen on.

"So, how can you afford it?"

"I'm selling my pearls. Your uncle is lending me some money and so is an associate of your brother. I intend to pay the loans off as soon as I can. When I die, the house will belong to all three of you but I'd like you to let Ernst continue living there as long as he needs to."

"And you're building a house from scratch?"

"Yes, Ernst has found a plot of land and a good architect. It's just a short distance from the school."

"So why are you moving exactly?"

Mutti sighed. "It's getting a bit too much at the Lauenstein. The children are getting a bit difficult to handle."

That didn't sound right. Mutti wasn't looking at her either. Käthe didn't think she was quite telling the truth.

"You love it there, though don't you Mutti?"

"I used to. But now they're asking me to do things I don't quite approve of."

"Oh?"

"Yes. Like allowing the children to help with the chores. Goodness, these poor creatures are tired out after trying to learn all day. What they need from me is a bit of mothering. Besides, they always take so long to do anything, and then do it wrongly so I have to do it again anyway." Mutti's face was quite red now and she was almost shouting.

"So what will you do with yourself in Stuttgart? Are you retiring?"

"Good heavens, no. I'm going to take in boarders. Teachers and students who can't get home during the week."

"Mutti. Really. Don't you think you should be taking it a bit steadier at your age?"

"No, indeed not. I'm so looking forward to being really in charge of my own home. When Ernst and I went on our little walking trip we came across the most delightful guest house. A lovely young woman ran it and baked delicious bread and cakes. I'm thrilled at being able to do something like that. It was going to the guest house that gave us that idea, actually."

Käthe couldn't help but chuckle. Mutti always loved her cake. "Listen, talking of cake, I'll go and get us some tea and cake, though I made it so I'm not sure how good it will be."

"I'm sure it will be lovely, dear."

Käthe was relieved to get a little time to herself. She got out some cake and got the tea things and the plates and forks ready. However, the water had almost gone cold again by the time she realised it had boiled. She was so engrossed in thoughts and worries.

It was handy having Mutti nearby to help with Renate. She didn't know what she would have done without her and Sister Greta when Renate had whooping cough. Then there was that time when she was keeping her and Hans awake all night when she was teething. Mutti had her over at the Lauenstein for one night and they were able to get some much needed rest. Mutti knew so much about little ones. Käthe hadn't really realised just how much until recently.

Talking of Renate, she would be bound to wake up any moment now. In fact, she suspected that the luxury of the little girl's afternoon nap would soon be over. She was sleeping for shorter and shorter stretches now.

Yes, she would miss Mutti but she was even more concerned about Rudolph Steiner and his weird teachings and about Mutti doing all of that work. Still, at least she would be living with Ernst and he would keep an eye on her. She hoped they weren't both becoming peculiar, though.

And she'd really have to be careful not to let Mutti think that she was jealous, because really she wasn't. Hans was looking after her very well. She had all that she needed here.

She heard Renate whimper. She would be waking up very soon. She must get this conversation with Mutti over.

She re-boiled the water and made the tea and then made her way back to the drawing room.

"It's a good idea, Mutti," said Käthe, as she poured the tea. She couldn't quite bring herself to look at her mother. If she was honest, she was terrified of not having her on hand.

"I'm so pleased you approve, dear. And of course you'll be able to come and visit." Mutti's voice wasn't very convincing either.

Käthe still avoided looking at her mother.

Neither of them said anything and they both just pecked at their cake and sipped their tea.

The door suddenly opened and in toddled Renate.

"Oh, no, you've done it again. What shall I do with you?"

"What's she done? Did Lotte get her out of bed?"

Käthe shook her head. "No, she's climbed out of her cot. She keeps doing that. We can't keep up with her." Then she noticed the nasty smell. "Oh, and she needs a clean nappy. What a tinker. What a stinker. Mutti, I'll make you some more tea after I've changed her."

Mutti got up on to her feet. "You go and make the tea and I'll change, madam."

If Käthe was honest, she was glad her mother had volunteered for the messier job. Oh, dear, she would miss her. She never thought she would ever say that.

The two women arrived back in the drawing room at the same moment. Mutti was deft at changing nappies and Käthe had had to boil the water twice as she found herself daydreaming again.

"There. A nice clean girl," said Mutti.

"And a nice cup of tea," said Käthe.

Renate was babbling to herself about something or other. Any day now, Mutti said, the little girl would utter her first words.

They both watched as she toddled about and occasionally sat down on the floor. She carried on babbling.

"Oh, I shall miss this little person," said Mutti softly.

There was a lump in Käthe's throat.

Renate suddenly propelled herself towards her grandmother and said loudly and clearly, "Oma – tea?" She then turned round and toddled over to her mother and said, "Mutti – tea?"

"You clever girl," said Käthe.

Renate threw back her head and giggled.

"She's so bright, isn't she?" said Mutti. "Anyway, you know what I think? I think…" She was interrupted as Renate launched herself at her knees and buried her face in her lap. "What are you doing down there?"

The little girl just giggled.

Mutti looked up at Käthe. "I think it will be much more fun staying than just visiting. You must come and stay with us often in Stuttgart and I shall come back to Jena to stay with you."

Renate straightened up. "Oma stay. Oma stay. Oma stay," she chanted. "Mutti stay. Vati stay."

Mutti laughed. "The words are coming thick and fast now. There will be no stopping this one. I can see a little chatterbox in the making."

Käthe smiled. Her daughter was growing up. Her mother was moving on. Life cycles, she guessed.

Renate came over to her and grabbed her hand. "Mutti Oma stay."

Didn't Mutti always say that children were very wise? Her daughter seemed to have got it. She knew she couldn't stop this happening. She must make it be all right.

Jena 1928

Chapter 34: no new buttons for the scum

"Is it far to the shop now, Mutti? Can I really have giraffe buttons? I like giraffes." Renate skipped ahead of Käthe, turned round and skipped back.

"I do wish you'd calm down a bit and let me keep up with you."

"But Mutti, I like skipping and I like giraffes. Will they really have buttons that look like giraffes at the shop? Is it far now?"

Käthe laughed. Renate always ran everywhere. She'd started running almost as soon as she'd started walking. Skipping made a nice change today. She hardly ever stopped talking either. She was obsessed with giraffes. Could it be because of their long elegant necks? She looked as if she was going to be tall herself.

"The shop's not far now. Now listen. You mustn't be disappointed if they don't have buttons that look like giraffes. If any shop's going to have them, though, it will be Frau Schneider's. She just might not. She will have something very nice, though, I'm sure."

"Frau Schneider. Mrs Cutter-upper." Renate giggled. "Mutti, I'm going to run to the corner and back again. It will make us get there quicker."

Käthe couldn't quite follow that logic but she guessed if her daughter was racing around having fun it would stop her constantly asking, "Are we nearly there yet?"

They weren't very far away at all in fact. Five minutes later Käthe was opening the door to the little haberdasher's. Renate seemed delighted by the bing-bong of the bell that was activated when a customer stepped on the doormat. She stamped on it several times.

"That's enough." Clara took her hand quite firmly. "Now, tell Frau Schneider what we're looking for today."

"I want some buttons that look like giraffes. Have you got any?"

Frau Schneider frowned and pursed her lips. "I don't think I do have but I think I have got something you might like."

Now Renate frowned. Käthe hoped she wasn't going to cause a fuss. These fashions at Kindergarten were becoming a bit of a problem.

"I'm getting a lot of requests like this." Frau Schneider rummaged through one of the drawers behind the counter.

"Andreas has elephants on his winter coat," said Renate.

"Oh yes," said Frau Schneider. "We've had elephants but I'm right out of them now. I've got a few tigers and lions. But no giraffes. I think their necks are too long to make them into buttons."

Renate was really pouting now and Käthe was afraid she a going to stamp her foot. "I'm sure Frau Schneider will find you something nice," she said.

Renate shook her head. The stamp was coming any second now. Just as she raised her foot, though, Frau Schneider turned back to them. "Yes. Here we are. What do you think of this then?"

Renate's eyes lit up when she saw the appliqué patch of a very handsome giraffe.

"Perhaps you could get Mutti to sew a pocket on to your coat and put this on the pocket and I've another idea as well." She pulled a large box from under the counter. "Why don't you take a look in here? I don't have any giraffe-shaped buttons but I do have some the same colour as a giraffe."

Renate turned to Käthe. "Can we do that, Mutti? Can we put the giraffe on a pocket on my coat? And can I pick the buttons myself?"

"I don't see why not. Mind they're all the same size though."

Renate started to sort through the box, poking her tongue out as she concentrated.

Frau Schneider smiled and nodded. "She's doing well isn't she?" she whispered. "Though I can see she's handful. She certainly knows what she wants, doesn't she?"

Käthe rolled her eyes and nodded.

The shop bell bing-bonged and a young woman about the same age as Käthe came in. She was very sombrely dressed and Käthe recognised straight away the black uniform of the Jewish Hausfrau.

The clothes may be dull but they were of extremely good quality. Well her own clothes were also excellent quality but they were far more fun and she chose them herself. Neither Hans nor Mutti and certainly not Oma Clara would dare tell her what to wear. The young woman, Käthe expected, would be getting plenty of advice from her mother and her mother-in-law. Her husband would probably more often than not accompany her on shopping trips to make sure that he approved of any clothing she bought. He wasn't here today, though. That might be a good sign. Or was she just after a few shirt buttons?

The woman nodded at her and Käthe smiled. Thank goodness Mutti and Vati changed religion or that might have been her now. Not that she wanted any sort of religion. It was all nonsense. There was no big man in the sky looking after us all. It was all just an accident of nature. A pretty clever one, yes, but an accident all the same.

Frau Schneider looked up from helping Renate to sort through the buttons. She saw the woman standing there, blushed and looked away again very quickly.

"Hurry up now," said Käthe. "This lady is waiting."

"Don't you worry, my love," said Frau Schneider. "You take your time. The lady can wait."

Had she imagined it or had Frau Schneider put a strange emphasis on the word "lady"?

"It's all right," said the woman. "Perhaps I can come back again later."

"Perhaps you should," said Frau Schneider. "Perhaps you shouldn't come back again at all, in fact."

The young Jewish woman blushed and hurried out of the shop.

Käthe was happy that Renate was so engrossed in searching through the buttons that she hadn't noticed what had just happened. Probably she was too little to understand, anyway.

"They make me sick," said Frau Schneider. "Coming in here with their airs and graces. They always take such a long time to choose anything and they always argue about the price. Then when I offer them something cheaper they complain about the quality. You get what you pay for, don't you?"

Käthe's mouth went dry. Probably Frau Schneider didn't realise that she came from a Jewish family. "Do you get many coming here?" she asked.

"Not so much anymore."

"Oh. Why not?"

"We're trying to put them off."

"We?"

"All of us shop keepers in this row of shops. In fact lots of shops that belong to the Guild are doing the same."

"But if they're spending good money, what's the problem?"

"They're not though. They're pushing down the prices. And they're taking our children's jobs and their houses. My husband says they're controlling the banks as well. We'd really be better off without them."

The room was beginning to swirl around and Käthe could see black patches floating in front of her eyes. Renate was wobbling her arm. "Mutti. Mutti. Why do you look so funny?"

"Oh my goodness, Frau Edler. You've gone quite pale."

"I don't feel too well."

"Come and sit down." Frau Schneider lifted up the hinged part of the counter and came round on to the customers' side of the shop. She led Käthe to a chair in the corner. "I'll go and get you a glass of water."

The chair was near the door which Käthe pushed open to let some air in. She started to feel more herself and by the time Frau Schneider came back with the water the black patches had disappeared.

"You look a bit better." Frau Schneider handed her the glass. "I hope my little outburst didn't upset you."

It had though. She would have to tell her. "You probably don't realise – why should you – but I come from a Jewish family. My parents became Evangelicals when I was a child."

Frau Schneider put her hand in front of her mouth and frowned. "I didn't know that. I am so sorry. I didn't mean to cause offense. You've always been a good customer, Frau Edler. And as you say, you've changed faith. You're just like us now."

198

"Yes, but my mother still has a lot of Jewish friends. These people you're talking about are my mother's friends."

Frau Schneider sighed. "I'm really sorry but it's true that they try to exploit us."

"I'm so sorry. I didn't realise. They shouldn't do that."

"Well, you don't anyway. Are you feeling better, now, Frau Edler? Or should we get you a cab?"

Käthe stood up. "I'm quite all right now thank you. If you'd be so kind as to parcel up the buttons and the patch I'd like to settle up and then we'll be on our way."

"Yes, certainly."

There was an awkward silence as Frau Schneider carefully wrapped the appliqué patch in tissue paper, put the buttons into a paper bag and folded the top over firmly.

Renate put her arm round Käthe's legs. Käthe looked down and stroked her child's hair. Two rich brown eyes looked up at her. Jewish eyes. Eyes just like her own and like those of the young woman who had come looking for shirt buttons.

Without waiting to hear the price, Käthe handed over a note and waited while Frau Schneider sorted out the change.

Käthe picked up her parcel. "Thank you and good day," she said, taking Renate's hand firmly.

"I really didn't mean…"

Käthe didn't stop to hear Frau Schneider's repeated apology.

She gripped Renate's hand tightly and the little girl seemed to understand that there would be no running ahead on that trip home. Her Mutti had something on her mind.

Käthe walked as fast as she could. The people who worked in these shops hated her mother's friends and some of her own relations. Her grandparents wouldn't be allowed to buy things here. This was frightening. Well, anyway, if that was the way they wanted it she would comply: she wouldn't go anywhere near their shops in the future. She would shop instead in one of the new department stores.

It was only after she'd told the whole story to Hans and he had guffawed and told her not to be so sensitive and that the Schneider woman was a fool, that she realised that although the giraffe patch was safely in her handbag she had left the buttons on the counter. There they would have to stay. There was no way she was going back there. No buttons for the scum, then.

Chapter 35: exciting plans

Käthe jumped. The front door had just clicked to. Hans? Was that Hans? What was he doing home so early? She had just made some coffee but had then decided Renate ought to have an early bath. What did they get up to at Kindergarten? She was really dirty. Perhaps it would be better when she started school properly next autumn. She was half way up the stairs now.

"Käthe? Renate? Lotte?" called Hans. "Where are you? I've got something to tell you?"

"I'm just taking Renate up to the bathroom. There's coffee. Help yourself."

Renate wriggled and got away from her. "I want to see my Vati."

"That's my girl." Hans held out his arms ready to pick her up and swing her round in the air.

Renate dashed back downstairs. Käthe held her breath and waited for the reaction.

It came. Hans pushed his daughter away and looked up at Käthe. "What the heck, Käthe? She's filthy. She's like an urchin."

"Send her back up, then, and I'll get her washed."

"Get Lotte to do it. There's something I've really got to tell you."

Käthe felt sick. What could it be? He hadn't lost his job had he? Or something else equally bad?

Lotte had already come out of the kitchen. "It's all right, Frau Edler. I'll see to her."

Renate stamped her foot. "I want to know Vati's secret."

"It's not a secret. I'll tell you over supper. Only if you're a good girl mind."

Renate pulled a face as she went upstairs with Lotte. She was still chuntering, though.

Käthe relaxed a little when she met Hans in the hallway. At least he was grinning.

"Let's grab that coffee," he said.

They went into the lounge. Käthe poured the coffee and offered Hans a piece of the walnut and coffee cake. "Well," she said, "what is it?"

His stuffed his mouth full of cake before he could answer. Then he licked his fingers and grinned, swallowed the cake and took a slurp of the coffee. He put his cup down and waved his hands in the air. "You are now looking at the new manager of the defence unit. I'm being promoted and we're being asked to move to Nuremberg."

"Nuremberg?" Käthe almost dropped her cup.

"A lovely town built inside a castle. They've even found a partly-built house for us. We can buy it cheaply. It's surrounded by woodland but also not too far from the railway so that we know we're near civilisation."

"We'll be nearer to Mutti?"

"An advantage, surely?"

He had a point she supposed. But it was a lot to take in. "I think I need a breath of fresh air," she said.

"Why don't you tell Mutti how grand it's all going to be?" Hans held a forkful of spinach up to Renate's mouth.

Renate pushed the fork away. "Will I still have to go to the proper school there? Will I still have to eat spinach?"

"Oh, I'm sure it's just like here in many ways." He offered the fork again. Renate took a mouthful of food.

Käthe twiddled her hair around her finger. "So, why can't we stay here?"

Hans sighed and put the fork down. "Because the work they want me to do isn't here. It's there. It's nearer to your mother as well. And as your mother gets older..."

"My mother is going to live for a good many years yet."

"I don't mean that. She just may need a bit more care as she gets older." He shovelled another forkful of spinach into Renate's open mouth. The child was frowning and whimpering. Käthe was vaguely aware that Renate was doing her hamster trick again – filling her cheeks with food she didn't want to taste. There would be consequences. That didn't seem so important though now. This conversation was more urgent.

Hans sighed. "Oh Käthe. It's a beautiful city. You'll love it once you're there. I know you will."

Renate suddenly started coughing. Her face went very red. She spluttered.

"God, Hans, she's choking."

Hans leapt to his feet, sprang over to where Renate was sitting and thumped her on the back. She coughed again even more violently this time. Soggy, unchewed spinach spread itself all over the white tablecloth. The wretched child had done it again. Käthe wanted to slap her but she was determined never to smack her child. She couldn't help being irritated, though. "Renate, that is really disgusting."

Hans was beginning to titter.

Renate looked shocked. Then she burped loudly. Soon she was giggling too.

Hans started roaring.

Käthe couldn't help it. She had to see the funny side. She started chuckling as well.

"You know," said Hans after he had eventually gathered some control again, "maybe we should stop trying to force her to eat spinach."

"Good idea, Vati."

"She has to eat her greens, Hans." Käthe was so worried their daughter might be struck by the same weaknesses that had made her father suffer. Spinach, she knew, was rich in iron.

Hans shrugged and shook his head. "She'll probably acquire a taste for it when she's older."

Renate pulled a face and pushed the rest of the spinach to one side of her plate. She carried on eating the rest of her food.

"Good girl." Hans nodded as he watched Renate eat. "And you know what else is a good idea?" He raised his eyebrows at Käthe then turned back to Renate. "Going to live in Nuremberg. It's the best town for toys in the whole world."

Renate stopped eating. Her eyes grew round.

Hans nodded.

Käthe knew exactly what he was trying to do. She wished he would stop.

Hans looked from Renate to Käthe and back again. "So don't you think it might be nice to go and live there. And. The whole town is built inside a castle. What about that, then?"

Renate clapped. "Can we go and live there, Vati? Can we?"

"I should think so. If Mutti agrees."

Damn the man.

At that moment, the door opened and in came Lotte. She put her hand in front of her mouth as she saw the spinach bedecked tablecloth. "Oh my."

"Don't worry," said Käthe. "I'll help you clear this up and put on a clean cloth on before we have dessert."

"You must join us for dessert," said Hans. "We have news. We're moving to Nuremberg. You must come with us."

So, it was settled then. They were moving to Nuremberg.

"As soon after Christmas as possible," said Hans. He grinned. "Just think. We'll be able to go skiing from there easily."

All evening, after Renate had gone to bed, he threw suggestions at her.

"Maybe you can take up science again."

"If you don't like the house, we can pick another."

"The job is really a good one. We'll be able to afford so much more."

By the time they went to bed she was almost convinced. She even began to look forward a little to the new house. If they were moving just after Christmas, she would have to start sorting out things now. Persuading Lotte to go with them. Finding a school for Renate.

"You see," said Hans. "It really is a good opportunity." He turned over, and in seconds he was snoring.

She drifted off herself eventually. A little later though she woke with a start. That was what was bothering her. Hans was going to be working for the defence department. Didn't that mean making weapons? And did that mean there would be another war?

"Hans! Hans, wake up."

"What's the matter?" His voice was thick with sleep.

"You're going to be managing the defence department?"

"Yes. It's an important job, Käthe."

"But defence. That must be weapons and war."

"You know we're not allowed to develop weapons."

"So why defence?"

"To protect. To be prepared. It's science really. Besides, I really think there will be another one."

"Another war? Surely not."

Hans was now sitting upright in bed. "We were unfairly treated after the last lot. Something has to give."

"Another war, though?" Käthe shuddered.

"Look, I'm wide awaken now. I'm going to make some camomile tea. Would you like some?"

Käthe nodded. Another war. That would be terrible.

Stuttgart 1929

Chapter 36: changes

"Look at the lights," whispered Mutti. "Don't they sparkle?"

Renate nodded her head and clapped.

Käthe couldn't believe what she was seeing. All of the children, even the disabled ones were carrying a candle. It was just getting dark. It was all very pretty, but surely it was dangerous. One slip and a fire could start so easily.

Renate seemed fascinated. Well, at last it was keeping her amused. The play had been very good. Who would have thought such young people could produce something so refined?

"So, you enjoyed that, did you?" said Mutti.

Renate grinned. "It's so pretty. I wish we could have candles at home."

No way. At last the school conceded to 20th century life and put on the electric lights as the play came to a close. Thank goodness.

"How would you like something to eat and drink?" said Mutti to Renate.

"Yes please."

Mutti took her hand and led her to the classroom where the food was being served. Käthe and Hans followed. Käthe was astounded once more. "How do you manage all of this?" she asked. "These days?"

It was quite a spread. There were Wiener Kipferl, Stollen, Strudel and Christmas shapes made from Lebkuchen. There was tea and coffee and warmed apple juice flavoured with cinnamon. There was even some cream though if truth be told it was really Quark, thinned with milk and flavoured with a little vanilla.

"We can do a lot when we pull together as a community," said her mother.

"Oma, will you teach me how to make Lebkuchen?" said Renate.

"Hmm. Lebkuchen are a bit tricky but we certainly can have a go at some Strudel or a cheesecake if you like."

"Yes please, Oma." Renate tried to wipe the sticky crumbs from her face but actually made it worse.

"Just look at the mess you're making, will you?" said Käthe, spitting on her hanky and scrubbing at her daughter's face.

Renate squirmed and wriggled. "Mutti, that hurts, and your spit smells funny. She pulled away from Käthe and almost knocked a plate out of a lady's hand.

"I'm so sorry," Käthe mumbled.

"No problem," said the lady but she looked annoyed.

Käthe was relieved when her mother suggested they should set off home. This school was just a bit too good to be real.

It was completely dark when they got outside. Despite the lamps they could see a sky that looked like dark blue velvet covered in sequins. The snow glistened in the lamp light. It was pretty. Käthe had to admit that. She just couldn't enjoy it. She was plagued by this overwhelming anxiety all of the time.

"Mutti, can I run to the end of the road then run back to you and Oma?"

"Go on then," said Käthe. Renate was already skipping along. Käthe couldn't work out how she managed to keep herself upright on the very slippery pavements. She and Mutti were walking very gingerly.

"Aren't you frightened she'll fall?" said Mutti.

"Not that one. She's more-sure footed than a mountain goat and even if she does fall – it doesn't happen very often, mind, she seems to bounce back on to her feet."

Mutti held her breath as she watched her granddaughter run backwards and forwards. She really was fast for such a little girl. She was relieved, though, when they arrived at the house and there had been no accidents.

"She can run, can't she?" said Mutti.

"Oh yes. Faster than anyone else in her Kindergarten group. No one else comes anywhere near her. Not even any of the boys."

By the time Mutti had overseen the preparations for supper and laid up a table for Hans, Käthe, Renate and herself in her private sitting-room, the little girl was very sleepy. It was really past her bed time.

As soon as supper was done, Renate laid her head in her mother's lap, stuck her thumb in her mouth and fell asleep.

"Goodness, she's worn out," said Mutti. "I'm not surprised, though, with all that running backwards and forwards."

"And the play. She enjoyed that but it tired her," said Käthe.

"She ought to go to bed," said Hans.

At the sound of her father's voice Renate awoke.

"Bed time," whispered Käthe.

"Can Oma put me to bed? I want Oma to, Mutti."

Mutti nodded at Käthe. "Yes. It's fine. Of course I'll read you a story. Come on and let's get you up those stairs."

Renate kissed her mother and father goodnight. Käthe and Hans were left alone.

"Do you really think it's going to be all right?" Käthe was exhausted. There had been so much to sort out. She was also worried that they hadn't told anyone else yet. What would Mutti's reaction be?

"It's going to be wonderful. You like the house, don't you?"

Käthe nodded. Yes, she really did. It was almost ready now and was much more modern than the one they had in Jena. The garden was lovely. It was going to be so nice for Renate. "The work, though?" That was the sticking point.

Hans laughed. "Käthe, you know I'm not going to be making or throwing bombs. They won't let us. It's all going to be pretend. Just science and fun."

Käthe sighed. "Unless there's another war."

Hans took another sip of his wine and shrugged.

They sat in silence. They really had nothing more to say to each other.

Mutti came down at last. "So you have managed to get everyone to call her Renate?" she said when she got back down to the sitting-room. "The Kindergarten people were all right about it?"

"Yes, though she's still Klara Renate on anything official. And we're resigned to spelling it the German way," said Käthe.

"I don't see why we should have to be," said Hans. "We should choose her name. Not some drunken priest."

"Well it's done now." Käthe tutted. "Anyway, we've got much more important things to discuss with Mutti. Shall I tell her or will you?"

Hans glared at her.

Käthe sighed. "Right. Listen, Mutti. We're moving to Nuremberg."

"Nuremberg?"

Mutti looked serious. She was clearly finding this difficult to process.

"I'm going to be working for Siemens," said Hans. "I'll be working on defence weapons."

Mutti shuddered. "You don't think there's going to be another war, do you?"

Hans shrugged. "Every nation must have its defence."

"Mutti, it's a well-paid job. It will help to secure Renate's future."

"I do hope you're right," whispered Mutti. "Oh, and by the way, she says she really likes the school here and she would like to come to it."

Käthe rolled her eyes. "Don't encourage her, Mutti."

Stuttgart 1932

Chapter 37: spots and science

Käthe was awake really early even though the journey from Nuremberg the day before had been more demanding than they'd expected. It should have been a bit easier really. The main problem had been Renate. She'd been whiny and clingy. What a good job they hadn't reminded her that it was her birthday. They would celebrate today instead. Hopefully she would have a nice day with Oma and Uncle Ernst. Then she and Hans ought to be back in time for a birthday tea.

She glanced at the clock. Quarter to six. It looked as if they were going to be able to get out of the house before Renate woke. Usually she was awake by now on these bright summer mornings. Perhaps she was still tired after the journey.

Hans was still snoring away. Käthe smiled. It was going to be their day today. She was going to accompany her husband to a science convention. It would be so good being amongst people who had a brain in their heads again. She was a little fed up of playing the housewife.

She shook him gently. "Wake up, you," she whispered. "How can you not be excited about this?"

Hans mumbled something then slowly woke up. He rubbed his eyes. "What time is it?"

"Time you were getting up."

"Oh no. Not already? It feels as if we've only been in bed five minutes."

Käthe shook her head and laughed. "You don't know how lucky you are. Come on. Get up and get dressed."

It was quite exciting washing and dressing quickly and quietly.

"Should we make some coffee before we go?" asked Käthe.

Hans shook his head. "No need. They'll serve Bretzel and coffee when we arrive. The quicker we get out, the better. We don't want young missy waking up or we might never get away."

Thirty minutes later they were shutting the door quietly behind them. Renate still hadn't woken. Käthe worried for a moment or two whether there might be something wrong. Was the child sickening for something? Oh, even if she was, it probably wasn't anything too serious. Mutti would surely know what to do if there was a problem. She certainly wasn't going to miss out on this.

"You won't expect too much, will you?" said Hans as they drove down towards the town. "It's a trade conference, not an academic one. Anyway, things have moved on in science."

"Are you saying I won't understand?"

"Some of it you won't but a lot of it you will. It just might not be what interests you."

"I expect I'll manage." The cheek of the man. Was he treating her like the little housewife?

"There's something else as well."

"Oh?"

"There probably won't be any other women there."

Ah. That again. "Do you think I'm not used to that?"

"Well, if you think the university was intolerant, you'll find these industrial people a lot harsher."

"Are you trying to put me off?"

"No. Just warning you. I don't want you to be disappointed."

"Well, I'll try not to disappoint you then."

"I'm sure you won't."

Hans slowed down and indicated left. They turned into a side street and there was the hotel where the conference was being held. Käthe's stomach started churning as she stepped out of the car. She wasn't going to let the people put her off, though. She would show them. She most certainly would.

The foyer was already busy and they had to queue for twenty minutes to register. Hans had been absolutely right; there were no other women here apart from a few of the catering staff. He was right too about the Bretzel and coffee and at least the queue for those was quite short.

"I'll have to go and work on the stand with the others," he said. "You can wander around as much as you like. Come and pick me up at half past twelve and we'll go and get lunch together. Unless you get too interested in something, in which case, meet me here at four o'clock. I've insisted that I leave then as it's our daughter's birthday. Sort of. Good excuse anyway." He shoved the last piece of Bretzel into his mouth, licked his fingers, slurped the last of his coffee and wiped his chin. He put his dirty cup and plate on a nearby table, waved hastily and set off in the direction of his display.

Käthe was left sitting in the middle of the foyer, not quite knowing what to do next. Well it was no good. She mustn't dither. Best look around, she supposed.

She finished her breakfast and set off determinedly in the opposite direction from Hans.

It was the same at every stall she visited. None of the men stopped their conversations to talk to her. Those who weren't talking to a colleague gave her a curious look and if she did catch eye contact with one of them for a split second, he would look away quickly as if embarrassed.

The information on the displays was all very easy to understand. Hans had been wrong there. Much of it though was hardly interesting at all. What did she care about these practical applications of what was really quite simple science? When would she see something that would excite her like Professor Einstein's ideas about time and relativity?

She was getting really bored. It was much too early for lunch. Should she wander outside and have a stroll around the town? Stuttgart was a quiet little place really. It lacked the busyness of Berlin and prettiness of Nuremberg. It was no worse than Jena though. Still she couldn't understand why Mutti and Ernst were so keen on it. And at that funny little school. Did they teach them science there? This wasn't really science here.

Suddenly a voice called out. "Käthe Lehrs. What are you doing here?"

She would recognise that voice anywhere. And she was using her old name. Käthe looked round frantically to try and see where it as coming from. Then she saw her. Trousers, waistcoat and jacket to match. Dressed like a man again. So, she'd gone back to that.

She rushed over to the stall where Gerda was standing.

"What on earth are you doing here?" Gerda hugged her.

"Hans is here. He's working for Siemens now. He's helping to look after their stand. I'm just here for a look around, really. What about you?"

"Duty calls. A bit boring for you, isn't it, though?" Gerda's eyes twinkled.

"Yes and no. It's good to get back to a bit of science."

Gerda laughed out loud then. "Oh I bet you're still a pure scientist, aren't you? Still stuck on relativity and all that?"

"Yes, I suppose so. I carried on you know. Studying under Professor Einstein. At a distance still. The academics in Jena weren't so inspiring, though. Then our daughter Renate came along. And that was the end of that."

"Come on then." Gerda came out from behind her stall and linked her arm through Käthe's. "We'd better go and get a cup of coffee."

A few moments later they were catching up in the coffee lounge. Gerda had now completed her doctorate at the local university. She had been sponsored by one of the nearby engineering firms and now worked for them.

"Of course I'm into applied science now. At least I can earn a living from that."

"They've accepted you in this world? Hans warned me there wouldn't be any other women here."

Gerda sighed. "It's all all right as long as I behave like a man." She held up her arms and pointed down to her suit.

"And you've not thought about getting married and having a family?"

Gerda roared with laughter. "Oh come on, Käthchen. You know that can never be." She leant towards Käthe and put her mouth to Käthe's ear, cupping her hand over her own mouth. "There is someone, though. She's a poet and we're sharing a house out in the suburbs."

"I see." Käthe felt her cheeks burning.

"No good you getting jealous, young lady. You had your chance but you chose your Hans."

"I'm not jealous. I'm happy for you."

Gerda leaned back in her chair when the waitress brought their second cups of coffee. "Have you heard that Professor Einstein is thinking of emigrating to America?" she said in a louder voice.

"Oh, why?"

"You know he's Jewish, don't you? He just thinks it might be safer with things as they are."

She had been vaguely aware that Professor Einstein was Jewish. She wouldn't have thought though that he would let that bother him. She was just about to remind Gerda that she was Jewish too but something stopped her. Had Gerda remembered that her family was Jewish? She'd always thought Gerda didn't really care but this was something they'd never discussed really. Back then it hadn't mattered so much. She shrugged. "Tell me about your work then."

"I could show you if you like. I'm off duty at 2.00."

"Well, as long as I'm back by 4.00." She explained about Renate's birthday.

It all worked out quite well. She skipped lunch with Hans. He'd have only bored her anyway with all the details of how successful his firm was becoming and what good contacts they'd made today. She spent a very pleasant couple of hours with Gerda talking pure science.

Her laboratory was so different from the ones they used to use in Berlin. It was modern and light and airy.

Käthe picked up some of Gerda's notes. They were very neatly printed.

"You've been putting your typing to good use?" asked Käthe.

Gerda laughed. "No, I have a secretary who does that for me. My hand writing is as bad as ever. If not worse. I have so much more to write these days. But Magda, bless her, can read my awful scrawl and gets everything typed up very quickly."

"It's all very impressive anyway."

"But the experiments aren't quite as exciting as the ones we used to do." She rubbed the back of her hand against Käthe's cheek. "Oh, my love. All that secrecy and the two of us alone together in those dark, cool laboratories."

Käthe flinched and Gerda pulled her hand back. "Don't worry. I don't want to steal you from Hans or anything. I love Szilvia to bits."

"Szilvia?"

"She's Hungarian. Incredibly beautiful and intelligent. But not a scientist and I always hoped that you and I would achieve great things together."

"Yes. A darn nuisance that I had to fall in love with Hans."

"It's a pity you can't carry on with your studies," Gerda said as they walked back to the conference. "Being married and having children shouldn't stop an intelligent woman like you."

"Oh, it's just not to be."

Hans was waiting impatiently when they got back. He gave Gerda a strange look when Käthe explained about them bumping into each other. Then he simply nodded and turned to Käthe. "Come on, hurry up. We mustn't let our daughter down."

"It's not as if she's going anywhere," said Käthe as she got into the car. Renate was probably thoroughly enjoying herself with that new friend she'd made last time they'd visited her mother. She probably hadn't even noticed they weren't there.

There was quite some tension in the car. Hans frowned and stared at the road ahead.

She wondered he knew about Gerda? About her having – well – different tastes? For goodness sake! It was just the science that interested her. She wasn't like Gerda. Then she began to wonder, though, what Gerda might think about her being Jewish now that this seemed to be such an issue. She shuddered when she remembered the incident in Frau Schneider's shop. That was almost two years ago now but it still bothered her. Now there seemed to be more and more people thinking the same way as Frau Schneider.

They stopped at a road junction. They had to wait for several cars to pass in front of them. Hans drummed his fingers on the steering wheel. "So what did you two women talk about?" He looked away from them.

"Oh, just some of the latest ideas. And about Professor Einstein."

"Einstein? What's new?"

Käthe couldn't believe that Hans wasn't keeping up with his former colleague's news.

"He's thinking of going to America."

"America?"

The road in front of them cleared and Hans was able to turn on to the main road.

"It's because he's Jewish and he doesn't know what might happen here."

Hans grunted.

Käthe felt sick. If Professor Einstein thought it was bad enough that he'd got to emigrate shouldn't she be thinking about that too? "Do you think we should make some plans?"

Hans tutted. "Overreaction," he muttered.

Perhaps he was right. He was frowning, though, and concentrating on his driving.

After what seemed like a long time they pulled up in front of the her mother's house in Schellberg Street.

"Anyway, you and your family don't look Jewish. He does. Because he's well known they'll notice him more. And you're not Jewish because you're Christian." He climbed out of the car. "Come on, we've got a daughter to see to."

It was oddly quiet as they walked up the garden path. She would have thought that on a nice day like today the two girls would be playing out in the garden and making quite a lot of noise.

"We're back," she called as they made their way through the front door.

"Where's my day-late birthday girl?" said Hans.

"We're up here. We have chicken pox," Mutti called.

Käthe exchanged a glance with Hans. "Chicken pox?" Then she remembered. "Oh, Hans you'd better not come up."

She ran up the stairs and into Renate's bedroom. "Hans has never had chicken pox," she said to her mother.

"He should stay away," said the doctor. "It can be very nasty in adults."

"It's not very nice in children," said Renate. "Please go away and leave me and my spots in peace."

The doctor frowned. Mutti tittered.

Something sank in Käthe. She would now have to nurse a sick child. Any plans she might be forming about being a scientist would have to be put on hold yet again.

AH Berlin 1932

He marched smartly along the Wilhelmstrasse. He was strong against the cold. It must be at least minus four degrees but felt reasonable as there was no wind. The sky was clear and the sun was shining brightly. The weather seemed to be in keeping with what was about to happen.

He arrived at the Reichskanzlei. An aide held the door open for him as he stamped the frost off his boots. The man saluted and he nodded briefly.

The President looked even older than his eighty-five years. It was such a burden that successive governments had failed to bring stability.

The old man shook his hand. "It's good that we can form a viable coalition at last," he said. "Now we can look forward to a brighter future."

It was his turn to speak now to the crowd gathered there. "I promise to uphold the constitution," he said. "I promise to govern with the good of the nation in mind. Always. I shall not rest until Germany is great again."

They clapped loudly, raised their arms and shouted, "Heil Hitler."

Yes, this was what he had been working towards for years now. His time had come.

Nuremberg 1933

Chapter 38: a new ruler

There was a tense atmosphere in the streets today. It was crowded but that wasn't unusual for a Saturday. Yet it wasn't the normal shoppers who were walking along the pavements. There were a lot more men than normal and their faces were pretty grim. The better dressed were making their way into the smarter guest houses and taverns. Those in working clothes were gathering on street corners, looking either worried or ecstatic as they smoked cigarettes or pipes.

Something was up and Käthe was surprised that Hans hadn't said anything about it. And why hadn't he wanted to come into town and talk to the other men? Whatever it was, he couldn't have known about it. He'd been very happy to let her come shopping. Renate needed some more play clothes and she herself needed a new blouse.

"Buy something charming," Hans had said. "But don't spend too much."

She wasn't all that interested in shopping, really. Now it looked as if something mysterious and exciting was going on. She'd better find out what.

There were even a few women walking purposefully along the streets. She smiled to herself. Perhaps women were becoming involved in the world after all.

There was a young man selling newspapers on the corner of the street. It must be a special edition. "Herr Hitler in charge now," he shouted. "Enabling Act has given him temporary powers."

She stopped to buy a copy.

"What's actually going on? What does that mean, the Enabling Act?"

The young man blushed. "I don't really know. I'm just using the words they told me to say. I think it means Herr Hitler is totally in charge now."

Käthe nodded. She expected Hans would be able to explain it all. No, wait a minute. She'd got a brain in her head, hadn't she?

222

She could figure this out for herself. There was a café in the new department store, wasn't there? She would go and buy herself a coffee and sit and read the newspaper. Her blouse and Renate's clothes could wait.

The café in Shocken was actually quite empty. Very odd for a Saturday. All of those men who really had to talk about the latest political happenings would go rather to the taverns and the coffee houses. Perhaps fewer women were shopping as the menfolk thought it better if they stayed at home.

There was another woman, though, and she was also reading the paper. Käthe sat at the table next to her. Maybe there would be a chance to get into conversation.

The waitress came and took Käthe's order almost immediately. The young woman looked up and smiled. She was a considerably younger than Käthe. A career woman, perhaps? Certainly single – she was not wearing gloves and there was no sign of any rings.

"Are your reading about Herr Hitler?" said Käthe.

"Yes. It's astonishing, isn't it?"

"I've not read the article yet. Do you understand what's happened?" Käthe felt her cheeks go red. Why had she said that? The woman would think she was an idiot.

"It's tricky, isn't it?" said the younger woman. "Especially if you're not able to follow all of it. Fortunately I've a degree in politics so I'm pretty au fait with what's been going on." The woman smiled.

Käthe nodded. This was so unfair. How come this bright young thing was using her degree and she wasn't allowed to? Oh, yes, that was right. She was a mother now and had to concentrate on her child.

"Basically Hitler's party got the most votes in the latest election but not a clear majority. Therefore the Enabling Act can be brought in. That allows him to be in charge for four years."

"I see." She didn't really but at least one thing was clear: Hitler was going to be their leader for a while.

The young woman nodded. "I actually think it's not a bad thing, really. He has some good plans that will make life better for all of us. He intends to make Germany great again."

223

Was that really true? Käthe wasn't sure. For some reason she couldn't quite explain she remembered the horrible incident with Frau Schneider and the buttons.

The younger woman stood up. "Do excuse me. I have to do an interview with the radio now. It was nice talking to you."

The waitress arrived with Käthe's coffee. Käthe opened the paper and began to read. Yes she'd understood that Hitler had in fact been Chancellor since January. That already gave him quite a bit of power but now he and his party were also in charge of the government. The Chancellor was in charge of the Reichstag and only had some limited powers. The real power was with the President and that was still Hindenburg. But that man's health was failing. This Enabling Act gave Hitler the right to act without consent from Parliament. He certainly was the Führer, the leader, now. Käthe felt grateful that Hindenburg was still there. At least he might be able to provide some balance.

It all puzzled her though. That young woman had said, hadn't she, that Hitler had some good plans. Yet she couldn't bring herself to like him.

She looked through a few of the other articles in the paper. Oh and here was something else interesting. Goebbels, who was named Reich's minister of propaganda – whatever that meant – was claiming that newspapers were outdated and that all news would probably soon be communicated better by the wireless. Well, at least perhaps she'd be able to listen and keep herself better informed.

It still looked, though, as if she would have to ask Hans about it after all.

She finished her coffee and paid her bill. Then she quickly made her way to the ladies' wear department, picked up a blouse in her size but didn't bother trying it on. It took her all of ten minutes to pick out half a dozen play suits for Renate in the children's department. Then she was able to set off home.

"So, have you spent all of my money?" said Hans when she walked into the lounge, still in her hat and coat and still clutching her shopping bags.

"Of course not. I've only bought what was necessary." She dropped the bags on the floor. "That's hardly important. Did you know about Herr Hitler taking complete control?"

"Naturally."

"And you let me go into town with all the drama going on?"

"Darling, it's nothing. Really it isn't. The man's an idiot. He won't last long. He'll soon make some really stupid mistake and he'll be out. That's if somebody doesn't assassinate him first."

"Some people think he's going to be good." That young woman she'd spoken to seemed incredibly intelligent. If she was taken with him wouldn't lots of other people be? "Well, there was certainly a lot of fuss going on today."

"You don't need to worry about that at all."

"Do you know how patronising that sounds?"

Hans tutted. "I didn't mean anything other than it's all so ludicrous that it won't last. You'll see."

"Hmm." She hoped he was right but she wasn't so sure. Some people had looked worried and others had seemed jubilant. They were all taking this very seriously. She sighed. "I'll go and put these things away and then we can have lunch."

Later, after lunch, she looked at the newspaper again. There was a very clear photo of Herr Hitler on the front page. Two very intense eyes looked at her. His mouth drooped slightly to the left, making him look a bit sulky. That silly little moustache made him look as if he was pouting. Why was this man so powerful? Why did people either love him or hate him?

She realised she felt neither emotion. She was actually scared of him. Those eyes frightened her.

If he scares people like that he's going to be very powerful, she thought. She'd heard that he was an incredibly good speaker, almost like an actor.

"Who are you exactly?" she whispered to the photo. She shuddered, folded the newspaper and put it in the bin.

Nuremberg 1935

Chapter 39: officially alien

Käthe could hear Hans talking to himself. Or rather she knew he was shouting at the newspaper again. He always did that in that half hour after breakfast before he needed to go out to work.

"What's Vati cross about now?" asked Renate. "He's always grumpy in the mornings. He's like a big angry bear."

She was right. He was like a very grumpy bear. Thank goodness it wasn't with her and Renate though. He was still always polite enough to them. Even if he was usually dismissive whenever she asked him what bothered him about the news. She took Renate's hand. "He's not cross with us, sweetheart. Best not disturb him though because then he night be."

"Käthe, come here," Hans growled suddenly. "You've got to read this." This was something new. He actually wanted to discuss the news with her. She exchanged a look with Renate. "You go and get ready for school," she said. "I'll tell you about it later."

Renate nodded and started looking for her school things. Käthe made her way into the conservatory.

"It's preposterous. You should read the nonsense they're saying. There will be no more Heil Hitlers from me. From now on it will be Heil Edler. I don't care what anybody says."

"Isn't that a bit dangerous?"

"Don't care if it is. I will not be dictated to by that horrible little man. Not now."

"So, what's happened?"

"Apparently persecution of the Jews has become official. We are allowed – nay – expected to persecute them openly. We must persecute them assertively not passively as we have been doing. What on earth do they mean? What are we expected to do? Ransack their houses? Kidnap their children? Steal their furniture? They are good hardworking Germans like the rest of us."

Käthe felt faint. This would just not go away, no matter how rational they tried to be about it. She sat down quickly on the nearest chair.

Hans folded his paper and looked at her sternly. "Oh come on, Käthe. They can't possibly mean you, can they? Daughter of an eminent businessman? That business is still running successfully so you and your family must be respected. Your brother got the Iron Cross. And you're as German as can be. You even look German."

"Even my eyes?"

"Lots of Germans have brown eyes. And you come from a Christian family."

"I've never been christened, though."

"Well, why don't we do something about that? Which would you like; Catholic, Evangelical or Lutheran. Maybe someone at Renate's school would know what to do."

"Do you think they would help? Or might it be dangerous even to mention it?"

Hans laughed. "Well, they wouldn't be very Christian if they didn't, would they? Just shows, really, what a lot of nonsense it all is. But yes, if it makes you happy, let's get you baptised."

"Do you really think it will make a difference?"

Hans sighed. "There is really no need for any help. You mustn't worry so much. I must go. There's no more time to talk about this now." He paused. "There is one thing though. We are short of secretarial staff. Why don't you apply for one of the positions? We can get a nanny for Renate. Make yourself useful and important. Be one of the modern young women. Then they'd never want to touch you."

"I don't know…"

"Well, think about it. I'll bring some details back this evening."

Then he was off.

She didn't need to think. She didn't want to be a secretary. If she could work on science again, then maybe yes, that would be a good idea. It was too late, though. She'd been away from it for too long.

The front door shut. She and Renate were alone. Hans didn't seem to understand how serious this all was. He was being much too flippant about it. What would become of her and Renate? She didn't feel at all Jewish, whatever that might feel like. He was right. It was all nonsense. The trouble was, people could be pretty stupid at times. Hadn't she seen that at the university in Berlin? Even more so in Jena. Her own brothers weren't above being idiots. And Mutti. Look at them spending all of their time with this new and slightly odd religion. Of course Mutti and Ernst and their friends wouldn't hurt anyone but suppose some people got to be just as crazy in another way?

She sighed. What would become of them? Ought they to be doing something?

"Ready, Mutti!"

Oh, God, Renate. She would be late for school if they didn't hurry.

Her daughter stood in the doorway. Yes, her hair was a bit dark and of course she had deep brown eyes like her own. But with her plaits like that and her satchel on her back she looked so German. They were not Jewish. They were not.

"Come on then, young lady. Best foot forward. We mustn't be late."

After a brisk march they neared the school.

"Good morning, Frau Edler," called one of the other mothers.

Renate skipped forward and joined a group of giggling girls who were making their way into the school building. She was so at home here, Käthe could see that. Surely they wouldn't make her go to a Jewish school, would they?

Everyone seemed so nice here. Perhaps she could talk it all through with the teachers. They really were decent. Surely she could trust them?

"Bye, Mutti," called Renate.

Käthe waved.

Yes, she would do that. Just not today, though. She must think out very carefully what she was going to say. She would spend the rest of the day figuring it out. That would be a positive step.

She pulled up the collar on her coat. There was still a nip in the air though the sun shone brightly on this fine April morning.

Chapter 40: cremating the books

Käthe drew in a deep breath. The air was so delicious she must have more of it. It was one of those days that was warm and pleasant without being hot. She could smell the lilac blossom. Bees buzzed nearby. She almost felt as if she was on holiday. Renate wouldn't be home until much later: she was going on a trip with some friends after school. She was meeting Hans in town and they were going for a dinner before they collected their daughter from her friend's house. It would be like walking out again. She and Hans didn't have a lot of opportunity to do anything romantic these days. Anyway, she needed something like that to cheer her up. And she did feel cheerful this evening. Perhaps it was going to be all right after all.

As she crossed into the town, though, she noticed that the light dimmed a little. She couldn't see a cloud but the sun didn't seem to be shining quite so brightly. It wasn't going to rain, was it? Well hopefully they would be in the restaurant by the time it started. They could always take a taxi home. Renate would like that.

She soon became aware though that she could smell smoke. It wasn't a cloud at all. It was a fire. She hoped it wasn't a house fire and that nobody was getting hurt. It seemed to be coming from the next street.

She glanced at her watch. Yes, she had plenty of time. She would take a detour and see what was going on.

She turned at the end of the road and felt as if she was going to choke when she saw the people there. There were hundreds of them and some of the most officious and aggressive-looking men she had ever seen in their bright black uniforms. They and a lot of people in ordinary clothes were throwing things on to a fire.

Käthe somehow managed to make her way to the front of the crowd. She found herself standing next to a young woman about the same age as herself.

"What are they doing?" she asked.

"They're burning books," the woman whispered.

"Why?"

The woman shook her head. "Best to join in or they'll start asking questions." She passed Käthe a pile of books.

Käthe took them. "Why exactly are we doing this?"

"We're getting rid of any books written by non-German writers and even some that are if they're not so good for our development as a race."

Käthe didn't know what to say. She gripped the books tightly.

The woman shook her head. "I don't like it either, but it's best to go along with it. I hate seeing books being destroyed like this." She launched the pile she was holding towards the fire.

Käthe reluctantly took the books the woman passed her. She clung on to them for several seconds first though and just stared at the flames. Then even more reluctantly she threw them into the fire.

Every time a batch of books hit the burning mass it seemed to flare up. It actually fascinated Käthe to watch the pages curl, then char from the outside before the book burst into flames, even though it also seemed such a terrible waste. Some men with rakes pushed in any half-burned books.

"How many?" asked Käthe.

"Thousands. It will be thousands."

This was astonishing and terrible. How could they destroy books like that?

"I'm Käthe Edler, by the way."

"Best not to exchange names, really," said the young woman.

"I suppose not," said Käthe. She didn't really see why not, though.

It was getting very warm. She supposed she ought to make her way towards the restaurant.

She went to look at her watch. As she lifted up her arm she noticed the name of the author of the book she was holding. She gasped. A shudder ran through her body. Albert Einstein. It was one of Professor Einstein's books. She stroked the cover and opened it at a random page.

She was aware of the other woman staring at her again. She bit her lip as her companion pursed hers and shook her head gently. It was no good, though. Käthe could not bring herself to throw it on to the fire. She looked to see if anyone was watching. No one was looking at her. She quickly stuffed the book under her coat.

The woman touched her arm. "Take care," she whispered.

Käthe nodded and scuttled away.

Käthe was breathless and twenty minutes late when she arrived at the restaurant. Hans was scowling and looking impatiently at his watch. Before he had the chance to say anything, however, she started speaking. "I'm not hungry. You must look at this." She scanned the room to see if anyone was watching. The restaurant was crowded and the waiters were all busy.

"One of Einstein's books. I don't understand. Why are you giving me this? Where did you get it?"

"They're burning books, Hans. Any books by non-Aryan writers. Even worse. Any books by non-German writers or by any writer, German or not, who doesn't glorify the German people."

Hans went white. "It's serious then."

Käthe nodded. "Oh yes. Very serious indeed."

"Dear me."

"I've lost my appetite. I don't think I can eat. Let's fetch Renate and get home."

"I think you're right." Hans stood up and signalled that the waiter should bring him his coat.

The waiter arrived. "I hope we haven't caused any offense," he mumbled.

"No, not you. Not yet. My wife isn't feeling very well." Hans turned to Käthe as he pulled on his coat. "We'd better go home and think."

At least he was taking the situation seriously now.

Chapter 41: rallies

The leaves on the trees were beginning to turn. It would soon be the equinox and the days would be getting really short. A few weeks after that at Renate's school they would be getting ready for Christmas. Ironic really. All this fuss and there was their daughter celebrating a Christian tradition. Even more ironic: neither she nor Hans believed in any sort of religion and yet given half a chance she could be persecuted for belonging to the wrong one.

Oh, she should forget all that. It was a lovely afternoon. It was still mild. The garden was really beautiful now that the trees were mature. They were lucky with this house. Really lucky. She'd been such a fool to resist it when Hans had first suggested they should come here.

"Will these look right, do you think, Mutti?" Renate was waving some leaves and twigs at her. The child just loved making collages from things she found in the garden and in the nearby woods. She was really content this afternoon.

It was all wonderful. Or at least it should have been. Yet Käthe was afraid and she couldn't quite work out why.

"Well, Mutti? What do you think?"

"I'm sure it will look lovely." Käthe thought she was going to be sick. She couldn't be pregnant again, could she, not after all this time?

No, it wasn't like that. It was more like when you're nervous about an exam. But what had she got to be nervous about? She was getting ridiculous.

"What's that noise?" said Renate suddenly. She dropped her collection of bits and pieces on the ground. She had gone quite pale.

"What noise?"

"You must be able to hear, it Mutti."

No, she couldn't. But wait. Something odd was happening under her feet. The ground seemed to be shaking. It wouldn't be an earthquake, would it? They didn't have them here, did they?

Then she could hear it. A steady rumble. And in the distance music. A marching band. Of course. The rumble must be the steps of boots hitting the ground. Hundreds of people, perhaps thousands of people, marching.

It must be another one of those rallies. She'd never seen one before. She'd seen the big parade ground, of course, just from a distance, but she'd kept out of the way and she'd kept Renate away from them. Today, though, it looked as if one was coming their way.

Hans had said, hadn't he, that they were going to get bigger?

She made her way to the gate and looked up the road.

"Where are you going?" Renate looked as if she was going to cry.

"Nowhere." Not yet. "I just want to see what's going on."

Oh, good heavens, here they came.

There were soldiers, Hitler Youth boys, BDM girls and marching band after marching band.

"What is it, Mutti?" whimpered Renate. "What are they doing?"

"Just people who like dressing up in uniforms," Käthe muttered. "Putting on a display."

"I don't like it, Mutti."

"Go to Vati. Go on." She pushed Renate towards the door. "Hans. Hans!" she shouted.

He appeared in the doorway. He raised his arm.

Don't you dare, she thought. In the end she didn't hear whether he said "Heil Hitler" or "Heil Edler". The noise of the marchers and Renate's screams were too loud.

This was terrifying but it was fascinating. She just had to see it.

She waved to Hans and shouted, "Look after her. I won't be long." She started off down the garden path.

They shouted at her but she ignored them. She rushed out of the gate and started following the marchers. Just a little further along, in just those few minutes, crowds had gathered to watch them go past.

She managed to keep going forward by elbowing her way through the people. On and on she went, pushing her way through and getting along slightly faster than the rest of the crowd.

She was going to be covered in bruises.

Soon she was in the middle of town. Those parading slowed down slightly, turned their heads to the right and lifted their arms up to salute. And there he was. On his balcony at the Deutscher Hof Hotel. He was lifting his hand seemingly half-heartedly. She'd heard that he'd had that balcony especially made so that he could watch his people make their way to the rally ground. He seemed to be smirking.

Käthe shivered. *He looks like the devil admiring his kingdom.* She remembered, though, that she didn't believe in the devil or in God. Was this man about to change her mind on that one?

Then she was being swept along again. Her feet didn't even touch the ground.

They arrived at the parade ground. Then it really was impossible to move. Not even all of her expert pushing through could get her any further now.

She watched, fascinated, as group after group piled in through the gates. Fascinated and terrified. This was like a nightmare. They weren't people. They all kept perfect time in their marching. They were machines.

How more could they possibly fit it, she wondered. Yet they kept on making their way in. The big black swastikas now seemed like a threat yet she could remember Vati telling her when she'd seen it once in a book that the swastika was a religious symbol of good fortune. Now it just looked like the legs of a machine that was going to mow you down and kill you.

Eventually the last of the marchers walked through the grand entrance gates. The bands carried on though, now all playing the same tune. Everyone, including those outside, started singing along. The words made her shiver.

Just how big was this parade ground? She'd never been quite this close to it before. She'd never wanted to look. Now she looked to the right. And this was the shorter side, wasn't it? If you flew into space would you be able to see it, perhaps? How many people were in there now? Thousands and thousands, surely? It was a monstrosity. Why had they built this?

A car drew up at the gate. An officer saluted. Käthe looked at the face of the man in the car as it drove past. It was just a glimpse but she could clearly see that it was him again. That silly little moustache and the mean eyes. And a nasty stare.

"Heil Edler," she whispered to herself.

She was trembling and her mouth had gone dry.

A few moments later it became quiet within the stadium. Then he started to speak. His words echoed round the walls.

It was just empty rhetoric, grand-sounding words that don't mean anything.

The crowd inside the stadium erupted into a series of "Sieg Heil"s, each one louder than the one before. The people outside started joining in.

Heil bloody Edler, thought Käthe. Damn the man. If I'd got a gun I'd shoot him.

She turned and walked quickly in the direction of home. They really would have to come up with a plan soon.

Chapter 42: bakers all

"They shouldn't be long – at least I hope not," said Käthe as she showed her mother the room where she'd be sleeping. "Hans suddenly got it into his head that he should get her passport sorted out before the holidays."

"And you've told her this is for her trip to Italy? You're still letting her go?"

"We've said so, yes, and that she has to have her own passport as we're not going with her."

"Well, maybe…"

"I just hope it's not taking so long because there's any problem."

"Surely not… with Hans as her father…"

"You'd have thought so, wouldn't you?" Käthe's lips were pursed as she helped her mother to hang her clothes in the wardrobe.

The front door slammed. She could hear Renate's and Hans's voices. "Mutti! Oma! Are you here, Oma?"

"In the guest room," Käthe called.

Renate rushed up the stairs and into the bedroom. "Vati had such a row with the official but then we went to see Herr Müller – you know, he's Vati's friend – and he said I can have a grown-up passport and that next time I need one I'll be a proper young lady. It will be ready straight after Christmas."

"What's he been doing this time?" Käthe muttered almost to herself. Then more loudly to Renate she said, "Go and tell your father to arrange for some tea to be made and some of the biscuits we baked yesterday to be put out. Then he'll explain it all, I'm sure."

As soon as Renate had left the room Käthe flopped down on the bed. "He just doesn't know when to keep his mouth shut. He'll get us into such trouble one day." There were tears in her eyes.

"Let's see what he has to say first." Mutti rubbed Käthe's back. "I'm pretty well finished here. Tea and those biscuits sound good."

"He was an officious young man," said Hans, licking the crumbs off his fingers. "Goodness, Renate, you must take after your grandmother – these are pretty good. Your mother certainly can't bake like this."

"I can and I helped her," said Käthe. "Stop changing the subject. What exactly happened?"

"He wanted to put Klara Renate on the passport and I explained she was supposed to be Renata Clara. He just wouldn't have it."

"And when he said 'Heil Hitler' Vati said 'Heil Edler!' "

"Oh for goodness sake, Hans. I wish you would stop that. One day, one day…"

"Calm down, woman. Even Klaus does that."

"Then he'll get into trouble as well. And that young man was only talking common sense. You know that the passport has to say exactly what it says on her birth certificate. The man was only doing his job." She glared at Hans.

"He looked all of seventeen and he was far too sure of himself."

Renate giggled. "Vati roared at him. You know how he does sometimes."

Mutti shook her head gently and frowned. "But why did that mean she had to have an adult passport? I don't really understand."

"I think I did frighten him a little. And he was absolutely right: she is old enough to have an adult passport. She didn't have to, but she could. He just wanted to get rid of us as quickly as possible. I think he was a little bit afraid of me despite his bravado."

"And Herr Müller was ever so kind. How do you know him, Vati?"

"Oh we did some classes together in Berlin. When we were students."

"Well, it's a good job he was there and made you see sense. Renate, go and see if there are any more biscuits. It looks as if you and your father have finished the whole lot."

As soon as Renate had left the room, Käthe turned once more to Hans. "Do you think it might help her, having a full adult passport? Will there be anything on there that says she is Jewish? Will she be able to leave Germany more easily? Please tell me that that's why you did this and you just made the scene with the young man for Renate's sake? What does Klaus say?"

"No, it really all happened like we said. Klaus doesn't know anything about this. But I will ask him. I promise I will."

Käthe felt the tears forming in her eyes again. She was grateful that Mutti turned away as if she hadn't seen.

Mutti turned to Hans. "You don't think things are that bad, really, do you?"

Hans for once didn't look as if he was about to laugh. "All those rallies make it look serious enough. You should see them, Clara. They're terrifying. And you should see Herr Hitler sitting there at his window at the Deutscher Hof Hotel. As if he's some sort of god." Then he grinned. "But this can't go on forever. Sooner or later all we sensible Germans will realise he's just a madman and do away with him and his cronies."

"I'm sure you're right, Hans."

Renate burst back into the room. "Mutti, we'll have to make some more. There's hardly any left. Oh no." She ran over to her mother. "You and Vati haven't been arguing again, have you?" She turned to her father. "Don't be rude about Mutti's baking. Her apple cake is excellent and she can make biscuits."

Mutti laughed. "Tell you what. I'll make some more biscuits tomorrow." She smiled at Renate.

"Will I be allowed to help as well?"

Chapter 43: blood laws

"You can see it clearly in the diagram," said Ernst. "The black circles represent Jews. Look at the two columns on the right. If your family is like either of those, you are definitely Jewish."

"But we converted, didn't we?"

Ernst shook his head. "It's race, not religion, they're talking about. I hate to tell you but we're actually the far right column. Mutti and Vati both each had two Jewish parents. And look." He pointed to a black circle next to a white one. Underneath were the words "Marriage forbidden". "That means you and Hans. You two wouldn't be allowed to marry now. In fact, the next step might even be that they ask you to divorce."

Käthe shivered.

"Over my dead body," shouted Hans. His face went bright red.

Ernst sighed. "Mutti just won't get it. She won't have it. She's adamant that she's no longer Jewish."

"Yet she invited the shomer to Vati's funeral." Käthe remembered it only too vividly. It has seemed unbelievable that her mother had held on to those old ways. What had she been thinking?

"It also doesn't help that she still has so many Jewish friends and that she's still in contact with them."

"Would they know about that?" Käthe was finding it difficult to swallow. She quickly did an inventory of her own friends. How many of them were Jewish? She realised she didn't even know. It had really never mattered to her. They had always been just people.

"It's not even that simple with Mutti," Ernst continued. "She thinks it will all get better soon. That everybody will come to their senses."

Hans cleared his throat. "Let's hope the woman's right. A lot of it is very silly."

"You know that and I know that. Unfortunately a lot of ordinary people don't."

"Well, what can we do?"

"Moving's the only option. I'm no longer allowed to teach at the school. They still pay me but it's not fair. I can't expect them to carry on doing that. I've decided to go and work in the Netherlands. They're setting up new Waldorf schools there."

"You're going to leave Mutti?" Käthe couldn't believe that her brother would do that. "Well she must come and live with us, mustn't she Hans?"

Hans rolled his eyes.

Ernst shook his head. "She won't budge. She insists that she must stay behind and look after the house so that it stays ready for the boarders."

"But if the school's closing there won't be any boarders."

"She doesn't think it will be for long. And she just thinks that I'll be going away because the Steiner Foundation needs me to be in the Netherlands, not that I need to be there."

"What about Rudi?"

"He's making his own plans. He's looking for an academic position in the United States or England. Perhaps even Canada."

"So everybody's going away?"

Ernst nodded. "Except our dear mother of course." He touched Käthe's hand gently. "You should consider it too. You and Renate."

"Oh, stuff and nonsense." Hans stamped his foot.

Käthe bit her lip. "What about Renate? Surely she's safe. Her father's German for goodness' sake."

"I'm afraid she's not safe. Not at all." Hans pointed again to the chart that was still open on the table. "You see. She has two Jewish grandparents so she is a Mischling of the first degree. Blood, not religion."

Käthe stared at the chart. It was brutal. All those black circles indicating Jewishness. "It's such a horrible word." How could they label her daughter like that? A Mischling of the first degree. Horrid, horrid, horrid.

"It's actually even worse." Ernst pointed to a little box at the end of the page. "Look. She is a Sondermischling because both grandparents on one side are Jewish. I think they think that that somehow intensifies the Jewishness."

241

"She's no idea she's Jewish. She doesn't even know what that means."

"I think we'll keep it that way, don't you? I'd be very grateful if you would leave now, Ernst, instead of petrifying my wife and threatening my child." Hans was scowling.

Ernst shrugged and stood up. "Well I guess I'll get back to Stuttgart and see if I can get Mutti to see some sense." He nodded to Hans.

"I'll see you out," said Käthe.

Ernst turned to face her as she opened the front door for him. "Really. You must try and persuade Hans that this is very serious indeed. You have to think of getting out. You and Renate."

"I don't know how I'll manage without Hans. I'd really want him to come with us, if we do go, but I don't think it would be all that easy for him to find work abroad."

Ernst shook his head. "Oh, he could find work all right. The English would welcome him with open arms. I doubt whether he'd be able to get an exit visa, though."

"Why do you say that?"

"He's working for defence, isn't he? They won't let him out of the country with what he knows."

"But I thought it was only a game. That it was all theoretical."

Ernst sighed and shook his head again. "If only. But I don't think our dear Führer will stop until he's conquered the whole world. There will be another war, I'm sure of that. Take care, Käthe."

She closed the door behind him and took a deep breath. What should she do? She heard Hans come into the hallway.

"Käthe, darling."

She turned to face him. She was astonished to see that he had gone quite pale.

"Has he gone?"

She nodded.

"I am so sorry. I shouldn't have spoken to him like that. I wasn't angry with him. Just with the whole situation. It's ludicrous. But I love the pair of you so much I can't possibly do without you."

Had she heard correctly? He hadn't told her he loved her for months now.

"He's gone," she whispered.

"Well, I think it's high time we talked to Klaus."

"All right. If you think it's for the best."

"Yes. There's no point having a cousin in the civil service if you don't take advantage of him. And there's something else. Follow me."

She followed him into his study. She watched as he rummaged in the desk.

"Ah. Here it is." He pulled out a small pistol. "I think you should carry this around with you."

She stared at the small instrument. It looked like a toy or an ornament. It was tiny and very ornately marked. It was quite pretty really. It was a gun, though, wasn't it.

"A gun? You want me to carry a gun?"

Hans laughed. "It's not really a gun. It's just a lady's pistol. It could kill someone if used skilfully, however. It used to belong to my grandmother but it still works. I tried it out the other day on a magpie. Killed him with a single shot."

Good grief. She hoped Renate hadn't seen him doing that.

"I don't know how to use it, though."

"I'll show you. I would just feel happier if you had it with you at all times."

She took the pistol from him, looked at it, shuddered and then put it down on the desk.

He stepped forward and embraced her. "Please be safe for me," he murmured. He kissed her firmly on the lips and she suddenly felt excited. She wasn't sure whether it was because she was about to become the kind of woman who knew how to use a gun or because this was the first physical contact she'd had with her husband for a while now.

Nuremberg 1936

Chapter 44: talking to the teachers

"I'll come and fetch you this afternoon."

"Mutti, you don't have to. I'm perfectly capable of walking home on my own."

Yes, she was. But Käthe just didn't want anything to happen to her on the way.

"Well, I thought perhaps we could go and skate on the pond. And then maybe go and get a hot chocolate."

"Yes, all right then. But you'll have to remember to bring my skates."

"Yes, ma'am." Käthe saluted her daughter. She felt tempted to click her heels but something stopped her.

"Don't be silly, Mutti. And anyway. I can most certainly walk up the path into school on my own."

"Yes, but I need to see your teachers."

Renate's brown eyes grew round. "Why? Am I in trouble?"

Käthe shook her head. "No." But they might all be soon.

"So why do you want to see them?"

"Oh, just an idea I had. Nothing to do with you."

Renate shook her head and blew out her breath so that her lips trilled. "You're so funny, Mutti. See you later."

Käthe watched her daughter and the other children slipping and sliding their way into the building. It was bitterly cold and she would be glad to get inside herself. The children seemed to be enjoying the snow. Well, they would wouldn't they? To her, though, the cold seemed quite appropriate. She felt as if she and Renate, Mutti, Leo and Ernst and goodness knows how many other people were all being shut out in the cold.

She hesitated to go in. She tried to persuade herself it was because she was waiting for the children to settle down, for the other parents to depart or for the teachers to get organised. She really knew that it was because she was putting off this difficult conversation.

Her nose and fingers had gone numb. She heard the children singing their early morning hymn. She must do this. Now.

She braced herself, stepped forward and rang the doorbell.

A few seconds later Frau Fischer, the school secretary, opened the door. "Good morning, Frau Edler, how can I help?"

Well the woman still seemed friendly enough. Perhaps she didn't know about Renate and her. Or if she did she didn't care. Even better.

"I really need to talk to Renate's teachers. It's very important."

Frau Fischer smiled and nodded. "Come on in. I'll see who I can find."

She showed Käthe into the staffroom. "Hopefully I won't have to keep you too long. Make yourself at home."

Käthe settled herself on one of the shabby sofas. This room was typical of the school. A little worn at the edges but they'd obviously made every effort to make it as comfortable and as cheerful as possible. There were some lovely examples of the children's artwork on the walls and there were some pieces of the children's writing in a folder on a low table in front of her. She read through a couple of the stories while she waited. She was delighted to see one of Renate's there. The little monkey never even told her one of her pieces of work had been chosen for the visitors' book. This all helped to calm her nerves.

After a few moments, though, voices outside in the corridor warned her that someone was coming. She had to take a deep breath. Now she was going to have to put her cards on the table.

Frau Fischer, Frau Weber, the deputy head and Fräulein Mayer, Käthe knew was Renate's PE teacher, walked into the room. What a relief that it was people she already knew well. Or did that make it harder, actually?

"How can we help, Frau Lehrs?" said Frau Weber as soon as the secretary had left. Her warm smile softened her already gentle features further. She looked like everybody's favourite granny. The children loved her, Käthe knew.

"Well, you see... Renate and I... we're not..." She dreaded saying it. Once she'd said those words there would be no going back.

Frau Weber exchanged a glance with Fräulein Mayer and put

her hand gently on Käthe's arm. "We think we know what you're going to tell us. You and Renate are Jewish, aren't you?"

Käthe felt her cheeks go bright red. "How did you know though? Renate has no idea."

"Just a guess," said Fräulein Mayer. "Her eyes. Your eyes. And forgive us for jumping to conclusions, but although we've found your support of the school unending, we've noticed that you and your husband have not been that involved with the church."

Käthe shook her head. "We're scientists. We don't really believe in any god. My husband's Catholic, anyway, in theory. I've never been baptised. I was a bit too old, really, when my parents converted to the Evangelical faith. I'm sorry. I hope that doesn't offend you. Renate was baptised."

Frau Weber shook her head. "We can see you share our Christian values even if you don't believe in the same god. And that of course is ironic. The Jews' god is the same as that of the Christians."

Fräulein Mayer sighed. "These blood laws. Such nonsense."

"That's what Renate's father and grandmother say as well."

Fräulein Mayer nodded and frowned. "I suppose that's why Renate refuses to do the Hitler salute?"

"She does?"

"Yes. She won't lift her arm right up and she mumbles something incoherent."

Käthe shook her head. "My husband's bad influence, I'm afraid. He always says Heil Edler."

Oh she wished she hadn't told them that. They probably wouldn't approve at all.

But Fräulein Mayer and Frau Weber looked at each other and burst out laughing. "That is priceless," said Frau Weber, wiping a tear from her eye. "And tell me, Frau Edler, have you ever done the same?"

"Just once." Käthe shuddered as she remembered the parade ground.

"My, oh, my. I wish I could do that, but Weber just doesn't have the right sound."

"Neither does Mayer. But Edler. Who could spot the difference?"

"I hope the fact that I've told you about Renate and me won't make it difficult for you. We could take Renate away if you preferred." She dreaded the thought of the Jewish school though. Most Jewish people were fine but there were a few extremists she definitely didn't want Renate mixing with. And it would mean telling Renate she was Jewish.

Frau Weber's face became serious again. "There really is no need, Frau Edler. We will do all that we can to protect your daughter. I don't think it's going to be a problem. She seems so German, anyway. But I guess we'd better get her to do the Hitler salute properly." She smiled again and shook her head. "Heil Edler. So right!"

"There is another thought," said Fräulein Meyer. "Renate is such a good athlete that we could enter her for some of the competitions. That would take some of the pressure off and make her look even more German."

"Oh, I don't know…" She was sure Renate would succeed but wouldn't it expose her more? "Won't it bring a lot of attention to her?"

"Well, there's no need to make a decision yet. You can think about it. We won't be getting ready for the athletics programme until the spring." Frau Weber patted Käthe's hand again. "Rest assured, we'll take good care of your little girl and we won't let any harm come to her."

"Thank you."

"What about the BDM?" asked Fräulein Mayer.

Frau Weber bit her lip. "She's too young yet but she will have to join eventually. I suppose the other girls might notice something. Frau Edler, we may have to tell her at that point. Warn her to be careful."

Käthe swallowed the lump that had formed in her throat. This was so unfair. No way were either of them Jewish really.

"Never, mind, Frau Edler. We can cross that bridge when we come to it." Frau Weber sighed. "Though whether the school will still be here then, I don't know."

"Oh?" Surely they wouldn't think of closing this place. It was a wonderful little establishment.

Fräulein Meyer nodded. "We refuse to teach the Nazi doctrine. We are altogether too Christian."

Käthe shook her head. "This is all so difficult to understand. Why are they so against Christian values? When they're against the Jews who rejected Christ?"

Fräulein Meyer nodded. "Yes, and all this business of women being involved with children, cooking and the church. It doesn't make sense does it?"

Frau Weber stood up. She smiled warmly at Käthe. "Frau Edler, I promise you that we shall take good care of Renate for as long as we can. But if you will excuse me, I must now attend to several other matters."

Käthe got up on to her feet as well. "Of course."

The deputy head shook her hand. "Just one more thing. Have you thought of leaving? It might be an idea, you know. We think it's going to get worse. You might be safer in the Netherlands or England."

A few moments later Käthe was walking home through the snow. The sun was shining and water was dripping from some of the branches. Spring was on its way and Renate was safe for a while at least. She could relax a little now, couldn't she?

She looked up at the sky. Well, the sun might be shining but there were also dark clouds full of snow.

"It's not over yet, then," she murmured to herself. What were they to do?

Chapter 45: girls in bright uniforms

"Shall we get Zwiebelkuchen?" Käthe pointed to the large savoury tart on display in the baker's window.

Renate shrugged. "I'd rather have something sweet."

"We can do that as well. I was thinking we could have this with some soup for supper. It's a proper autumn dish. Now that the days are getting shorter, it might be nice."

"If you like. Have we got much more shopping to do, Mutti? I'm getting bored and I've got a lot of homework to do."

"I'll just get this and then we can get home. Do you want to wait out here or do you want to come into the shop?"

Renate shrugged again. Oh, she was getting so awkward. Yes, she was bored. It was partly her own fault for keeping the girl away from the others as much as possible. She didn't want them guessing who they really were.

"Look, I'll be as quick as I can. You wait out here with the other shopping bags."

Käthe went to go into the shop but was distracted by a sudden noise of chattering girls. Both of them turned to see what was going on.

The girls all looked a little older than Renate. They seemed so grown up. Most of them still had their hair in plaits but they were all wearing very elegant calf-length navy-blue skirts, crisp white blouses and a black tie. Most of them had on a khaki flying jacket though one or two of the girls were wearing a hand-knitted top. Some of the older ones were wearing the very smart great coat that Käthe knew went with this uniform. Those girls also had more sophisticated hair styles. Käthe smiled to herself when she looked at some of the footwear. Not all of them were wearing the most sensible black shoes and she guessed it wasn't just because their parents couldn't afford them. More likely they were trying to be fashionable.

She totally got it. These were girls from the Bund Deutscher Mädel and their lovely uniform was making them so proud of themselves. They really needed this, she could see that. To be able to wear such lovely clothes with so many of their fathers being out of work must be really encouraging. She just wished they hadn't turned up here and now. Renate was bound to be curious. And the girls would be curious about Renate as well. It was a good job it wasn't compulsory – yet.

There was a lot of excitement. The girls' voices got louder and louder. They giggled a lot as well. Yes, it did look as if they were having fun.

The two girls nearest to them suddenly stopped and the others coming up the hill bunched up behind them. The chattering got quieter. Soon all them were completely silent. They all stared at Renate. Renate was staring back and frowning.

Käthe grabbed her hand. "Come on, let's finish this shopping and let these young ladies get by." She pulled Renate and the shopping bags into the baker's shop.

The BDM girls continued to stare at Renate and Käthe through the window. One or two of them now seemed to be mumbling something and nodded towards Renate.

"Just ignore them," said Käthe. "Look away from them."

Renate did as she was told but Käthe could tell she wasn't best pleased. She just wished the girls hadn't turned up like that. And she hoped her daughter wouldn't ask any awkward questions.

Käthe made a big show of examining the cake display and out of the corner of her eye she saw the BDM girls move on. Thank goodness for that.

Of course it wasn't over. Renate was full of questions on the way home.

"Who were those girls?"

"What was that uniform they were wearing?"

"Why were they all staring at us like that?"

Käthe gritted her teeth. "Let's talk about it when we get home," she mumbled. That would give her time to think and would avoid anyone overhearing something that might harm them.

Renate refused to carry any of the bags. She marched off in

front with her hands in her pockets. Every so often she stopped, turned round and scowled at Käthe.

Really, the girl was getting so difficult now. Käthe knew she shouldn't let her get away with that. She just couldn't face an argument out in the open. Especially as it could be so dangerous.

"So this BDM, what does it stand for again?"

Renate was still looking a bit sullen. She was sitting on one of the kitchen stools and kicking the leg of it.

"Bund Deutscher Mädel."

"And who are they then, these girls?"

"They're all aged between fourteen and seventeen, so a little bit older than you. They do some interesting things from what I gather." *Please don't ask me to tell you what. You might find it a bit too interesting.*

"So why were they staring at us like that?"

"Probably because you look so old for your age. They most likely wondered why you weren't in uniform."

"The uniform's very nice."

"It is smart, yes." *Don't you go asking for one, though.*

"So, why did they think I should be wearing a uniform?"

"You have to join the BDM as soon as you're fourteen."

"Hmm. I wish I could wear a uniform like that. Isn't there a club for younger girls?"

"Yes, but the uniform isn't so nice and they don't have so much fun." *She'd better believe me.*

"Oh. Oh well. Can I go and play now?"

"Of course."

Renate jumped down from the stool and skipped out of the kitchen. That was over for a while, at least. They had a little time yet before she would have to join the BDM.

Then what would happen, though?

And why exactly had those girls stared so much at them? Had they noticed their eyes? They couldn't possibly have seen her rings doing their usual trick of twirling round the wrong way, could they? No, she'd had gloves on the whole time. Was it something about the way she walked? Was she too confident? Was she still the rich Jewish factory-owner's daughter?

Had those girls known that she and Renate were Jewish?

Renate had seemed satisfied with her explanation, at least.

She looked through the window and was pleased to see her daughter singing softly to herself as she made her swing go higher and higher.

Stuttgart 1937

Chapter 46: Heil Edler

"So, did you enjoy it?" Mutti said to Renate as they made their way out to the school yard.

It was their usual summer visit to Stuttgart and Mutti had insisted on them all going to watch the school play. Käthe had been dreading it but in the end she had had to admit that the students had put on quite a performance and the story had its merits.

"It was lovely," said Renate. "I wish we did shows like that at our school."

"Don't you have end of term concerts, though?"

"Well, yes we do. But we're all girls and the school is much smaller. So they can't be as much fun."

"I suppose you might have a point."

Mutti glanced at her. Käthe rolled her eyes and shrugged. But the girl was right. That little church school just didn't have the resources. "Well, anyway, it's no good you going on about wanting to come to Oma's school because it is going to close soon. And you'll be going to a new school soon anyway."

"Will she get into the Gymnasium?"

"She's got good marks. She should do," said Hans.

"I mean…"

Käthe shook her head and put her fingers on her lips. Mutti went to ask another question but fortunately Doctor Kühn turned up. He was going to talk to them about the Steiner Foundation.

"Heil Hitler!" said Doctor Kühn.

Mutti half-heartedly raised her arm. It was clear that she hated this as much as the rest of them. Käthe and Hans raised their arms without hesitation though.

Käthe said, "Heil Hitler!" loud and clear.

Hans though said, "Heil Edler!" Trust him. He would.

Renate stood there with her arms rigidly at her side. Käthe noticed a twitch of a smile on her mother's lips. Yes, Mutti was right. Renate was braver than the rest of them.

Doctor Kühn kept his speech quite short. Käthe was grateful. It was tiring standing out here in the sun without any shade at all.

Then it was "Heil Hitler!" again.

Hans's "Heil Edler!" was louder than ever.

She wished he wouldn't. Not here amongst strangers. It looked as if Mutti was going to burst out in a fit of laughter in a moment and Doctor Kühn was staring at her and at Renate who was still standing there with her arms at her side.

"You must do the salute," Mutti whispered, grabbing Renate's arm.

Renate pulled away from her and scowled. There was nothing to be done. Mutti scuttled away over to Doctor Kühn. Käthe followed her.

"I'm so sorry about my granddaughter," Käthe heard her say to him a few seconds later. "They must be more lenient in Nuremberg."

"In Nuremberg, of all places? Surely not."

Mutti blushed bright red.

"Don't worry, Clara. I don't blame the girl," said Doctor Kühn. "Good for her, actually. And I know you don't like this ridiculous saluting either. Neither do I, if I'm honest. But we have to be seen to be doing it."

Mutti nodded. "I know."

Doctor Kühn touched her arm gently and nodded to Käthe. "I don't think anybody important was watching today. And I actually don't think any of our more – what shall we say? – enthusiastic parents noticed. Go on. Go and enjoy your time with your family."

A few moments later they were on their way back to the house on Schellberg Street. Renate was as usual running on ahead and then coming back to urge them all to be quicker.

"Was I hearing things?" said Mutti to Hans. "Or did you really say 'Heil Edler'?"

"I did indeed," said Hans, grinning.

"Yes, and one day you'll get us all into trouble for it," said Käthe. "I wish you wouldn't." Damn the man!

"I think it's rather good, actually." Mutti giggled.

"Well, you would, Mutti."

Mutti suddenly stopped smiling and frowned. "But Renate...?"

"She's not German is she? Her teachers think she shouldn't be made to join in these things."

Mutti went to say something to her. Renate came skipping back towards them. Käthe stared at her mother. This conversation was over.

Later that evening Käthe and Mutti washed up after supper whilst Hans and Renate went for a short walk before Renate's bed time.

"I just hope he's not 'Heil Edlering' all over the place," said Käthe.

"Oh, the neighbours don't bother too much," said Mutti. "But how do you get on in Nuremberg?"

Käthe sighed. "We just keep out of everybody's way."

"Do you see anything of the rallies?"

"We hear them! When they're on you can hear them marching through the streets to get there." Oh yes. She couldn't get the frightening image of the one she'd attended out of her head.

"That sounds horrible."

"It is. Even the children have to march."

"Renate?"

"Well she's not old enough to join the BDM, and she doesn't have to go to the younger girls' group. So her teachers keep her away."

"Don't the other children find that strange?"

"Not really." Käthe put her dishcloth down and turned to face her mother. "We haven't told Renate she's Jewish. I don't think she would understand what that meant. Of course the other girls in her class don't know either. We want to keep it that way as long as we can. Her teachers know, though, and they protect her."

Mutti touched her arm but Käthe pulled away. She couldn't bear these signs of affection. But her mother kept her hand there. "And you? Do you consider yourself Jewish?"

Käthe closed her eyes. "No. Not at all. I'm German. Not even that. I'm just human. But you know, Mutti..." She opened her eyes again. She couldn't stop the tears forming. "If we go out anywhere, I'm sure people know. I'm sure they can tell when they look at me."

"Surely you get a lot of respect because of Hans's job?"

"Oh yes, of course." Käthe took up her dishcloth again and started scrubbing furiously at an almost clean plate. "The important man designing his clever weapons that will defend the German people. Yes, we are so respected."

The front door opened. Hans and Renate came in chatting and laughing. This conversation also was over for a while.

Nuremberg 1937

Chapter 47: afraid to go to the opera

Should she wear the blue silk or the grey satin? Both dresses were laid out on the bed. The fox fur or the mink? Hans had always said he liked her in blue, so perhaps it should be the blue. On the other hand, the grey satin was similar in shape to her wedding dress and it showed more of her cleavage and her shoulders. Hans always seemed excited by the opera. Maybe…

On cue the door opened and in he came.

"Not long now, darling. You need to get a move on."

"Well, what do you think?"

She picked up both dresses and held them up to her in turn.

Hans frowned. Then he grinned. "The grey one, I think." He kissed her shoulder. "Do you remember my study in Berlin?"

She giggled.

He put his arms round her waist. "And don't forget that perfume I gave you for your last birthday. Mmm. I'm really looking forward to this opera, but I'm looking forward even more to getting back home again with my beautiful wife." He pulled away from her. "Come on then, sweetheart. Chop. Chop. Things to be done. You can't go like that, semi-naked, much as I'd enjoy it. Can't have every man gawping at you. Perhaps you'd better wear the blue one after all." He fumbled in his pockets then he rushed out of the room. "Where did I put those dammed tickets?" he mumbled.

She pulled on the blue dress and sprayed herself with the perfume. It did smell rather gorgeous. She put on some lipstick and a little rouge on her cheeks. She never needed a pencil for her eyebrows. They were dark enough without. The mink would go better with that dress certainly. She pulled it on to her shoulders. She fetched the hat that went with it out of the hatbox on top of the wardrobe. There! That should be it.

She looked in the mirror and froze. A rich Jewish woman stared back at her. There was nothing she could do about the darkness of her hair and her eyes. Hans would expect the glamour of a woman who knew how to dress. But wasn't that one of the things that they all hated? The way the Jews flaunted their money. Oh, yes. They were comfortably off because of Hans's job. But she'd never wanted for money even before she was married and that had been because Vati had been, after all, converting to another religion or not, a hardworking, business-like Jew.

She couldn't go to this opera dressed like this. They would see her for what she was.

Hans came back into the room. "Oh yes. Very nice. But why are you sitting there staring? We need to get a move on or we'll miss the overture. Come on, woman."

"I can't go."

"What do you mean, you can't go?"

"Look." She pointed to her reflection in the mirror.

"A beautiful woman, glamorously dressed. Why shouldn't you go to the opera?"

"Because I'm a Jewish woman, expensively dressed, and they'll hate me."

"You are talking such nonsense, my dear." He put his hands on her shoulder. "Come now. Let's get going."

"No, please, Hans. I don't want to go."

"You're not going to let them get the better of you, are you? Come on. You are the amazing wife of clever old Professor Hans Edler. Why wouldn't they respect you?"

"No. It's no good. I just can't do it." Käthe stood up and took off her hat. "I've got a bad headache anyway. You go."

He stared at her for several seconds and then tutted. "Oh, very well then. You're just being silly, really. This is no way to stand up to them." He marched briskly out of the room and slammed the door.

She'd really annoyed him now.

As she slowly undressed again she remembered the story she'd read in the newspaper some weeks ago. A Jewish man had not only been asked to leave a performance at the State Opera House in Berlin but had been taken away somewhere and never been seen again. Well, he had been foolish enough to wear his kippah, but

261

why shouldn't he? That little skull cap really marked him as Jewish, though, and if he was still wearing it, he probably was really Jewish not just according to the race laws like Renate and herself. At least he could have avoided it though. There was nothing she nor Renate could do about their eyes. And that other silly thing too, with her rings. They kept slipping that way even though she kept on twisting them back. So many other Jewish women talked with their hands a lot. People said they were deliberately showing the jewels in their rings in the palm-side of their hands. That couldn't be right could it? Wasn't is just the shape of their hands that made that happen? Was there something her hands that marked her as Jewish as well?

She realised she'd thought of "other" Jewish women. Did that mean she was admitting that she really was Jewish?

She sighed. Perhaps she should have a bath. That might calm her down.

Soon the bathroom was full of steam. She added some bath salts and slid into the comforting water. She thought of Hans and hoped he was enjoying himself at the opera. Should she make herself beautiful for when he came back? Beg his forgiveness? Then seduce him?

No. It was useless. The mood had gone.

And what if Ernst had been right that they would be forced to divorce? Should she and Renate move away? Where would they go? The Netherlands? England? America? Neither of them spoke Dutch or English. Had it been wrong to opt for Renate to learn Italian at school rather than English?

Oh, this was all such a mess. If they went away, Hans would not be able to come with them. It would be the end of their family life. She knew as well that this having lovely clothes and a beautiful home, having constant hot water like this was just making her put off the inevitable moment.

She howled. Then she sobbed. The tears streamed down her cheeks and tumbled into the water. It was such a relief to let go of all these terrible feelings. Perhaps she would feel better soon.

She did begin to feel a bit better, in fact. She decided that she must talk to Hans properly. They really must make a concrete plan. Perhaps they could find a way of keeping in touch even if she and Renate had to move away. And maybe Hans and her mother were right. This could not last forever. One day it would all be over and they could live in peace.

The water was beginning to cool down. Time to get out.

Then there was a knock at the bathroom door. Had Hans come back? Lotte? Was there something wrong with Renate?

"Just coming," she called.

She dried herself quickly and pulled on her dressing gown. She glanced in the mirror. Her face was a little red and puffy but that could easily be because of the hot water and the steam. She opened the door.

"Mutti, I heard someone crying. Were you crying? Why is your face all red?"

"Oh, no, sweetheart. I was listening to the wireless in the bath."

"Vati says you mustn't do that. It's dangerous."

"Well, he won't know. And you won't tell him, will you?"

Renate shrugged. "I suppose not. You do look as if you've been crying, though."

Käthe shook her head. "I think I've got a bit of a cold."

"Is that why you didn't go to the opera after all?"

"Yes, that's right. But I'm feeling a little bit better now. The bath has done me good."

"Will you tuck me in then?"

"Of course."

She'd got away with it this time. But sooner or later she was going to have to tell Renate the truth.

Chapter 48: a good markswoman

It was annoying her. All it did was make her handbag heavy. She didn't feel particularly safe just because she was carrying it around with her. In fact, quite the opposite. If anything she was rather afraid of it. What if she accidentally shot someone or something?

"Don't be silly," Hans had said repeatedly. "The safety catch is on."

"So what's the point?"

"It's a deterrent."

She wasn't convinced. What was she supposed to do? Point it at someone and shout "Bang!"

"Will you show me how to use it properly?"

"Yes, someday soon."

The trouble was, "someday soon" had never arrived.

Still, it was a beautiful little thing and she imagined that Hans's grandmother had rather enjoyed carrying it around. She wished she could enjoy owning it but what it actually represented filled her with horror.

Hans came into the bedroom. "Oh, you're fiddling with that are you?"

"Well, don't you think I should learn how to use it properly?"

"I'm rather hoping you'll never need to use it."

Here we go again.

"Well, in that case, I'm not going to carry it around anymore."

"Käthe, you must."

"No, I mustn't. I'll only make a complete fool of myself if I try to use it and fail. You either teach me or get someone else to teach me otherwise I'll stop taking it everywhere with me."

"I don't know... We might get into trouble if we're caught."

"Sooner or later Renate and I are going to get into trouble. A lot of trouble. Another bit can't hurt."

"It's a matter of finding the right time and the right place."

"Well, what about the woods?"

"There's nearly always somebody there."

"It's usually quiet on a Wednesday morning." She folded her arms across her chest and frowned at Hans.

He sighed. "All right. I suppose so. Okay. Let's go out into the woods on Wednesday morning. And let's hope that it's quiet enough."

He walked out of the room, muttering to himself.

She felt sick. She was about to learn to do something that might enable her to take another life.

It was very quiet when they arrived at the middle of the woods. The children were at school and even those with younger children were occupied with domestic tasks at this point in the week. It was drizzling slightly and that was keeping even the dog walkers away. She'd half hoped that Hans would decide there were too many people around and would cancel the lesson. But now, conditions, it seemed, were perfect.

"So there, then," said Hans. "It's loaded and the safety catch is off. So. Hold the gun firmly with your proper grip, i.e. your most natural grip." He showed how he did this. "Align the sights on the target. Place the centre of the first pad of your trigger finger on the trigger. Begin pressing the trigger rearward, smoothly, without moving anything else or while moving everything else as little as possible." He shot at the piece of wood he'd set up as a target. There was a loud bang and the wood split into two.

She was astounded at how much noise that small and rather delicate little machine could make.

"Do you want to have a go?"

Käthe shook her head. She was quite content just to watch for now.

He went through the whole procedure again and once more the piece of wood he'd used split neatly in two.

"Come on. Your turn now."

Her hand trembled as she took the pistol off him.

"Hold it steady now."

She tried to hold it the way he'd shown her. She fumbled a bit at first but then got it.

"That's right. That's what we call your proper grip. Good. Align the sights."

She concentrated at looking at the middle of the piece of wood.

"Now press the trigger. Yes, that's right. Use just the top part of that finger. Try not to move anything else."

She pressed the trigger. There was a loud bang and she felt herself jolted backwards. She'd missed the piece of wood completely but she'd managed to hit one of the branches on the tree behind. A few leaves flurried to the ground.

Hans laughed. "Remind me to keep well out of the way when you're doing your target practice."

She tried twice more. The second time she hit another branch. The third time she did manage to hit the piece of wood but not in the middle like she was supposed to.

"Hmm," said Hans. "I think we need a new strategy."

"I'm sure we do," Käthe mumbled.

"Do you think it might help if you thought about exactly why you're doing this?"

"What do you mean?"

"Think about somebody attacking you and really hating you. Think about protecting yourself and Renate."

Käthe shrugged. "I'll try."

Hans found another piece of wood. He propped it up in the branches of a tree. "That's about the height of an average-sized man's head. Always go for the heart or the head."

She lined up the shot again. She pressed the trigger. The shot rang out loud and clear but missed the piece of wood completely. She tried a couple more times but still didn't manage to hit the wood in the middle though the last shot did skim the top and made the target fall to the ground.

"That would be dangerous," said Hans. "You might wound him but he could still call for help. Come on Käthe. You must try harder."

She was trying her best. This wasn't easy.

"Think of someone you really hate."

That might just be him at the moment. But then she had a very good idea. A very good idea indeed.

She stared at the wood until she could convince herself that she could actually see him.

Yes, that hateful little man. She could see his mean eyes and his stupid little moustache. She could even hear his voice. The way he went on, shouting almost hysterically. She would like to shut him up once and for all.

She took her time. She found a spot on the piece of wood that represented the middle of his forehead just above his nose.

She pulled the trigger back slowly. She'd get it this time. Her fingers didn't tremble like they had before. She closed her eyes just before she let the trigger go. She just knew she was going to hit the target.

There was a loud crack. The piece of wood split in two and fell to the ground.

"Hoorah! You did it. Try again." Hans found another piece of wood.

She did it six more times and then Hans declared that that would do for today.

"What made you suddenly so confident?" he asked as they walked home.

"Oh, you know. I just imagined I was face to face with the Führer."

"Well, well, well. It seems I have an excellent markswoman for a wife. I hope you never have to use that thing." He chuckled. "Though it would be quite good if you put a bullet in the bastard. Heil Edler!" He kissed her on the cheek.

Nuremberg 1938

Chapter 49: no Mostviel

She just didn't like this. Supposing they came for Renate? It would be so easy for them to go to the hostel and take her away from the other girls. Yes, the teachers had said they would never let anything like that happen but what could they do if some big brutal men came along and demanded that Renate should go with them?

"Should I pack the brown shorts or the black ones, Mutti?" Renate was holding both pairs.

Good question. Which one would make her look more German? The brown ones? Didn't Jewish women wear a lot of black? But then again, weren't the BDM sports uniform shorts black? "Why don't you take them both? Your teachers might tell you which would be best to wear."

"Mutti, there isn't room in my rucksack for two pairs."

"Well, I hope you don't rip them or get them dirty. The black ones I suppose then. They won't show the dirt. And put in a couple of jumpers."

"Yes, Mutti." Renate rolled her eyes and shook her head.

Käthe's stomach flipped over again. Could she think of some excuse to keep her daughter at home?

Renate suddenly stopped what she was doing. She wrinkled up her nose and shut her eyes. She took a couple of gulps of air and then sneezed loudly. She fumbled for a hanky in the pocket of her skirt. "I thought that cold had finished," she said as she found the hanky and wiped her nose with it. "I'd better pack a few more hankies."

"Take some of Vati's big ones. They'll be more use."

"And I'll look incredibly silly."

"But you'll be glad of them. They'll be more useful if you're going to keep on sneezing still."

"You know, Mutti, I think it was only fluff. That cold finished days ago."

"Go on. Just go and get some of your father's handkerchiefs. He won't miss them. He's got dozens."

Renate sighed. "If you insist." She stamped her way out of the room.

Käthe looked at the pile of clothes on the bed and rucksack next to it. Yes it would be a bit of a squash but it should all fit. But what if she never saw those clothes again? What if they did come to get her? She picked up the green jumper and held it up to her face. Renate had worn it yesterday evening when they'd sat out in the garden until late. It smelt of fresh air and of her daughter.

The bedroom door opened again and made her jump.

"Here, they are then. Mutti, what one earth are you doing with my jumper?"

"Just thinking how nice and soft it is."

"Really? I think it's a bit scratchy."

"Oh?"

"Mutti, I'm so glad that nasty old cold has gone. I'm really looking forward to Mostviel this year. Fräulein Meyer has asked me to organise some athletics activities for the younger girls. We're going on a long hike on Tuesday. And we're going to be allowed to stay up for an extra hour after the other girls have gone to sleep. I can't wait!"

She would have to. But what on earth could Käthe do stop her going?

Then she had it. "Are you sure you're really over that cold?" She put her hand on Renate's forehead. It was a bit warm. Just a little bit. It was probably because she'd been busy and it was still quite hot today. "You're still burning up." That was a gross exaggeration. She hated herself for lying but she really had to do this.

Renate shook her head. "I feel fine. I really am sure I only sneezed because of the dust or pollen or something. And anyway, even if I've still got a cold, a cold's nothing."

"I don't know, Renate. It can be very damp in those hostels. That can make a simple cold turn into something else. I don't want you getting really ill."

"Oh, Mutti. Don't fuss so. You or Vati can always come and get me if I get worse again."

"That wouldn't really be fair on the other girls and on your teachers."

"What are you saying?"

"I don't think you should go."

"You can't mean that? It will be my last time at Mostviel with the girls. And Fräulein Meyer is going to make it such fun this time."

"I'm sorry, Renate. I don't just think you should go."

"Mutti, you are so mean. I hate you." She ran out of the room, tears streaming down her face, and slammed the door.

Dear God, she had to do it. Käthe's own tears started.

The day didn't improve. Renate continued to sulk. She refused to eat or to speak to Käthe. Hans wasn't too pleased either when he came home to find so much tension in the house.

"It's bad enough that they're all so worried and arguing all the time in the office," he said. "It would be really nice to come home to some peace and harmony. Why won't you let her go, anyway? Fresh air is always good for a cold."

"It's not really the cold I'm worried about." She stared at the floor. She couldn't bring herself to look at him.

He put his hand under her chin and lifted her face so that she had to look at him. "Oh?"

"What if they know, Hans? What if they come to get her?" Tears were stinging her eyes again. She really wished that she wouldn't keep crying like this but it was all so awful.

He sighed and looked thoughtful for a minute or two. Then he pursed his lips and nodded. "Yep. You're right."

The door burst open and Renate rushed in. "Vati, tell Mutti. She's being silly. I'm perfectly well enough to go to Mostviel. Who's afraid of a stupid cold? Especially one that's almost over?"

Hans frowned. "I'm afraid I agree with Mutti. It wouldn't be right for you to go as you're not completely well."

Renate's lower lip quivered. "I hate you two. You're really mean. And Mutti, I don't know what you're crying about. I should be the one who's crying."

She stamped out of the room again, slammed the door and stamped her way upstairs.

Damn that horrible man.

Chapter 50: news

"At least she wouldn't have been there all that much longer anyway." The strain of it all was now showing on Hans's face as well. His cheerful words didn't quite ring true.

She looked at the letter again.

Dear Professor and Frau Professor Edler,

We are writing to inform you that we shall be shutting our doors for the last time at the end of this term when we break up for the Christmas holidays. The staff here cannot deliver the National Socialist curriculum now being demanded. The school may open again after Easter but it will no longer be as a Lutheran school. It will be a state school run on National Socialist principles. None of our staff will remain here.

We urge you therefore to make other arrangements for Renate. It is actually only a few months early for her: I have every confidence that she will get a place at the Gymnasium. Even though there they will also have to teach the new curriculum, I would imagine the breadth of subjects they will surely study there will even it out a little.

You will of course have to make some arrangements for the time between Christmas and next September though I believe it may be possible for you to teach her at home for this short period. Do get in touch if I can be of any help with the paperwork for this.

Yours sincerely,
Corrine Weber

Käthe folded the letter back up. "What shall we tell her? Should we let her know that she's Jewish now? Is it time?"

"Not yet. Let's leave that until we really have to."

Käthe nodded. "But we should tell her about the school closing?"

"Yes, we'll have to. Everybody will soon know, I expect. Oh, let her think she can stay on in Stuttgart after Christmas. Listen I've got some more news."

"Oh?"

"I met Klaus at lunchtime."

"He's still working at the government office?"

Hans nodded. "He asked to see me actually. He said it was urgent."

Käthe felt sick. She just knew something bad was coming. "What did he say?"

"Well, he's got a lot of inside information. But he thinks you and Renate should really get out now. As soon as possible."

"What about you? Will you come as well"

"You know I can't." Käthe thought she could see tears in his eyes as well.

"He says he can help to get you an exit visa. It will cost, but we can afford it naturally. You will have to go and meet him and you may have a long wait but he can definitely get it for you."

"And Renate?"

"I think it's best that you both go to England. Ernst and Rudi are there aren't they?"

"Yes... but Renate."

"Write to them. See if they can find a job for you and a foster home for Renate. Maybe one of the families from Ernst's school?"

"Yes, maybe." Käthe's voice was hoarse. Her world was falling apart.

"You won't get an entry visa for England unless you have a job lined up. But it will be easier for Renate."

"How?"

"There is an organisation called the Kindertransport. That's one of the things that Klaus wanted to tell me about. They're taking children who are not wanted here to England by train. Jewish children. They're asking English families to sponsor them. This means taking them in, looking after them and paying £50.00 – that's roughly 6000 RM – to cover their journey back when it's all over. We can easily cover that and if we can find a private foster family it will all be sorted out nicely. I think it will be so much better if Ernst and Rudi help you with this. We'll be able find a really good family for her over there before she even sets off."

Käthe felt faint. "I hate to think of her living with strangers. She can't speak English."

"I'm sure you'll get to see her a lot and she'll soon pick up the language. Remember how bright she is."

"So we're going to send her on her own? On the train?"

"It's for the best. You'll be able to join her soon afterwards." Hans suddenly guffawed. "You do realise don't you, that farce with her passport is probably going to make it all easier. At least she's got a valid adult passport."

Käthe managed to smile. "Well, let's get it all arranged as quickly as possible then. And I should talk to Mutti as well."

The door burst open. "Get what arranged? Talk to Oma about what? What's going on?" Renate was standing there in her pyjamas. She should have been asleep ages ago. Perhaps she'd been worried about the school closing. Just exactly how much had she heard?

Hans grinned. "Oh, your Mutti and I were just talking about the Christmas arrangements. We thought perhaps now that you are such a grown-up girl you might like to go and stay with that friend of yours."

"Really?"

"Yes, really. There's more as well."

Renate jumped up and down several times and clapped her hands. "What, Vati?"

"How would you like to go to Oma's school for a few weeks? Just until you can come back here and go to the Gymnasium?"

"Really? Can I?"

Hans nodded.

Käthe's heart plummeted.

"You shouldn't make her promises we can't keep. Or tell her lies. Mutti's school's closed as well. It's going to make it all the harder when we tell her the truth."

"But so much better this way, don't you think? She'll be happy thinking about the lovely Christmas she's going to have. It will stop her asking about what she's going to do about school. And most importantly, it will stop her giving herself away."

"Oh, I suppose you're right. Look, I'm going up now. I've got a terrible headache."

"I'm not surprised. I'll be up shortly."

Another lie. She hadn't really got a headache. She just wanted to rest in the dark and think all of those things through. She hated all these lies.

Stuttgart and Nuremberg 1938

Chapter 51: an obstinate woman

Käthe sat in her mother's lounge nursing a cup of camomile tea. She was still trembling from the journey. It had been horrific. It had taken more than six hours as the train had made several unscheduled stops. She'd had to show her identity card three times. She was sure the other people in the carriage knew she was Jewish. They'd been friendly to start with then after the first check they'd become decidedly cold. How could they know? Her maiden name didn't sound particularly Jewish and she doubted they'd been able to read her ID card that closely anyway. Was it the way she looked? She'd deliberately not worn her smartest clothes. Those eyes though. They all had them: Mutti, Renate and she herself. The menfolk not so much. Vati had looked very German and so did Ernst and Rudi.

"Come on," said Mutti. "Drink that up before you even attempt to tell me why you've come. Though I'm guessing it must be important – or at least you think it is – for you to want to come here without Hans and Renate."

Käthe sighed and took a sip of her tea. She wasn't the greatest fan of camomile tea but she knew that her mother was right about its calming affects. It warmed her as well. She hadn't realised how cold she'd been on the train despite how crowded it was. It didn't make sense. Perhaps it was the fear. She had to admit the tea was also soothing her.

Mutti slipped out of the room without saying a word. Käthe looked around. It was so clean and comfortable. The windows gleamed and there wasn't a speck of dust anywhere. How could Mutti be so fastidious about housework at times like these? The couch on which she was sitting was so comfortable she could almost fall asleep.

A few moments later Mutti reappeared carrying a plate of biscuits. She held it out to Käthe. "Come on. You should eat."

Käthe shook her head.

Mutti insisted. "They're beautifully fresh. I made them just

278

yesterday evening. You should recognise these. You loved them when you were a little girl."

Käthe took one and bit into it. Oh, yes. That taste. Vanilla and lemon. It took her back to when she was about nine. She was constantly out in the fresh air then and coming back starving. Mutti always had something delicious to eat but these had been her favourites. How could Mutti be so focussed on this when all these terrible things were going on around them? No matter. The biscuit melted in her mouth. Bliss.

"Well?" said Mutti as Käthe swallowed the last piece of biscuit.

Suddenly Käthe didn't want to break the tranquillity of the moment. This wasn't going to be an easy discussion. "So, how are you filling your time now that the school's closed?"

"I'm helping Karl Schubert with his special class if you must know. But I don't think that's what you really came to talk about." She pulled the plate of biscuits back so that it was out of Käthe's reach. "Now, tell me what you want to discuss with me." Mutti was looking straight at her. There was no getting out of it now.

She took a deep breath. "Renate and I are going to go away. It isn't safe here anymore for Jews." There. She'd said it.

Mutti had gone pale and Käthe could see that her hand was shaking as she covered her mouth with it. Käthe held her breath.

Mutti took a deep breath, stood up and put her hands on her hips. "We are not Jews. We may have been once but we never will be again."

Käthe now also jumped to her feet. "But, Mutti, you know what Ernst showed us. They don't see it like that. According to the blood laws we are Jewish through and through. Renate even has the horrible label of being a Mischling of the first degree."

Mutti frowned. "It's all such nonsense."

"It may be but it's what they're doing." She thought it was ridiculous too but this couldn't be ignored.

The colour came back into Mutti's cheeks. She walked over to Käthe and put her arm around her shoulders. "We can't let them win. If we give into them they will win."

Mutti was right. They shouldn't let them get away with it. But she had to think of Renate.

Mutti hugged her. "They're bound to come to their senses sooner or later."

"I hope so."

"Anyway, I have to look after my special class. I can't leave them and Karl Schubert or this beautiful house." She gestured to the walls of the room they were in. They both sat down again and took another biscuit each.

"Why are you doing this? Why are you so keen to help these people?"

Mutti tutted. "It's not obvious?"

Käthe shook her head.

"Because of your father. He wasn't whole either but look at what he did. I want to help these poorly-equipped young people to get the best out of life. It was the same at the Lauenstein."

"And what about Steiner and his crazy ideas?"

The door opened at the moment and Mutti was not able to answer. Käthe could see that she'd annoyed her though.

Karl Shubert walked in. Käthe had met him a couple of times before and she actually quite liked him though she couldn't understand why he was so enthusiastic about these children.

Karl's eyes lit up. He rubbed his hands. "Your vanilla biscuits Clara. May I?"

"Of course."

"Thank you." He took a biscuit. "I won't stay. I can see you have company. Good day to you, Frau Edler."

Käthe smiled. "Good day to you too."

Mutti shook her head after he'd left the room. "That man. He works so hard." She looked deeply into Käthe's eyes. "And I won't have a word said against Rudolph Steiner. His teachings are completely sound. You can see the miracles that are happening here. Your brother was right."

"So, we can't persuade you?"

Mutti shook her head. "I'm staying put and I will protect these children. You must do what you must do. Don't worry, though. You have my blessing. I suppose Hans can't go with you?"

Käthe shook her head. She felt the tears pricking at her eyes.

Mutti came over to her and put a hand on her shoulder. "It will work out all right. You'll see."

It was just getting light when Käthe finally arrived home. Hans was about to have breakfast. He poured her a coffee. "Well?"

Käthe shrugged and pursed her lips. "She just won't move. She refuses to think about it."

"Then there is nothing more you can do. Sit down and have your coffee. Eat something."

She sat down. She felt dirty and she could hardly move. Two difficult train journeys in just under a day had left her exhausted.

She ignored the food but sipped the coffee. It revived her a little.

"Get some rest. I'll see that Renate gets to school. I'll arrange for you to see Klaus tomorrow."

"The sooner the better, surely?"

"You need a clear head."

Käthe nodded. "At least there's one thing. She absolutely accepts Steiner now. And actually, I think his ideas are all right, really. No worse than the conventional religions at least and he seems to be doing some good."

"So you must concentrate on yourself and Renate now."

Indeed she must. And is seemed there was no place for him.

Renate burst into the dining room. "Mutti, you're back. Please don't go away like that again." She started howling. It was years since Käthe had heard her cry that way.

AH Nuremberg 1938

He looked in the mirror. Now there was a dictator. There was a mature man. The moustache suited him. The lack of animal products in his diet was making him glow with health. What wasn't there to admire? His most glorious hours were now just around the corner. He straightened his tie and then turned back to his desk. He looked again at the plans they'd made and smiled to himself.

Oh yes. They'd been right back then, at Landsberg. He was good at making speeches. He'd persuaded them all: the big generals, the politicians and the little housewives with their children, church and cooking.

Weren't the boys in his youth movement glorious? As for the girls, he'd bed them all if he had the time and strength. Whoever had designed that uniform had known what they were doing. So sexy. Just what all the hardworking men wanted to come home to. Aryan babies would easily be made.

Now it was time to act.

He knew that in a few days' time there would be a massive assault on the scum. The good German people would burn down their places of worship and lute their places of business.

Then there was that pressing matter of getting more breathing space for his people. The Treaty of Versailles was shite. Germany would show them. Germany would be great again. Germany would take up her place in the world.

He turned back to the mirror, raised his arm and clicked his heels. "Sieg Heil!" he whispered.

Now, he must hurry to that meeting. That would be the real beginning.

Nuremberg 1938

Chapter 52: facing the Führer

Six thin red flags, each adorned with a deep black swastika, stood either side of the main entrance. They waved lightly in the December sun. They made her shiver. It wasn't the cold, although the day was bitter enough. It was bright and sunny, as well, and that seemed at odds with what she and Renate were now facing. She'd put off this meeting with Klaus time and time again but he'd contacted them yesterday and said that they didn't have much longer. She must come and see him in his office and they must get this paperwork done.

The building seemed to lie as well. It looked like a fairy-tale castle. It should be full of romance instead of which it was just occupied with bureaucracy and some nastiness as well. It seemed evil to her. More like the home of the wicked fairy.

She must do this, however.

She pushed open the big heavy doors and found herself in a draughty hallway that had black and white marble tiles on the floor. *Cold, cold.* She wished she didn't have to be there.

"May I help you, madam?"

Käthe looked at the speaker. It was a young woman in a smart grey uniform. She was sitting behind an elegant mahogany desk. Her blond hair was wound into neat plaits that were coiled over her ears. Her lipstick was bright red and her eyebrows were heavily pencilled black. Her blue eyes stared icily at Käthe. Could she tell, Käthe wondered, by just looking at her that she was one of the scum?

Käthe trembled as she went to speak. "I'm here to see Doktor Klaus Edler. My name is Käthe Edler."

"Do you have an appointment?" There was no warmth at all in the young woman's voice.

"Yes. He's expecting me at three thirty."

"Very well. I'll let him know you've arrived."

Käthe watched the woman pick up the phone and ask for Klaus. She was put though within seconds. "Frau Edler is here to see you. Oh, I see…. Yes, I'll get her to wait."

It sounded as if there was a problem. She could do without this.

"Frau Edler, Doktor Edler is going to be a little late. Will you follow me, please?"

The young woman's heels clattered as she walked along the corridor. Käthe could barely keep up with her and she had flat shoes on. How could she walk in those?

The corridor seemed to go on for ever and ever. Then they turned into another one and then another. Was she being kidnapped? Was Klaus in on this too? Surely not.

At last the young woman stopped in front of a pair of double doors. She opened one of them and signalled that Käthe should go in.

"Doktor Edler has asked that you should wait for him here. He says you are to make yourself comfortable. He will arrange for some tea to be sent. He thought you might like to look at some of the books. He will be with you in about one hour."

"Thank you."

The young woman nodded curtly at Käthe and left the room. Had Käthe imagined it, or did she click her heels?

It was quite a nice room and reasonably comfortable. There were some softly-upholstered chairs and a smart parquet floor. The last of the sunlight shone through the long windows, each of which was flanked by heavily-embroidered curtains. There was a lot of blue in the décor, though, and it made the room seem cold.

There were several bookshelves, yes, but she didn't think she would be able to concentrate enough to read. It would probably all be propaganda anyway. She gazed at some of the titles on the shelf nearest to her. *Jahrbuch des deutschen Heeres 1937.* What would she want to know about the German army? *Handbuch der Judenfrage.* Oh come on. A handbook about the Jewish question. *Mein Kampf.* Hitler's book? What was Klaus thinking? Or had he done this deliberately? If he'd made out that she would be delighted to read these books, wouldn't that make her look like a good German citizen?

Oh, anyway: she really couldn't concentrate on reading now.

There were some very big paintings on the wall. One showed

a knight in armour rescuing a maiden is distress. Another quite modern one portrayed Hitlerjugend boys and BDM girls marching smartly. They'd made them look really glamorous. Surely it wasn't their job to be glamorous, was it? A picture of the Bavarian mountains was far more pleasant, but that was probably propaganda too. No doubt they were trying to show how beautiful the fatherland was. Well it was, clearly, but so were many other places in the world.

She sat down. She wasn't going to look at pictures or books. She rummaged in her handbag. Yes it was still there. The safety catch was on but it was otherwise ready to fire. She touched the pistol as if to reassure herself that it was real. She imagined how quickly she could get the catch off, aim and shoot. She felt sick at the thought of having to do that. Hans always said, "Be prepared for the worst but hope for the best."

Worst-case scenario today: she would have to use the gun but it would all go wrong and she would be arrested. Well, at least she would have tried. Best case scenario: everything goes well with Klaus, she gets the exit visa and also manages to find a job in England quickly. Even better if all of this would stop but that didn't seem likely.

She carefully rearranged the contents of her bag so that the pistol was near the top.

Oh, come on, Klaus. Do hurry up. Would he actually be able to help her anyway? Her stomach carried on churning. She would be glad when today was over.

Someone fumbled with the door at the far end of the room. At last. Now maybe they could get down to business.

The door seemed to be sticking. Perhaps she could open it from this side.

She got up out of her seat and marched towards the door. "I've got it," she called as she grabbed the handle.

It was stuck. Well and truly stuck. "Try turning it the other way from your side," she called.

Klaus did not reply.

The fumbling carried on.

She grabbed the handle again. "Let me have another go."

She felt the person on the other side of the door let go. She turned the handle once more and suddenly there was a loud crack as the door flew open. "Klaus, at last," she started.

Except it wasn't Klaus. Another familiar face looked back at her, though. She could never mistake that wild look, that silly moustache and those mean eyes. Closer up he looked smaller than she'd imagined. He blinked at her like a frightened rabbit.

His arm twitched.

She started to raise her arm. I must remember to say "Hitler" and not "Edler", she thought.

He dropped his arm back to his side though and he carried on blinking at her. He swallowed, blushed, mumbled something and half clicked his heels.

She dropped her arm as well and pulled her handbag closer to her body. She could feel the outline of the pistol pushing into her chest.

She realised she was trembling.

Chapter 53: shooting Hitler

I fumble in my bag. I know exactly what I must do. He's watching me. Is he scared? I manage to release the safety catch without taking the pistol out of my bag. My mouth's really dry now. There's a lump in my throat. But I manage to stop the trembling.

I now pull the pistol out of my bag and point it right at him. I remember the time in the woods with Hans when I managed to get my motivation right, Well, I don't need to imagine today; the actual target is here in front of me. I aim. Shall I go for the heart or the head? I decide on the heart. If I miss I might still get him in the throat or the head.

I use my natural grip, just like Hans showed me. I pull the trigger and fire. There is a loud bang and I feel the shock of it in my arm, right up to my shoulder. Even though it's such a little gun it's a powerful machine.

He falls in slow motion to the floor. He looks at me as if he can't believe what I've just done. There is blood all over his chest. His eyes stare. I think I've killed him.

There are loud footsteps in the corridor. People are shouting. The door is thrust open. Klaus is the first to come in. He see me and goes white.

"What have you done?" he whispers.

The young woman from earlier is here. She has her hand in front of her mouth. I think she's going to vomit.

A couple of men in uniform start shouting orders.

I feel perfectly calm now. It was the right thing to do, wasn't it?

It doesn't take long for them to come for me. The Gestapo arrive and I am handcuffed and led away.

I am put into a small cell and have to wait. Will I ever see my husband and my daughter again? Will this stop the war? Or will it make his cronies all the more angry with people like me?

I expect they'll kill me. I wonder whether I'll be hanged, shot or decapitated? What will that feel like?

She'd thought about this thousands of times since that day in December 1938.

London 1976

Chapter 54: face to face with the Führer

Käthe's coffee had grown cold. Served her right for daydreaming so much. The past was the past. There was nothing she could do about it now. She looked at her watch. The man was late. He was due ten minutes ago. She really couldn't stand unpunctuality. It was rude. It was disrespectful to the person you'd agreed to meet. You shouldn't waste their time like that.

She spotted a young man coming through a revolving door at the side of the foyer. Could that be him? What a peculiar way he was dressed. Jeans and a smart jacket. Plus shirt and tie. He looked as if he was about the same age as her grandson. He liked to dress that way, too.

"It's called 'smart casual' Oma," he always said when she commented. "It's what we all do nowadays." Well perhaps it was better than when he used to look like a long-haired hippo. Oh, and he's corrected that as well.

"You mean hippy, Oma. A long-haired hippy."

Thank goodness the fashion now was for shorter hair. So much smarter. Yes, that young man looked very smart – if you ignored his jeans.

She watched him speak to the young girl at the reception desk who pointed towards where she was sitting. That must be him then. Seconds later he was coming towards her and was already beginning to smile.

Just why had she agreed to do this? She now felt almost as nervous as she had that day.

"Frau Edler?" he asked as he arrived at where she was sitting. He was holding his hand out.

Käthe struggled to get out of her seat. Drat these low chairs. You would think they'd know better. Obviously it would be mainly older people who came to a place like this. The youngsters just wouldn't be able to afford it. Low chairs and old people didn't go together.

"Please," said the young man. "Please don't bother to get out of your chair." He held out his hand to her.

She took his hand. What an incredibly firm handshake he had for a young man.

He sat down beside her. He took a business card out of his pocket and handed it to her. "Donald McQuire. Please call me Don."

"Katharina Edler. You may call me Käthe." She tucked the card away in her handbag. It might be useful one day.

"So, Käthe, do you mind if I record our interview?"

"Not at all. As long as you don't broadcast the recording anywhere and as long as you let me see anything before it's printed."

Don laughed. His bright blue eyes sparkled. "I can see you know what's what, Käthe."

"I should think so. I've worked in the media since the end of World War II and I'm still working there now. So I do indeed know what's what."

"Good for you. I can see that I'm not going to be able to pull any wool over your eyes. Not that I'd want to of course."

"Hmm." Käthe couldn't put her finger on exactly why but she liked this young man. Although what he was saying sounded like the usual journalistic banter there was something about him that seemed genuine and trustworthy.

"So. I'll just get this set up, and then we'll begin."

She watched him plug the microphone into the recorder. Really amazing, what could be done these days. She wondered what Professor Einstein would make of it or even Hans. Not that they could make anything of it. They were both long dead.

"Right." Don looked up and grinned. "We can make a start. Ready?"

She nodded.

"So, tell me what happened that day?"

"I'd been invited to the department of emigration by my husband's cousin, Klaus Edler. He was going to help me to secure an exit visa. I was hoping to find work in England. We had already looked at getting a place for our daughter, Renate, on the Kindertransport and my two brothers were looking for a foster family for her."

"That must have been difficult."

"It was. It was horrible."

"So how come you met Adolph Hitler that day?"

"I think either he or I had been shown into the wrong room. I waited ages and ages for Klaus. Then I heard someone struggling with the other door into the room. I went to help, thinking it was Klaus. Only it wasn't. It was the Führer himself."

"How did you feel? Were you scared?"

Käthe laughed. "Not really. I was more surprised than anything. I think he was too. Neither of us managed to do the Hitler salute. Not properly."

"What was he like then? Tell us how he reacted to meeting you there."

"He stared. He looked like a rabbit does when you get him in the car headlights. Totally bewildered. And you know what? He was actually much smaller than he ever looked in photographs or on films. It was useful to remember that afterwards."

"So what happened next?"

"I found the pistol in my handbag, released the safety catch, and pointed it at him."

"A pistol?"

"Yes my husband insisted that I carry it with me always. He taught me how to shoot. I was quite a hot shot, really."

Don laughed and scribbled something in his notebook. "Did you actually shoot him?"

Käthe shook her head. "I pulled the trigger but it didn't go off. It jammed."

"What did he do?"

"He turned round and left the room. A few seconds later Klaus arrived."

"And there were no repercussions?"

"None at all."

"And why do you think you got away with it?"

Käthe shrugged. "I'm not really sure. I'm guessing it was because he was too scared to admit that a woman had pointed a gun at him and he'd just run away. It made him look such a coward. It sort of became our secret. Mine and the Führer's."

"And did you feel safer after that? You'd faced Hitler and made him run out of the room, hadn't you?"

"Not really. I thought they might come looking for me any moment. It was actually a relief when I left Germany. But at least I had even less respect for him than before and I was quite confident that one day he would disappear."

"If you had shot him, what do you think would have happened?"

"I doubt that I'd be talking to you now. Or that I would have ever met my grandson. Or that I'd have led the interesting life that I have had."

"What do you think would have been the consequences for everybody else? For our society? For German society?"

"Hard to predict. I suppose World War II might never have happened. Whether things would be better now, I've no idea." She paused. "Was that young man still hanging about in the doorway when you came in?"

Don nodded.

Käthe sighed. "It seems that problem won't go away."

"Indeed. So, Käthe can you tell us a bit about what your life was like after you didn't manage to shoot Hitler? Tell me about that life that you lead after you escaped from Nazi Germany."

"Renate and I were lucky – compared to others. My brothers found her a really good family and I came over to England a couple of months later. We both learned English quickly. We've both become English."

"So, it all went very smoothly then?"

"Well, there were difficulties. We were both classed as enemy aliens. Renate had a nervous breakdown when she was still quite young. She didn't know who she was and she was worried about me living in London being bombed by the Germans and about her father, stuck in Nuremberg, being bombed by the Allies. Oh, and that was ironic." She chuckled. "We managed to bring across some good china and silver. It was stored in a warehouse that was burnt to the ground. It was hit by an incendiary bomb. There went all of our worldly wealth. All that we had left were a few nice white linen tablecloths. My grandson's wife now enjoys hosting tea parties with them."

"Your mother didn't make it. That's right, isn't it?"

"Yes, you're right. She was murdered in Auschwitz." *Her own fault, though for being so obstinate.* She wouldn't mention this, of course. It wouldn't make such a good story. A lump formed in her throat as she thought about Mutti. She didn't think she would be able to speak for a moment.

"That must have been very hard for you. She was a very brave woman from what I've gathered."

Käthe nodded. "She was," she managed to whisper.

"And what about your husband? Did you keep in touch?"

"Well obviously he couldn't contact us during the war. He was working on defence, you know. In fact, he worked on the V2. Renate has since told me that he and the other engineers deliberately worked very slowly on it. They didn't like what the Nazis were doing. He did carry on supporting us financially after the war was over. He remarried, though, you know."

"That must have been harsh."

Käthe shrugged. "I didn't blame him. He didn't know whether we were alive or dead. The Nazis forced a divorce. You couldn't have a good Aryan German married to the scum. I was too preoccupied trying to make life work for me and Renate to have any time to think much about him at all. I'm glad, though, that both she and my grandson managed to maintain a good relationship with her father. And people have been very good to us here."

"Thank you, Käthe. That's all very interesting and you are certainly a very feisty woman."

"That's what they said when I studied science at Berlin University." She winked at him. "Under Albert Einstein, you understand."

"Goodness me. I'll have to include that."

"And you might like to add that I was the first woman in Jena to get a driving license."

"Wow. Even more."

Don scribbled another note. "Now, I really have to go." He

packed up his things, shook hands with her again and made his way out of the hotel.

"Goodbye, young man," Käthe whispered as she watched him disappearing out of the main door. "I hope you can make a good story out of that."

Chapter 55: troubled society

Käthe supposed she'd better get going. She'd need to pay for her coffee of course. Was there a waiter or waitress around? That was the trouble with this sort of place; they were always so reluctant to bring you the bill. It was almost as if they were hoping you would order something else. And she would have to pay for a coffee she hadn't even drunk. What a waste!

She was English through and through now. In England most cafés were self-service. She liked that. It saved so much waiting around.

She was careful with money because she'd lived through some difficult times. She really resented that cold coffee.

There was a biscuit in the saucer. She looked around to see if anyone was watching. No. She wrapped it up in her paper napkin and slipped it into her handbag.

Now. About getting that bill paid. Ah, there was someone coming. She waved at the young girl dressed in black and carrying a tray.

"Would you like another coffee, madam?" The girl was already clearing away the cup of cold coffee.

"Oh no. I think I'd better be getting on. I'd just like to settle my bill."

"There's nothing to pay, madam. Blue Echo magazines are paying. They also said you were to have as much coffee as you liked."

"It's very kind of them but I really must go now." She found her purse, took out a £1.00 and gave it to the girl. "There, that's for you."

"Thank you, madam. Have a nice day now."

She pulled on her jacket and made her way towards the exit. She would be glad of some fresh air, actually. She pushed open the heavy main door. The cold air hit her, making her feel slightly dizzy. She hadn't realised just how stuffy it had been inside the hotel.

She was sure it wasn't really necessary, overheating the place like that. Oh, and there was that poor man still, slumped in the doorway. He was wrapped up in a thick sleeping bag now. Had he had that earlier? She couldn't quite remember. Maybe somebody had given it to him while she was still inside. That was something, at least.

He opened his eyes suddenly, closed them again, then looked up at her with just one eye open, the other screwed up against the sun. "Spare a few coppers, ma'am?" He held out his hand.

"I did give you something earlier, actually. You were asleep, though so you probably didn't see me."

The man shrugged.

Then she remembered the biscuit. "Wait a minute, though. Perhaps you'd like this." She took the piece of shortbread out of her handbag and handed it to him. It wouldn't be very nutritious, she knew, but the sugar in it might give him a bit of energy and it might just take some of the hunger away.

He stared at the biscuit.

"Go on. Take it. It will do you good."

He scowled. "What the fuck? Bog off, you silly old cow." He slapped the biscuit out of her hand. It landed in a puddle.

Käthe's cheeks started to burn. Why was the man so ungrateful?

"You do know they really want cash, don't you?"

She turned to see who was speaking. A middle-aged man in a smart uniform faced her. The doorman.

"They're homeless because they've got a drug habit. They're not interested in food."

"I am here you know. You leave my drug habit out of it. It's none of your business." The younger man was now climbing out of his sleeping bag and gathering his things together.

"That's right, sonny. Time to get going."

They watched as the young man made his way down the street. He was limping. He really was in a bad way. "Where will he go now?" she asked.

"There's a centre just down the road for the homeless. They

find things for them to do during the day. They can get a shower and a haircut. And a bite to eat."

"That's good."

"Yes. Mr Henderson – he's the owner of this hotel – set it up. They try really hard there to get them off the streets." He sighed. "But while they're still addicted it don't do no good. I wish he wouldn't tolerate them sleeping in our doorways. It makes the place look so untidy."

Thank goodness he did. And even if it's because they're addicted you have to ask yourself what made life so bad that they got into drugs in the first place. She smiled. "Thank you for enlightening me."

"My pleasure, ma'am." He touched his hat.

Käthe set off, trying to keep the young man in view. She was looking for something to do now that, at the age of eighty-seven, she was about to retire at last from her job with a London media firm. Would they welcome volunteers at this centre?

She thought back again to that day when she'd gone to meet Klaus. What if she had managed to shoot Hitler? Would that have that stopped World War II happening? And that awful "Final Solution"? Tears came to her eyes as she thought again of her mother murdered at Auschwitz. *Why did you have to be so obstinate, Mutti?*

And what if the Germans had won the war? What if Hans and his colleague hadn't dragged their feet with the V2s? There probably wouldn't be any people living rough. Hitler would have had them put down as if they were rabid dogs. One almost ought to be grateful that there were people living on the streets. And ashamed as well though. People like that young man she was following should not exist. They should be given hope and motivation. Life was abundant and glorious.

Käthe smiled to herself as she thought of the big lie she'd just told to the journalist. Lies didn't bother her quite so much now that she'd worked all those years in advertising. The opposite of truth was just another truth. No, it had all happened so quickly that she hadn't even remembered that she had a pistol in her handbag, even though she could feel the shape of it as she'd pressed the bag to her chest. She certainly hadn't thought to use it. No matter. It made a good story.

The young man turned off the street into an old church. By the time Käthe had made her way in he had disappeared completely. A young girl sat at a reception desk. She looked friendly enough. "Can I help you?" she asked.

"Yes. I've heard about the really good work you do. I'd like to volunteer, if you'll have me."

"Oh. It's quite strenuous work."

Oh, they were going to get all ageist on her, were they? "My dear. I've studied under Einstein, survived the hyperinflation in the 1920s, the depression in Germany in the 1930s and World War II. I'm Jewish and the Holocaust didn't get me. I was the first woman in Jena to get her driving license and I even learnt how to repair my own car. Back then. I know how to work a gun and I'm an excellent markswoman as well. Not that I'd ever dream of using one. And…" She raised her index finger and waggled it. "I met Hitler once. I wasn't a bit scared of him. He was just a wimp really. So I don't think a few homeless ladies and gentlemen will be too much of a challenge."

There. This time she hadn't told a single lie.

The girl grinned at her. "I think you would be most welcome. Let me show you round."

About the Author

Gill James writes novels and short fiction for children, adults and young adults. *Face to Face with the Führer* is the fourth novel in her Schellberg cycle of novels that are set mainly in Nazi Germany. She has also written a science fiction series for young adults as well as occasional short stories and flash fiction series.

She is published by Chapeltown Books, Tabby Cat Press, The Red Telephone and Butterfly. She is a part-time Lecturer in Creative Writing and she formerly worked as a senior lecturer. She has published several academic papers.

Her stories are published on *Litro, CafeLit, Alfie Dog, Ether Books* and in several anthologies.

She offers workshops on creative writing, book-building, creative writing in other languages and the Holocaust and life in Nazi Germany.

Reviews by Gill can be found in Armadillo Magazine, IBBY, Troubador and on her own web site.

Member of the Society of Authors, the Society of Children's Book Writers and Illustrators and the National Society of Writers in Education, Gill has an MA in Writing for Children and PhD in Creative and Critical Writing, thesis title: *Peace Child, Towards a Global Definition of the Young Adult Novel.*

She edits for Bridge House Publishing, CaféLit, Chapeltown Books and The Red Telephone.

Before becoming a writer and an academic she taught modern languages for 23 years in various schools and has continued to make school visits as a writer of fiction for children and young adults.

How the Project Came About

In 1979, Renate James (nee Edler) received a mysterious package in the post. It had come from Germany. She didn't recognise the name on the package nor on the letter that came with it. Then, as she began to read she started to recognise some names mentioned in the letter. Slowly she remembered the school she attended until the age of 13. She left that school to come to England on the Kindertransport on 28 January 1939. The school was closed anyway, shortly afterwards, as it was a Church school that did not promote Nazi idealism. Some of the girls in Renate's class decided to write letters in an exercise book. They included their class teacher, Hanna Braun, in the "Rundbrief" (literally "round letter".) Each girl wrote her letter in the book and then posted it to the next on the list. Three volumes were written in total and one volume with letters dating from May 1942 to November 1944 had been found in the loft by one of the "girls". That girl made it her duty to track down every single member of the class and invite them to a school reunion in June 1980.

Renate Edler did not know she was Jewish until 22 December 1938. She was 13 years old. She was only Jewish according to the 1935 Nuremberg "Reichsbürgergesetz" and the "Blutschutzgesetz". She had been christened as a catholic and her mother had been brought up as Lutheran Christian. The blood was tainted, however, and as she had two Jewish grandparents, she was a "Mischling" of the first degree. A further irony is that the only living grandparent, whose blood had tainted her, was Christian and had also become an anthroposophist. Her teachers all knew about this and protected her. Neither she nor her mother ever wore the Star of David, though they were being quite illegal in not doing so. It was not easy for Renate Edler. She had little solidarity with other Jewish children as she did not share their faith. On the other hand, she was luckier than many. Her uncles were already in England and found a very kind and generous foster family for her. Her mother was able to find work with the same family and joined her later. After the war ended, she was able to resume contact with her father and meet his new wife with whom she had an immediate empathy. There is further irony here: her father was not allowed to leave Germany as he was already working on the war effort. He was eventually involved with the design of the V2 bomb.

Clara Lehrs, Renate's grandmother, could not get out of Germany in time. She was eventually murdered at Treblinka on 27 September 1942, after spending some time in a ghetto in Rexingen and then being transported to Theriesenstadt on 22 August 1942. In 1939, she was forced to sell the house that she and her son had built in Stuttgart. She managed to sell it to a family friend who was also a colleague of her son. Prior to this, she and a teacher from the nearby Waldorf School, had opened this house to the "Hilfsklasse" (children with severe learning difficulties) from the Waldorf School. The class kept going there secretly until the end of the war and carried on openly almost as soon as the peace was declared. No one is quite sure how that could happen, especially as it was a Jewess who was protecting them for much of the time. The novels offers possible explanations.

The novel brings these three strands together. Though it does not replicate the letters from the German girls entirely it retains their spirit and their story is told in letter form. Renate Edler had started writing her autobiography prompted by the reunion in 1980. Sadly, she was diagnosed with cancer shortly afterwards and died in 1986. Just over twenty years later, it seemed appropriate to finish off what she had started. However, there were many questions and the research conducted in order to answer those questions led to further questions and further content for the novel and beyond.

This site unpicks the issues that the novel raises further and gives more insight to them and much of their background.

The Research

To date this has taken several forms.

Much of it has, in fact, been simply writing. Using a few known facts one writes and the imagination fills the gaps. Experienced writers are good observers of life and are often able to work out how something might have happened or how someone might behave in given circumstances. Sometimes the writing itself asks other questions. For example, just which cut flowers might be available in September in 1939?

There has also been some more traditional research.

An important step was to interpret the letters of the German girls. My mother-in-law had both transcribed and translated about half of them. I've had to do the rest. The handwriting is extremely hard to read and this was quite a slow process. However, being forced to take this slowly made me get to know each individual girl well.

These letters, just like the writing of the story, have also raised several questions. In order to answer these questions, it has been a matter of finding generally-available resources, which point to good secondary resources and reliable primary resources. The Holocaust is now generally well-documented though the German girls' letters add greatly to the information about civilian German attitudes at the time. In order to understand what they were saying it was important to find out much about the background – what were food shortage like, what was the BDM all about and what was expected of girls that age. All of this information is shared on this site but contextualised to the story.

There are many accounts of Holocaust survivors and from the Kinder who came over on the Kindertransport. However, many of these are told through a veil of memory and though useful and certainly interesting, they do not give as much clear information as diaries, letters, newspapers available at the time and photographs.

Newspapers have to be read carefully however. The critical reader has to cut through the propaganda to uncover facts. Often it is the small ads and the letters to the editor that give the best information.

There are also some excellent tertiary resources available: other interpretations in fiction of related events. These are also listed in the bibliography.

What has also been extremely useful is what I call secondary writer's research – creating an experience similar to what the players in the novel might have had.

Find out more on the web site The House on Schellberg Street:
    http://www.thehouseonschellbergstreet.com/

Glossary

Apfelkuchen
Apple cake.

Apfelstrudel
Apple pastry – lots of apple and a very thin pastry. The pastry should be so thin that you can read a newspaper through it.

BDM
Bund Deutscher Mädel. This was the main youth movement for girls aged 14-18 and it was compulsory. They wore a very smart uniform. They did many of the same activities as the *Hitlerjugend* and similar to our own Guide Association. There was also some Nazi indoctrination involved.

Bienenstich
Literally 'bee-sting'. A cake made of slices of almond topped pastry sandwiched together with honey-sweetened creamy custard.

Blutschutzsgesetz
This was one of the race laws passed in Nuremberg in 1935. It was made in order to keep the German race pure. It forbade marriage between Jews and Germans. It also defined being Jewish as having three or more Jewish grandparents. If you had two German grandparents you were *Mischling*. Mischlings were also not allowed to marry Germans.

Bretzel
A knot-shaped, salted bread roll.

Dampfkesselüberwachungsverein
Literally the "steam boiler regulatory society". This was actually the body that issued driving licenses at the time that Käthe got hers.

Freidrichbaumachinentechnik
Frederick Engineering Technology – this is the name of the factory.

Hausfrau
Housewife.

Hitlerjugend
This was the main youth movement for boys aged 14-18. They did many activities the same as the Scouts. There was also some Nazi indoctrination involved; a training ground for the SA and the SS.

Jawort
When you say "yes" in the marriage ceremony.

Kaffeeklatsch
This is the slightly mocking name for a group of people, usually mainly female, who meet to gossip over coffee.

Käsekuchen
This is a cheesecake made with *Quark*.

Kippah
A small hat/head-covering worn by Jewish men.

Konditorei
Cake shop.

Lebkuchen
A type of gingerbread, often covered with a thin layer of icing..

Mischling
A Mischling is a person who has two Jewish grandparents. They are too Jewish to be considered German but not Jewish enough to be considered Jewish. This was determined by the *Blutschutzsgesetz* that was established in Nuremberg in 1935, leaving many people, including Renate, without a clear identity.

Mutti
Mum, mummy.

Oberleutnant
First lieutenant.

Oma
Grandmother, granny, nana.

Quark
A type of unripe cream cheese. It is often used in Germany to make cheese cake.

Reichskanzlei
The office of the Chancellor of Germany.

Reichstag
This is where Germany's parliament met.

Sauerbraten
Meat pot-roast in vinegar.

Schnapps
A clear German spirit, distilled from fruit, without added sugar.

Sekt
Sparkling dry white wine made in Germany by the champagne method.

Sondermischling
People were Mischlings if they had two Jewish grandparents. If both were on the same side of the family you became a Sondermischling – a special Mischling.

Stollen
A yeast-based cake, a little like a fruit loaf. It contains dried fruit and often has marzipan in the middle. It is eaten at Christmas.

Strudel
Pastry that is rolled so thin that you can read a newspaper through it.

Vati
Dad, daddy.

Wiener Kipferl
Small crescent-shaped vanilla-flavoured biscuits. They are usually covered in icing sugar. A variant recipe replaces some of the flour with cocoa powder.

Zwiebelkuchen
A type of onion quiche, usually eaten in the autumn.

The Schellberg Cycle Workshop

Rationale

The Schellberg Cycle workshop presents a unique view of Nazi Germany and the Holocaust. It explores how normal decent people can become involved in something so horrific.

The Cycle includes the true stories of some feisty women and the men around them, including those of a young Jewish girl who comes to England on the Kindertranpsort, her grandmother who puts herself in danger in order to save some disabled children, her mother who has a dramatic encounter with Hitler himself and some ordinary German young women who are at first taken in by the glamorous life that the Nazi regime offers.

Nature of workshop

The workshop includes:
- Board games
- Creative writing exercises
- Role play exercises
- Discovery packs
- Reading material
- Discussion

Preview the teacher's notes at http://eepurl.com/cJOvRT. You can purchase your kit here for £50.00.

Please Leave a Review

Reviews are so important to writers. Please take the time to review this book. A couple of lines is fine.

Reviews help the book to become more visible to buyers. Retailers will promote books with multiple reviews.

This in turn helps us to sell more books... And then we can afford to publish more books like this one.

Leaving a review is very easy.

Go to https://bit.ly/3WUVG67, scroll down the left-hand side of the Amazon page and click on the "Write a customer review" button.

Other Publications by Chapeltown

The House on Schellberg Street

by Gill James

Renate Edler loves to visit her grandmother in the house on Schellberg Street. She often meets up with her friend Hani Gödde who lives nearby. This year, though, it is not to be. Just a few weeks after a night when synagogues are burned and businesses owned by Jews are looted, Renate finds out a terrible secret about her family.

At a time when the world is at war and the horrors of the Holocaust are slowly becoming apparent, Renate has to leave behind her home and her friends, and become somebody she never thought she could be.

The house on Schellberg Street needs to stay strong. Will it and those who work in it be strong enough? Will Renate ever feel at home again? And what of those left behind?

"This is a great cross-over book with an appeal to teenagers and adults alike. It gives an insight into how people's lives were torn apart by the war and how they managed to adjust and survive. A must-read for anyone studying World war II. Anyone who enjoyed *The Boy with the Striped Pyjamas* will love it." *(Amazon)*

Order from Amazon:
ISBN: 978-1-910542-23-1 (paperback)
978-1-910542-24-8 (ebook)

Chapeltown Books

Clara's Story: a Holocaust Biography

by Gill James

Clara will not be daunted. Her life will not end when her beloved husband dies too young. She will become a second mother to the young children who live away from home at a rather special school – a particular class of disabled children growing up in Nazi Germany.

Clara's Story: a Holocaust Biography is the second story in the Schellberg Cycle. It might be described as a tragedy or it might be described as a story of survival. In the end it is up to the reader or even Clara herself to decide.

"The social history starting before World War 1, and continuing to the present day, was extremely interesting and Clara herself had the attitude that where there's hope there's life. A well-written and thought-provoking book." *(Amazon)*

Order from Amazon:
ISBN: 978-1-910542-33-0 (paperback)
978-1-910542-34-7 (ebook)

Chapeltown Books

Girl in a Smart Uniform

by Gill James

Girl in a Smart Uniform is the third book in the Schellberg Cycle, a collection of novels inspired by a bundle of photocopied letters that arrived at a small cottage in Wales in 1979. The letters give us first-hand insights into what life was like growing up in Germany in the 1930s and 1940s.

It is the most fictional of the stories to date, though some characters, familiar to those who have read the first two books, appear again here. Clara Lehrs, Karl Schubert and Dr Kühn really existed. We have a few, a very few, verifiable facts about them. The rest we have had to find out by repeating some of their experiences and by using the careful writer's imagination.

"The book is well written and easy to read. The girl's home life is complicated and there are some moving developments involving her brothers. Thoroughly worth reading!" *(Amazon)*

Order from Amazon:
ISBN: 978-1-910542-10-1 (paperback)
978-1-910542-11-8 (ebook)

Ingram Content Group UK Ltd.
Milton Keynes UK
UKHW020713210423
420559UK00015B/866